I0426337

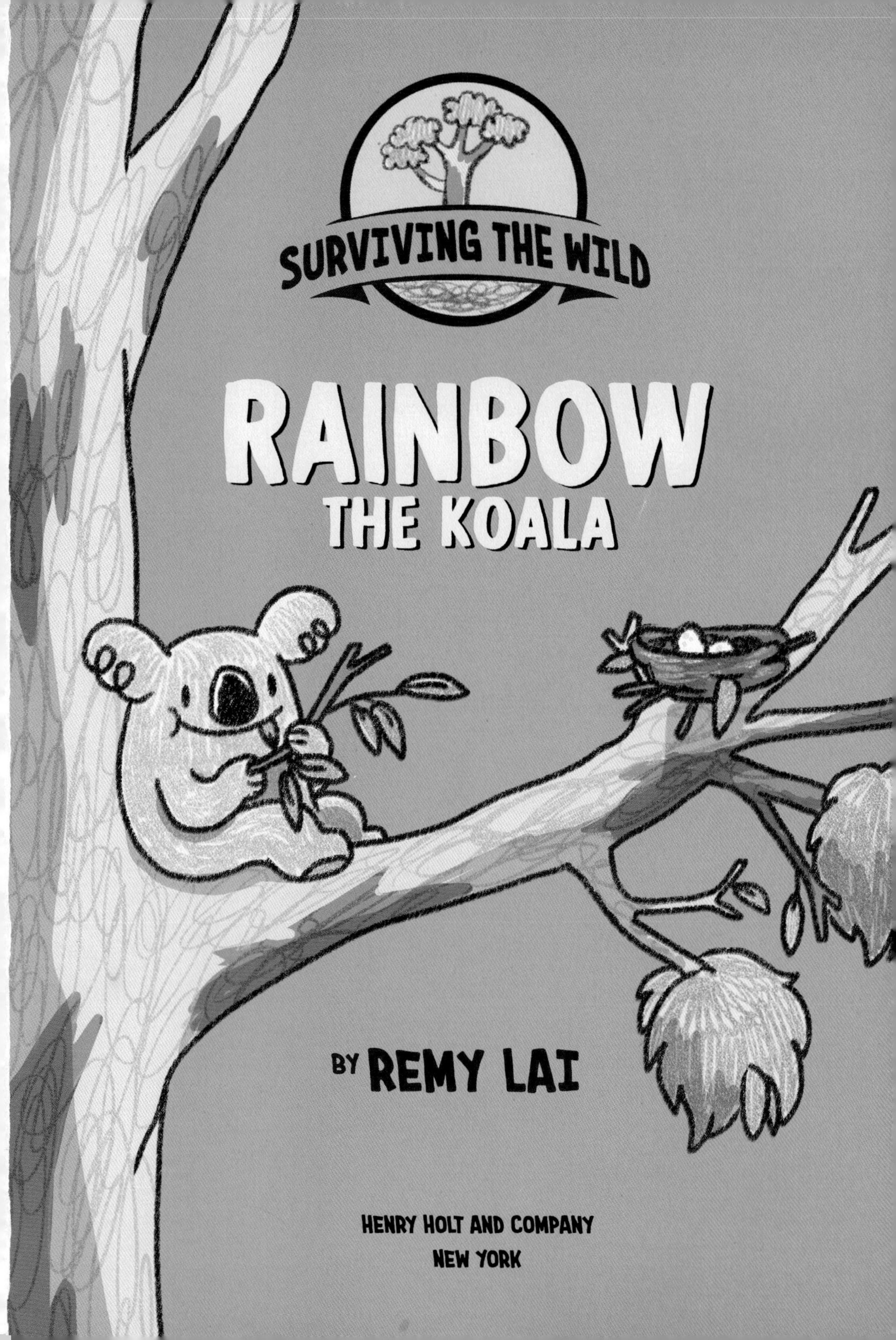

SURVIVING THE WILD

RAINBOW THE KOALA

BY REMY LAI

HENRY HOLT AND COMPANY
NEW YORK

I ACKNOWLEDGE THAT THIS BOOK WAS
WRITTEN AND ILLUSTRATED IN BRISBANE, AUSTRALIA,
ON WHICH THE TURRBAL AND JAGERA PEOPLES ARE THE
TRADITIONAL CUSTODIANS OF THEIR RESPECTIVE LAND.
I PAY MY RESPECT TO THEIR ELDERS,
PAST, PRESENT, AND EMERGING.

HENRY HOLT AND COMPANY, PUBLISHERS SINCE 1866
HENRY HOLT® IS A REGISTERED TRADEMARK OF MACMILLAN PUBLISHING GROUP, LLC
120 BROADWAY, NEW YORK, NY 10271
MACKIDS.COM

OUR BOOKS MAY BE PURCHASED IN BULK FOR PROMOTIONAL, EDUCATIONAL, OR BUSINESS USE.
PLEASE CONTACT YOUR LOCAL BOOKSELLER OR THE MACMILLAN CORPORATE AND
PREMIUM SALES DEPARTMENT AT (800) 221-7945 EXT. 5442
OR BY EMAIL AT MACMILLANSPECIALMARKETS@MACMILLAN.COM.

LIBRARY OF CONGRESS CATALOGING-IN-PUBLICATION DATA IS AVAILABLE.

FIRST EDITION, 2022
DESIGNED BY LISA VEGA
PRINTED IN CHINA BY 1010 PRINTING INTERNATIONAL LIMITED, KWUN TONG, HONG KONG

ISBN 978-1-250-78544-2 (HARDCOVER)
1 3 5 7 9 10 8 6 4 2

FOR C

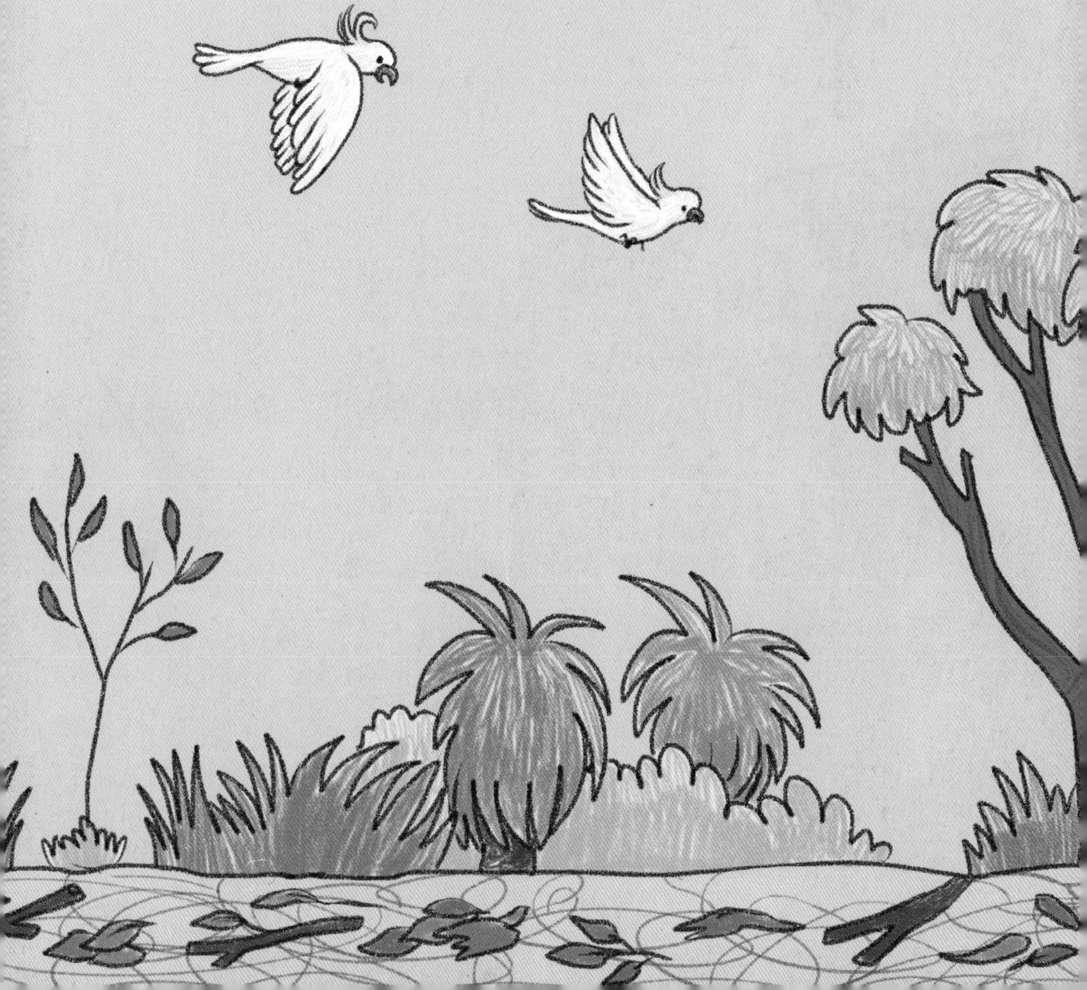

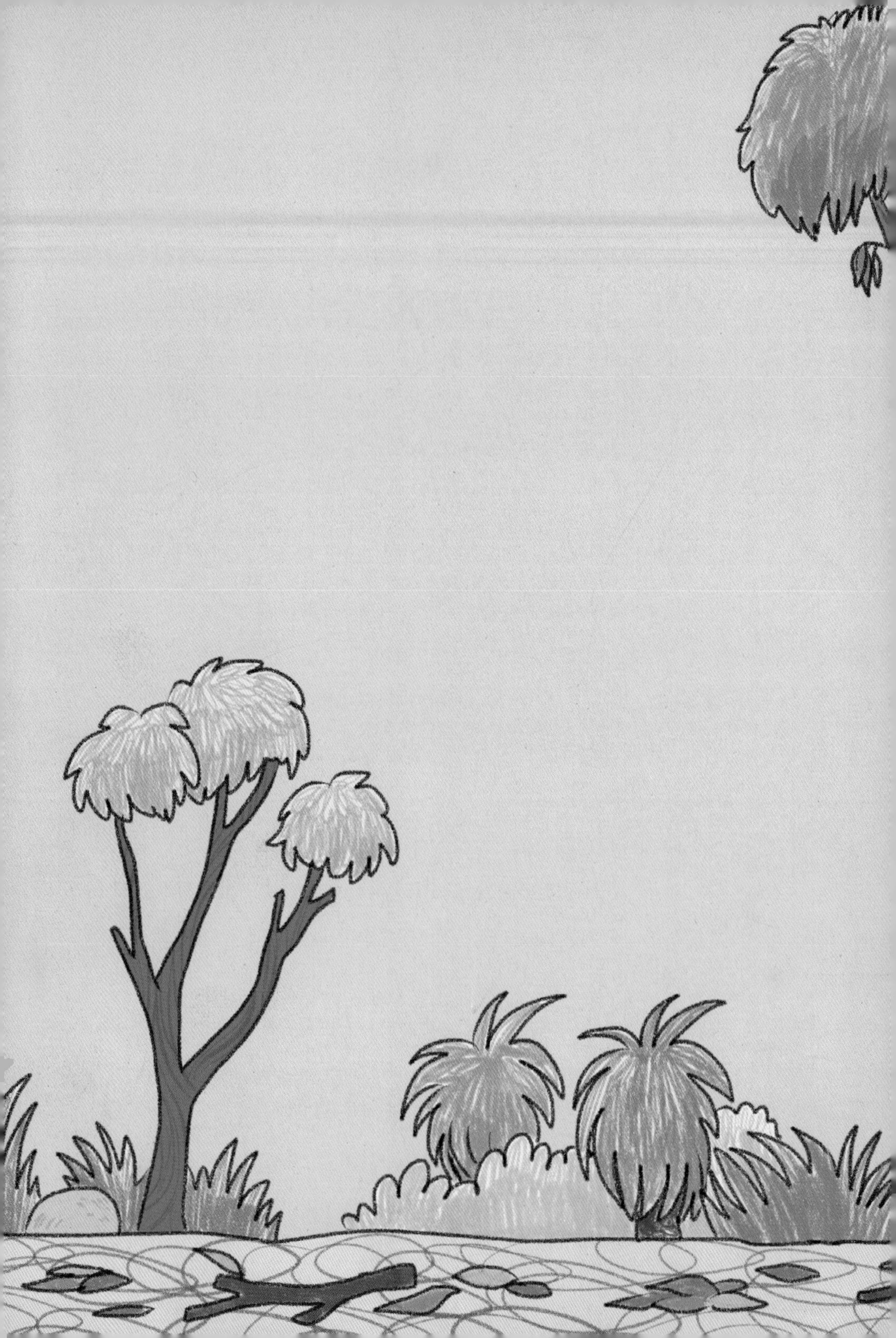

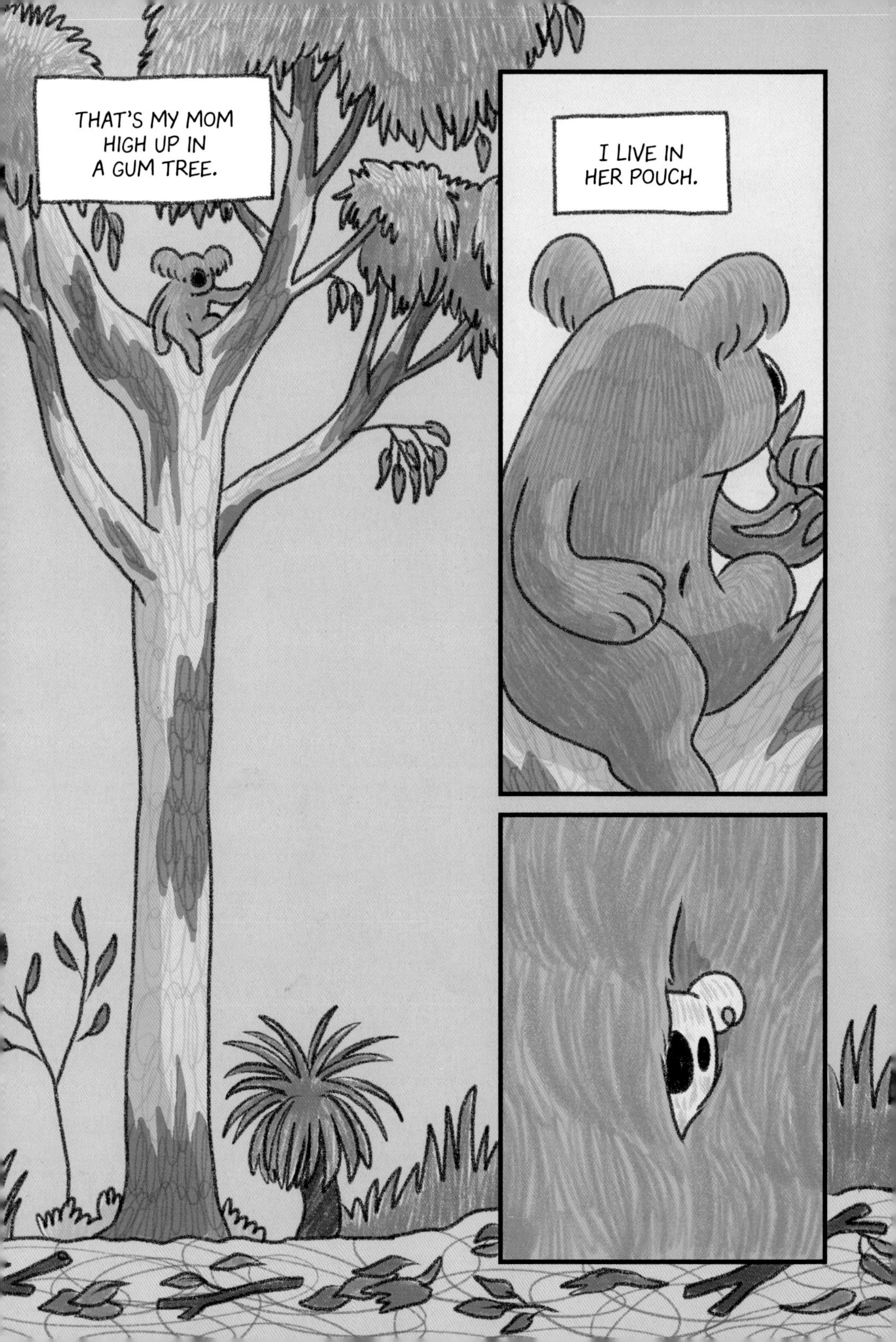
THAT'S MY MOM HIGH UP IN A GUM TREE.
I LIVE IN HER POUCH.

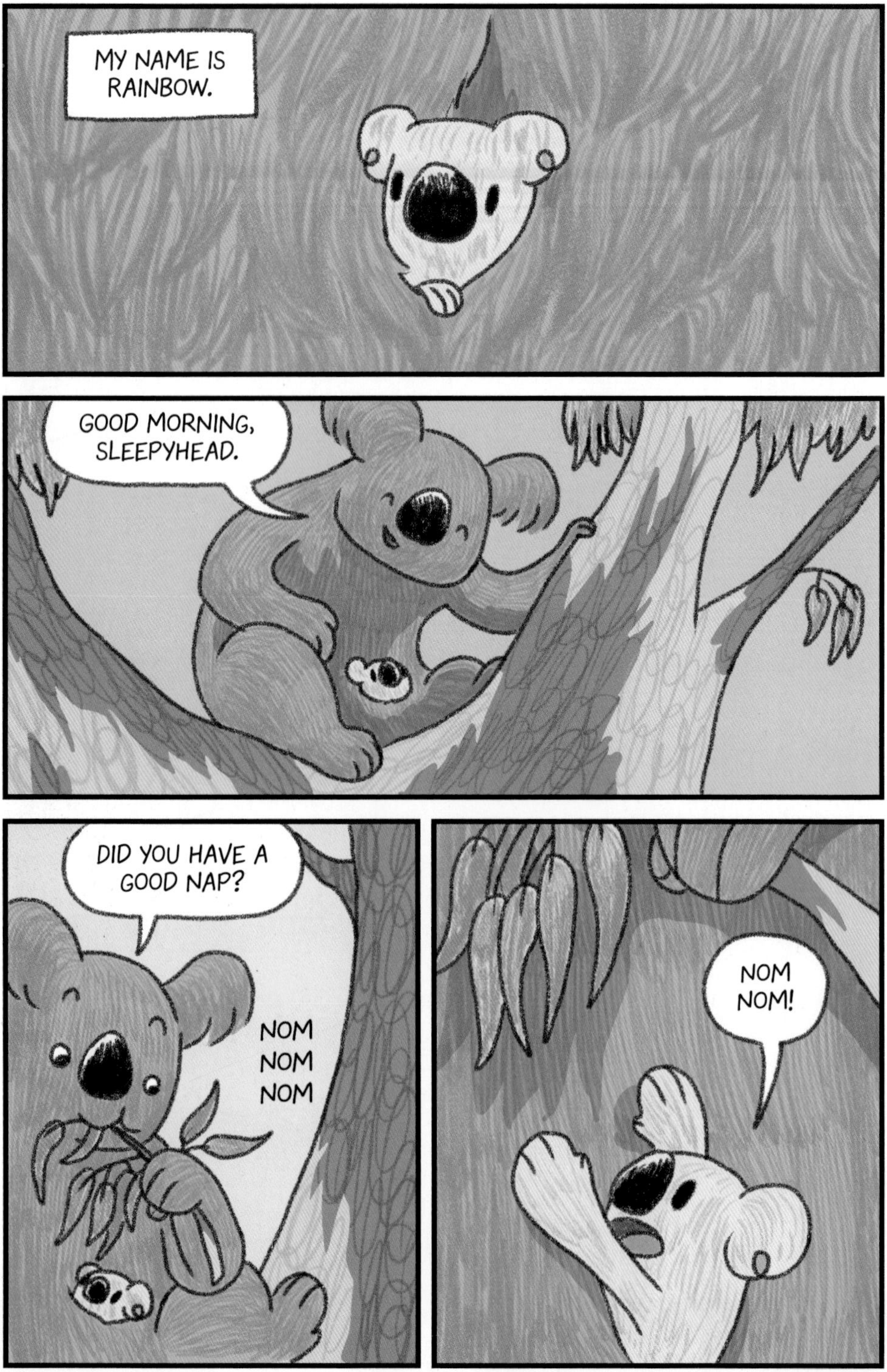
MY NAME IS RAINBOW.
GOOD MORNING, SLEEPYHEAD.
DID YOU HAVE A GOOD NAP?
NOM NOM NOM
NOM NOM!

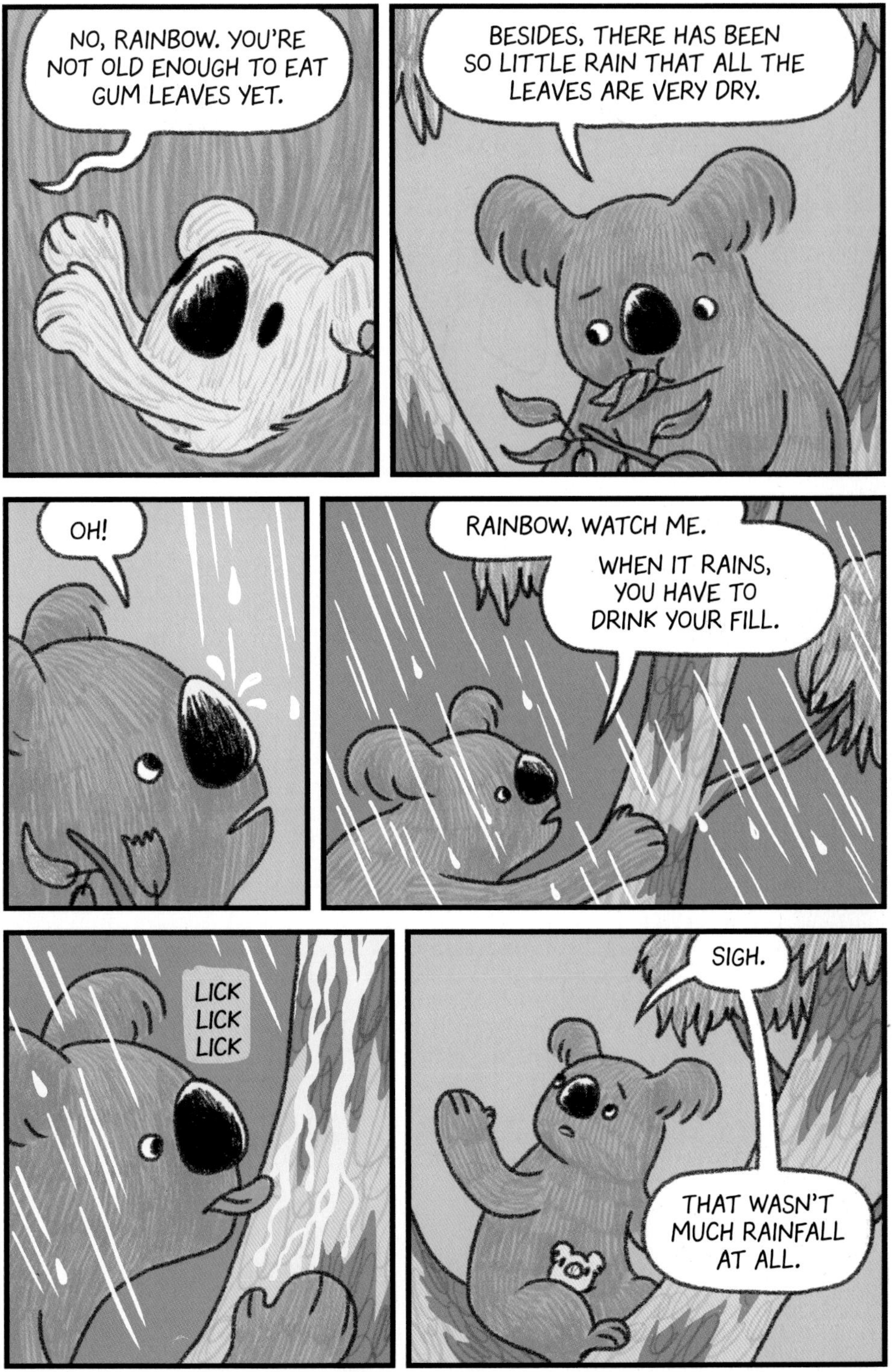
NO, RAINBOW. YOU'RE NOT OLD ENOUGH TO EAT GUM LEAVES YET.
BESIDES, THERE HAS BEEN SO LITTLE RAIN THAT ALL THE LEAVES ARE VERY DRY.
OH!
RAINBOW, WATCH ME.
WHEN IT RAINS, YOU HAVE TO DRINK YOUR FILL.
LICK LICK LICK
SIGH.
THAT WASN'T MUCH RAINFALL AT ALL.

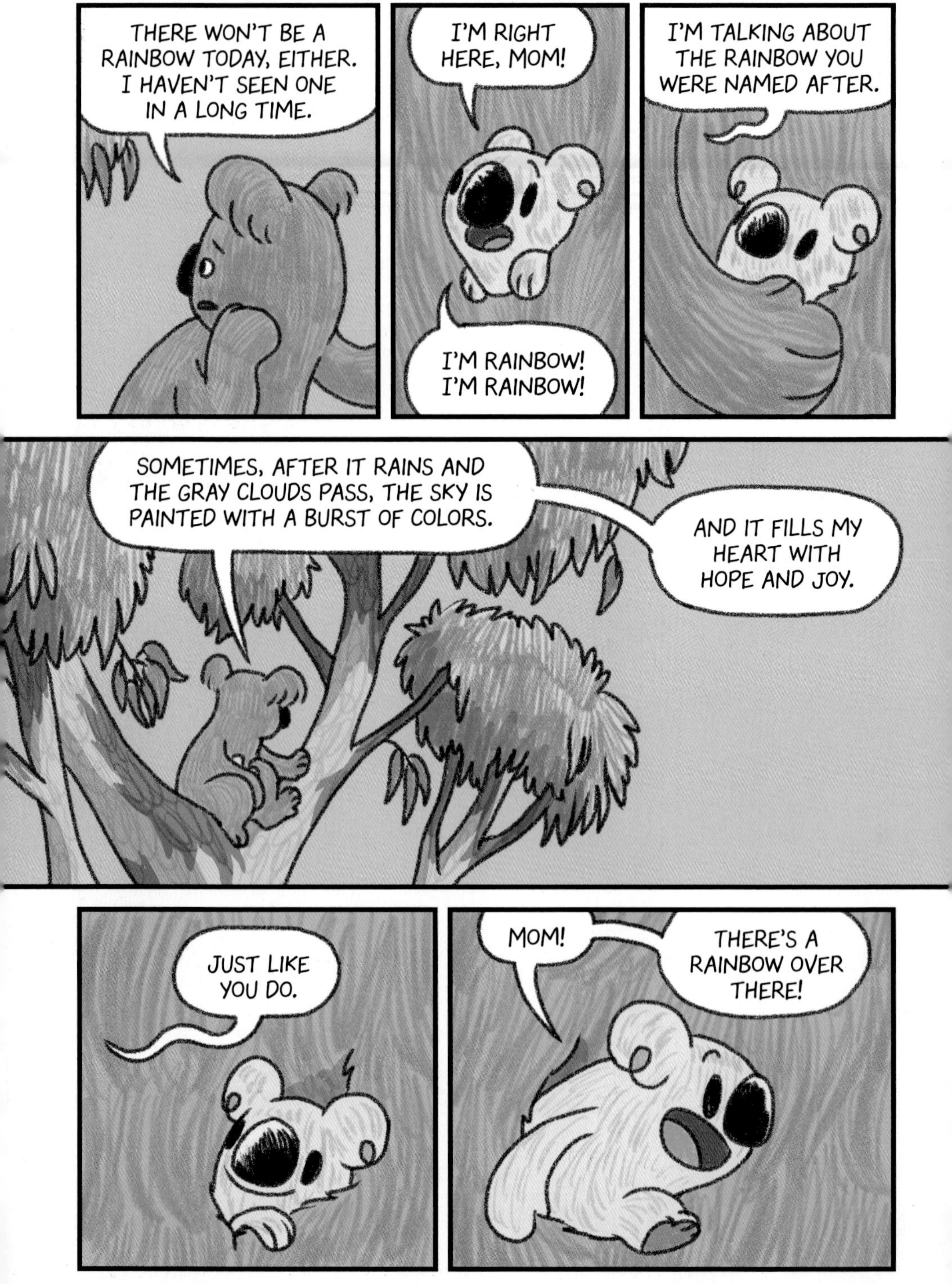
THERE WON'T BE A RAINBOW TODAY, EITHER. I HAVEN'T SEEN ONE IN A LONG TIME.
I'M RIGHT HERE, MOM!
I'M RAINBOW! I'M RAINBOW!
I'M TALKING ABOUT THE RAINBOW YOU WERE NAMED AFTER.
SOMETIMES, AFTER IT RAINS AND THE GRAY CLOUDS PASS, THE SKY IS PAINTED WITH A BURST OF COLORS.
AND IT FILLS MY HEART WITH HOPE AND JOY.
JUST LIKE YOU DO.
MOM!
THERE'S A RAINBOW OVER THERE!

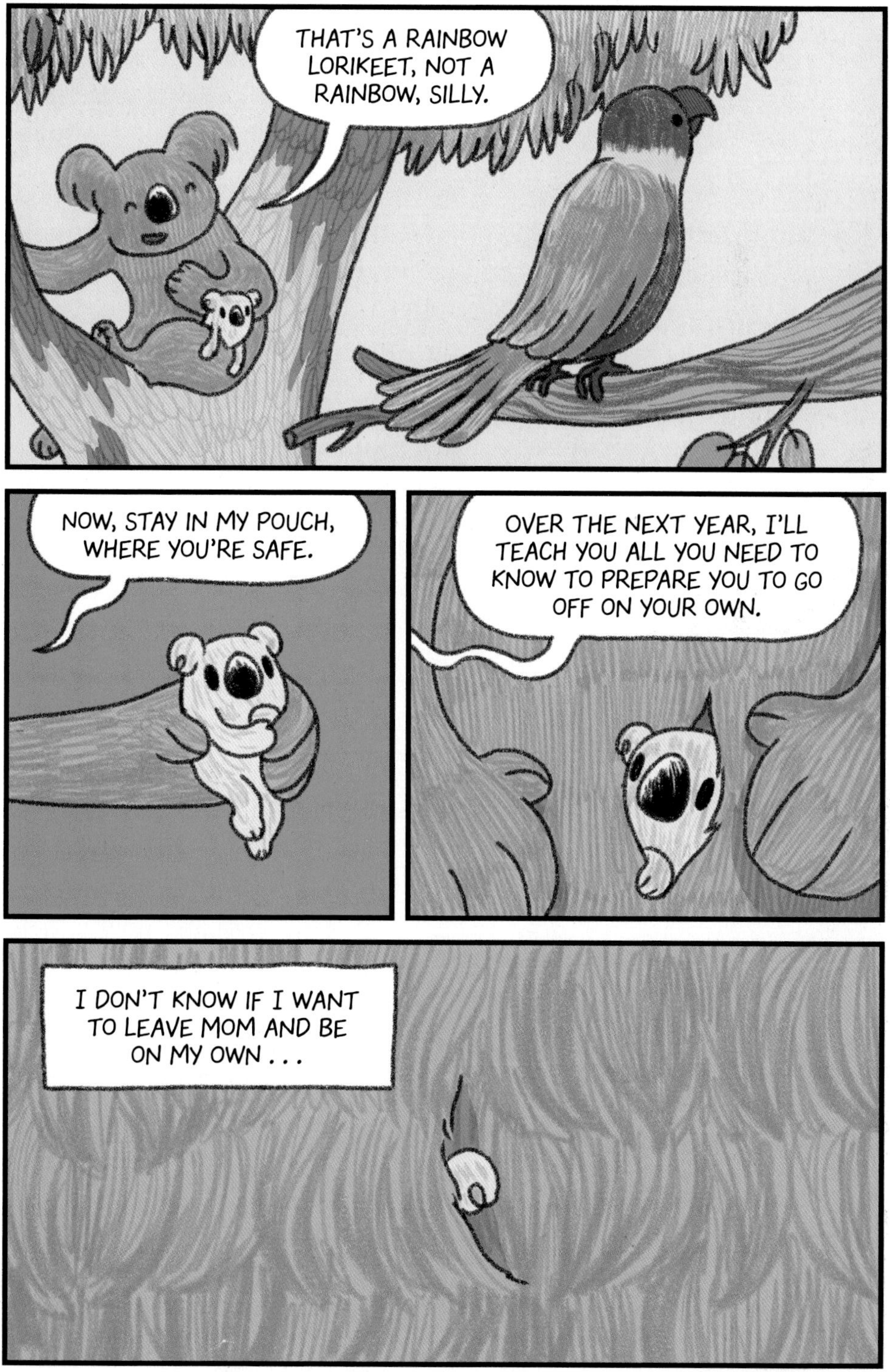
THAT'S A RAINBOW LORIKEET, NOT A RAINBOW, SILLY.
NOW, STAY IN MY POUCH, WHERE YOU'RE SAFE.
OVER THE NEXT YEAR, I'LL TEACH YOU ALL YOU NEED TO KNOW TO PREPARE YOU TO GO OFF ON YOUR OWN.
I DON'T KNOW IF I WANT TO LEAVE MOM AND BE ON MY OWN . . .

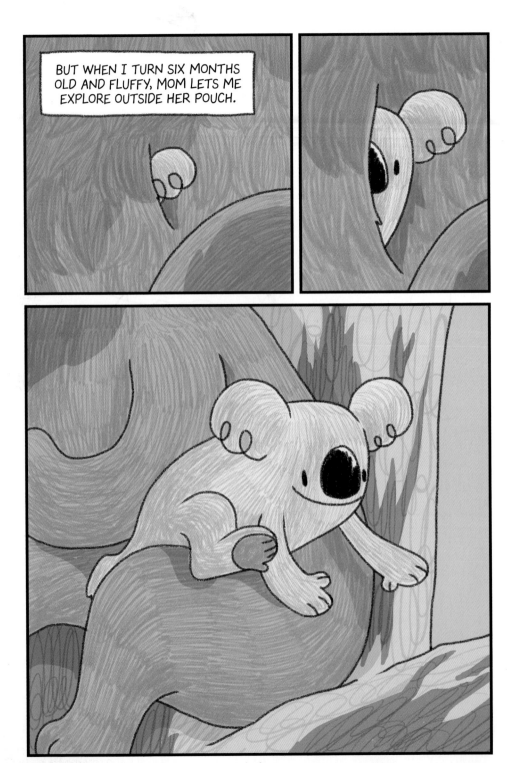

BUT WHEN I TURN SIX MONTHS OLD AND FLUFFY, MOM LETS ME EXPLORE OUTSIDE HER POUCH.

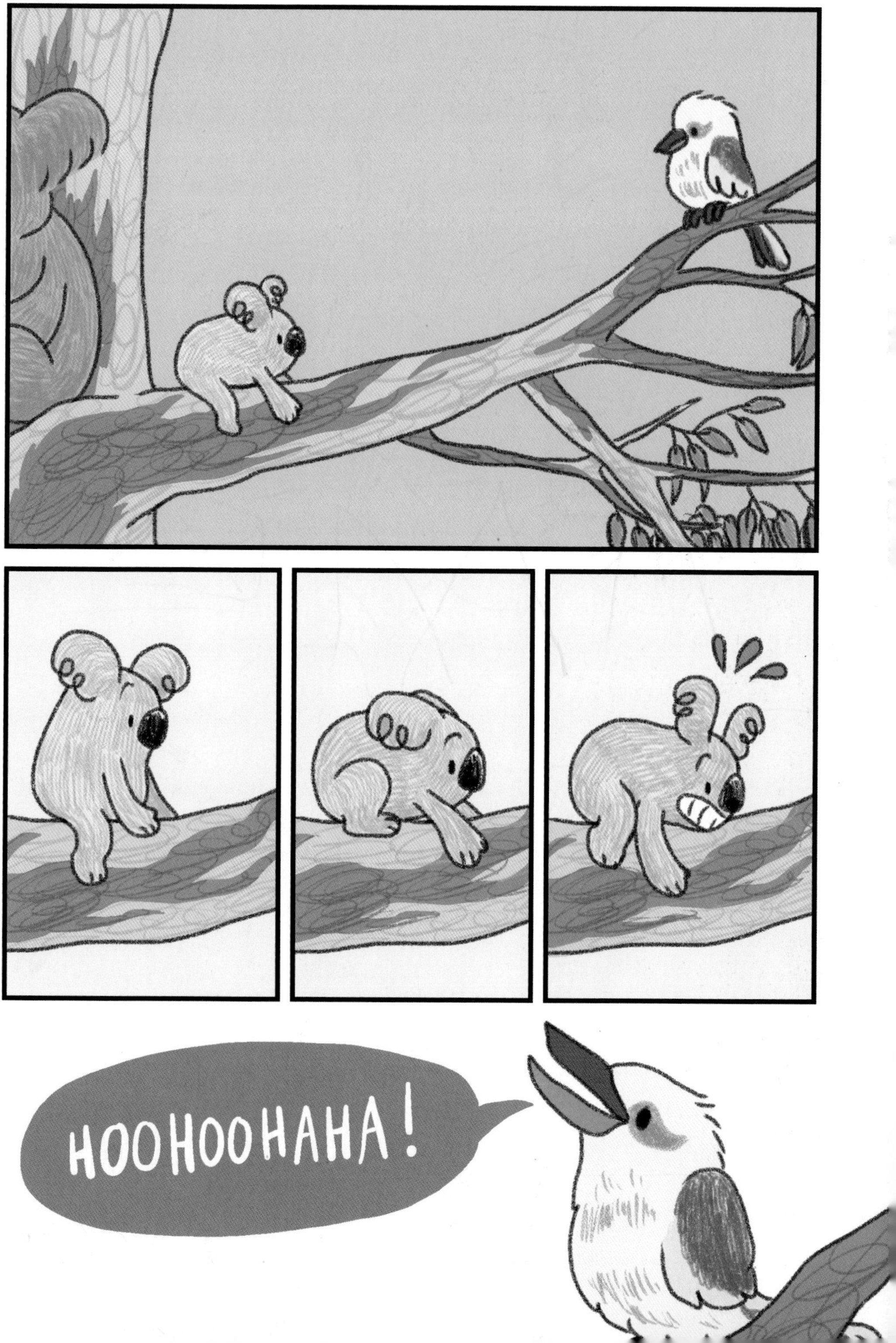
HOOHOOHAHA!

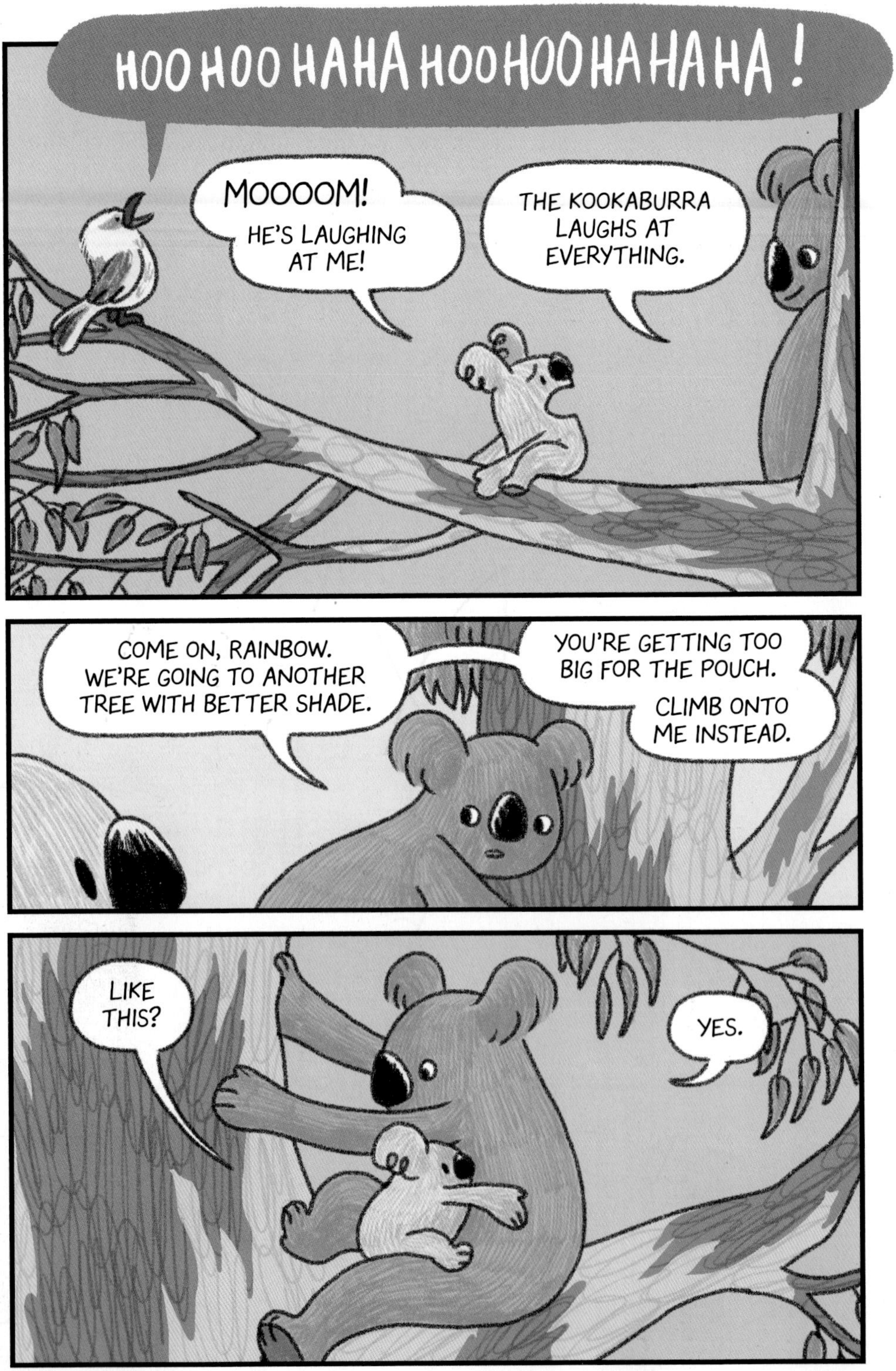
HOO HOO HAHA HOO HOO HA HA HA!
MOOOOM! HE'S LAUGHING AT ME!
THE KOOKABURRA LAUGHS AT EVERYTHING.
COME ON, RAINBOW. WE'RE GOING TO ANOTHER TREE WITH BETTER SHADE.
YOU'RE GETTING TOO BIG FOR THE POUCH.
CLIMB ONTO ME INSTEAD.
LIKE THIS?
YES.

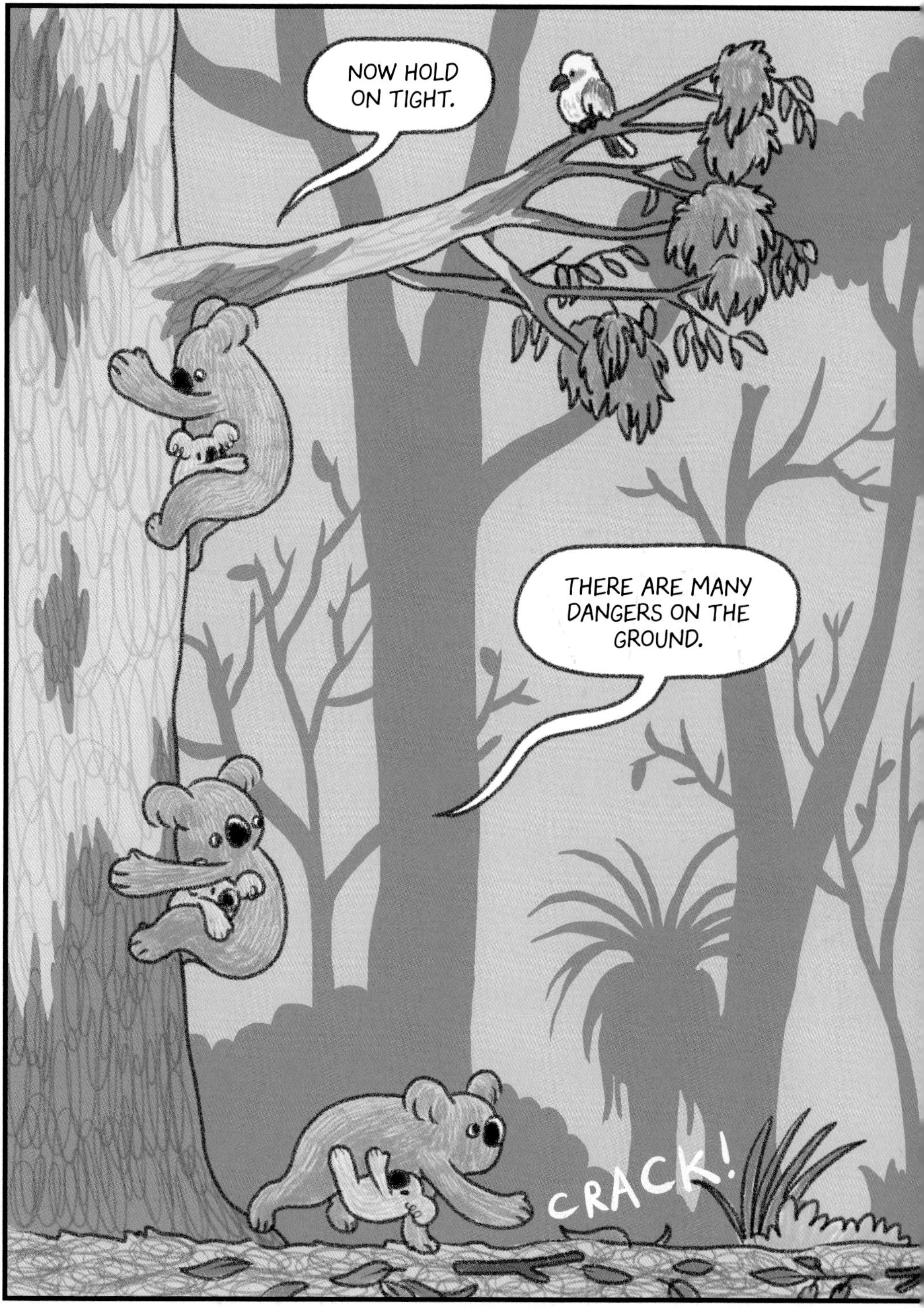
NOW HOLD ON TIGHT.
THERE ARE MANY DANGERS ON THE GROUND.
CRACK!

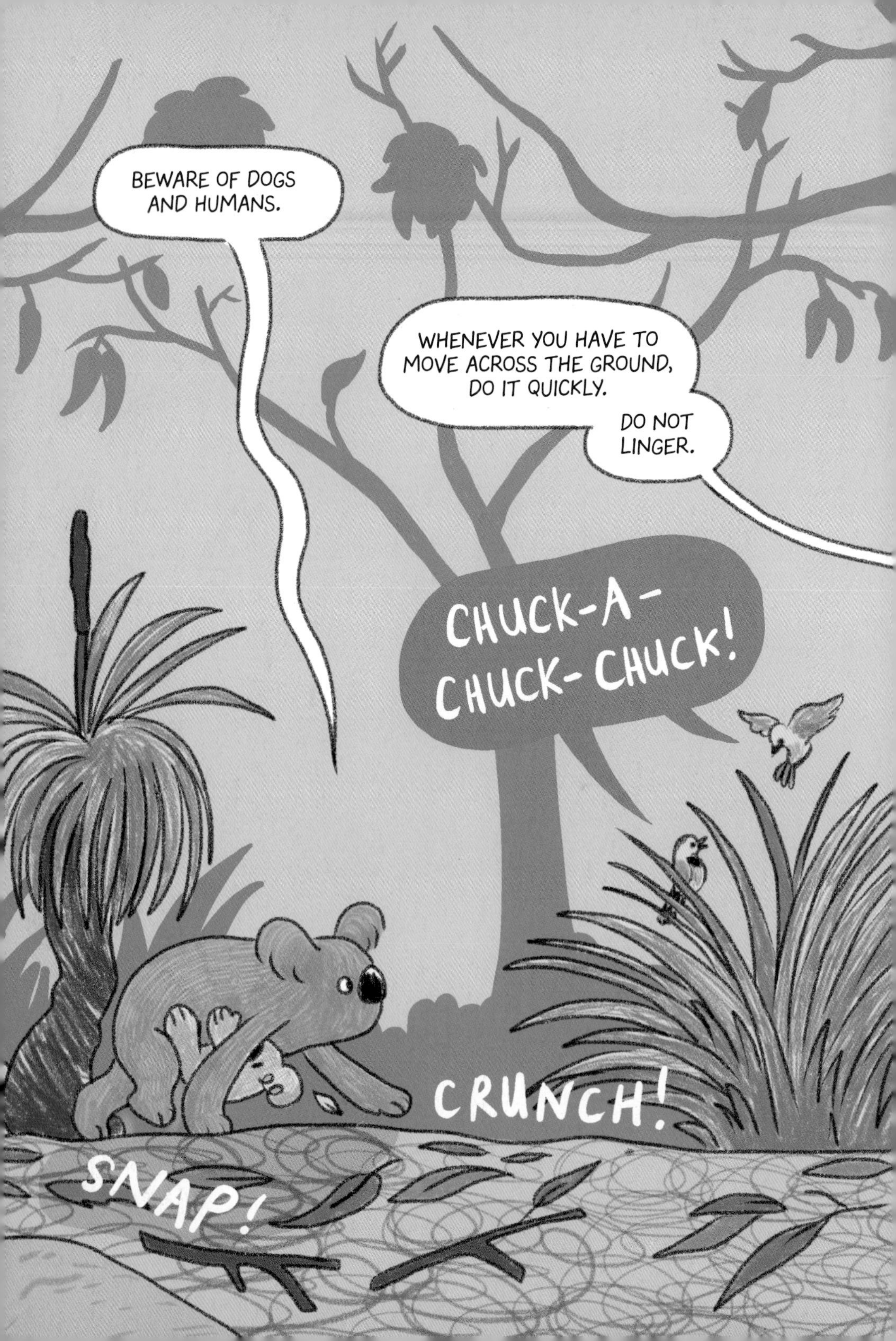
BEWARE OF DOGS AND HUMANS.
WHENEVER YOU HAVE TO MOVE ACROSS THE GROUND, DO IT QUICKLY.
DO NOT LINGER.
CHUCK-A-CHUCK-CHUCK!
CRUNCH!
SNAP!

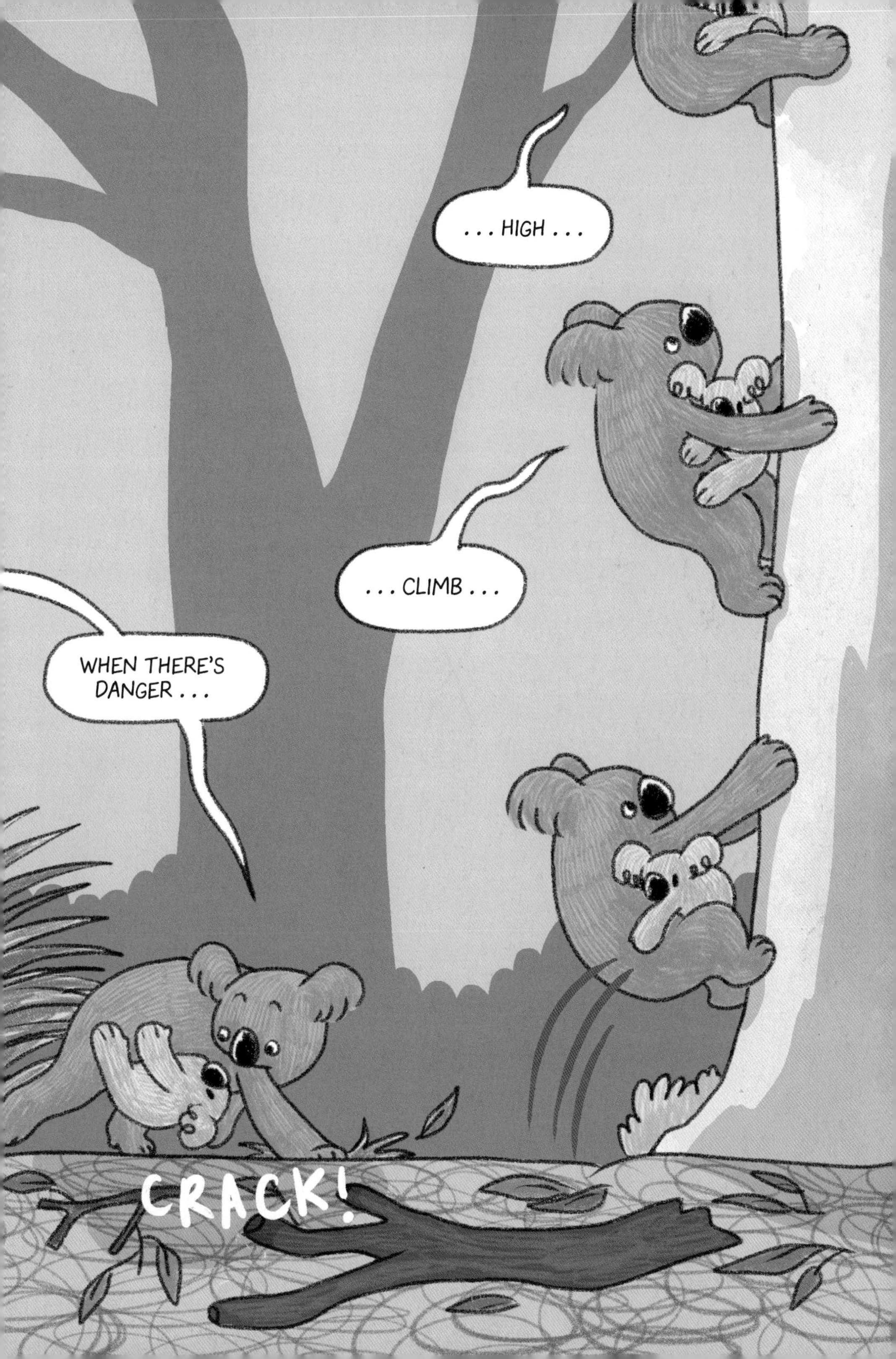

WHEN THERE'S DANGER . . .
. . . CLIMB . . .
. . . HIGH . . .
CRACK!

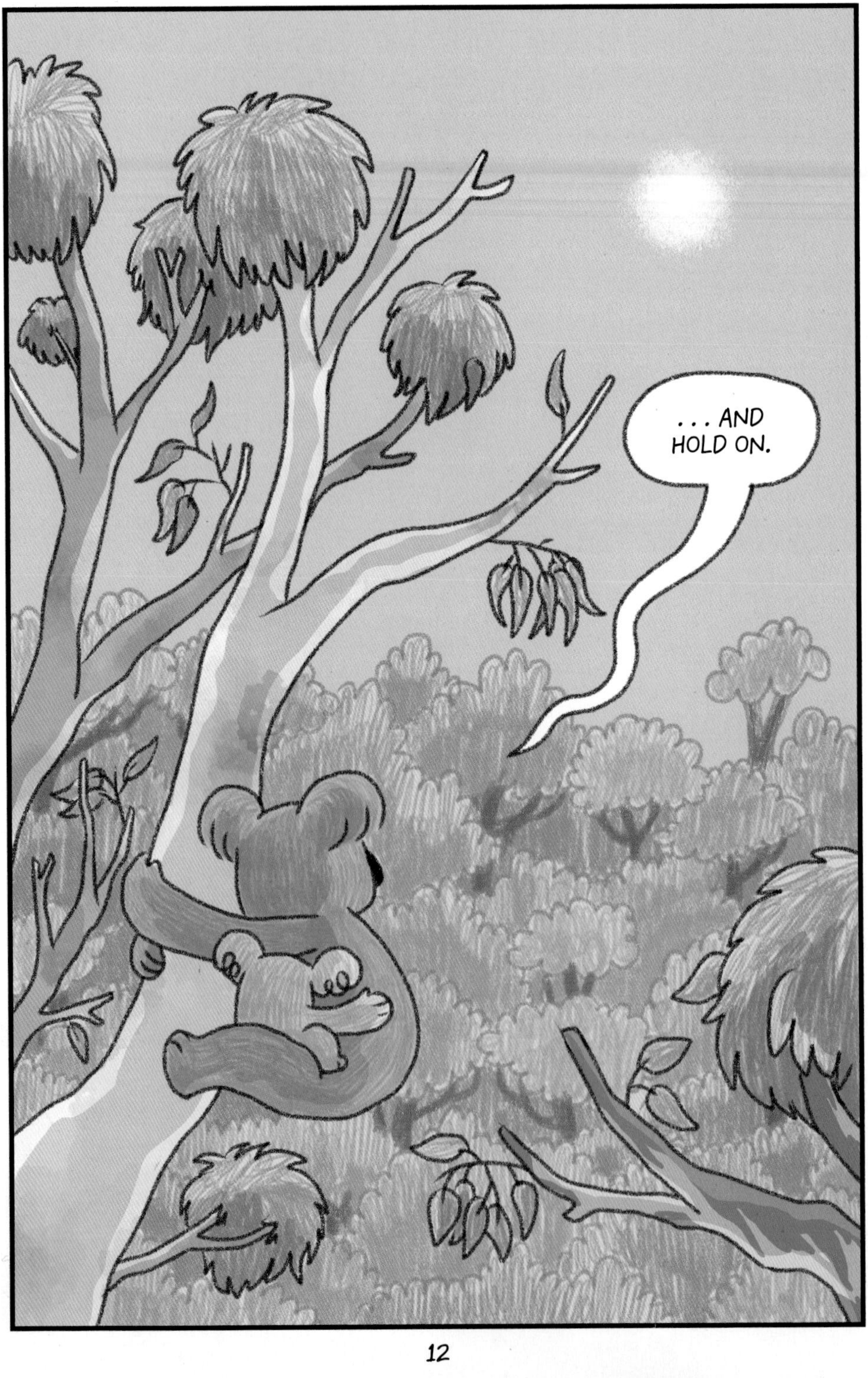
. . . AND HOLD ON.

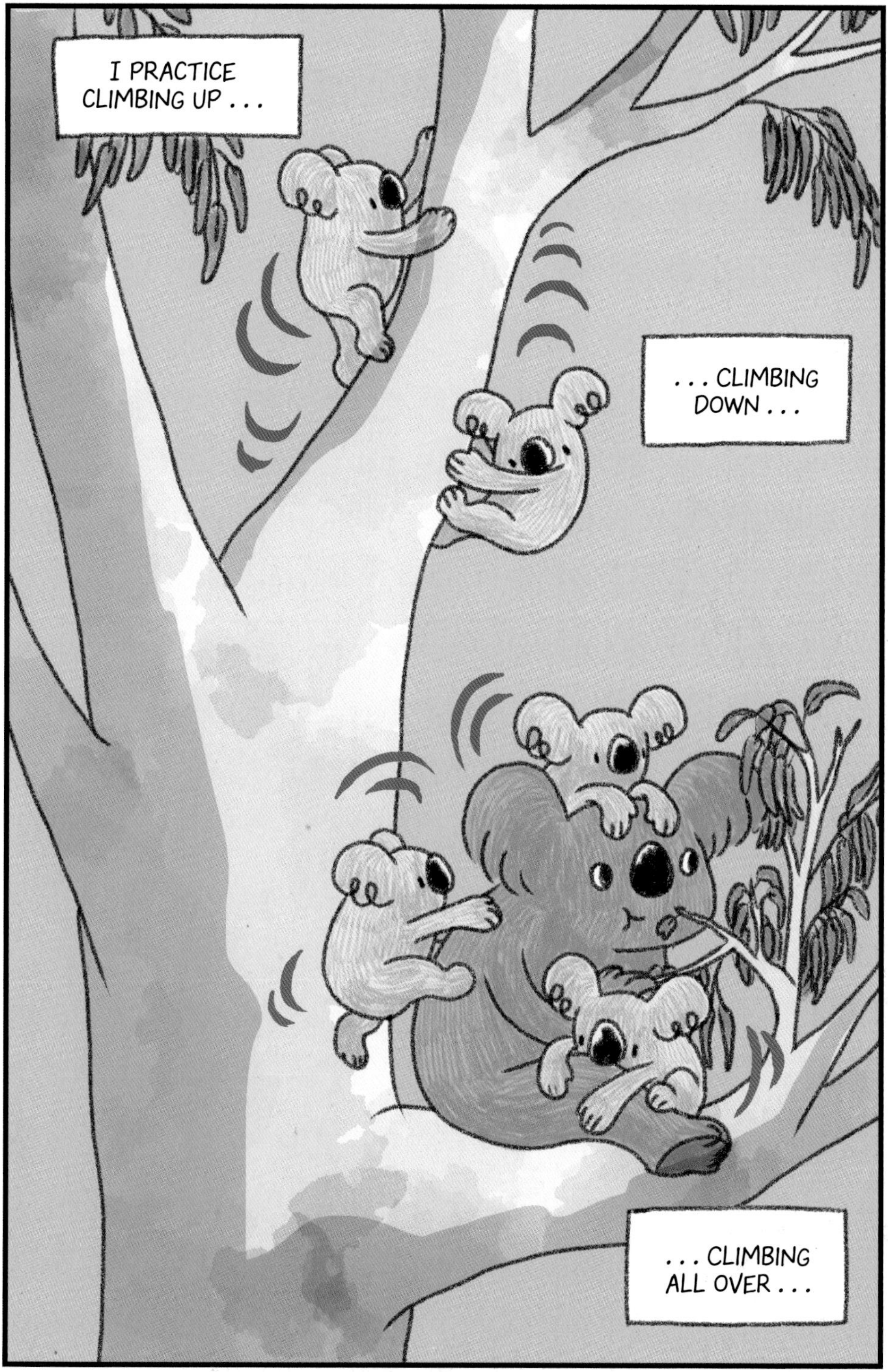
I PRACTICE CLIMBING UP . . .
. . . CLIMBING DOWN . . .
. . . CLIMBING ALL OVER . . .

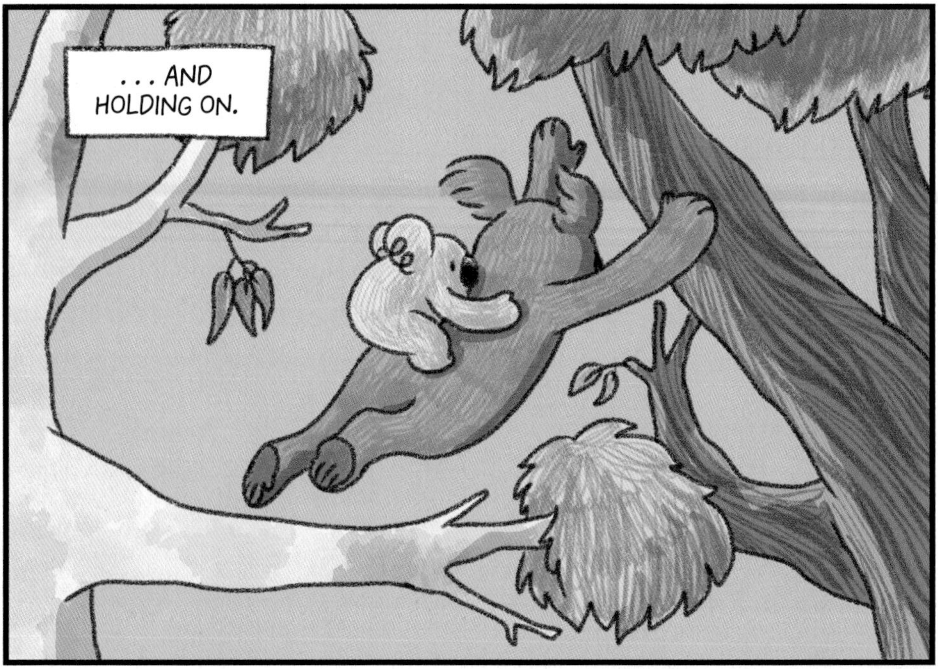
. . . AND
HOLDING ON.

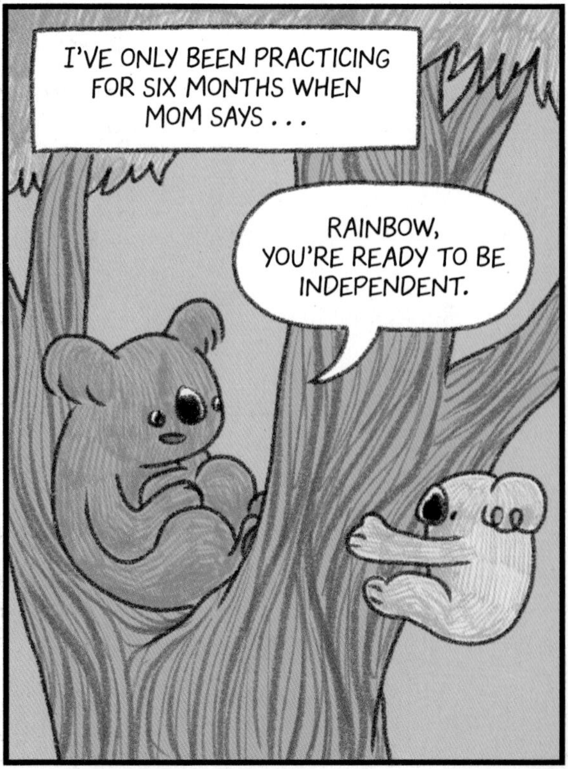
I'VE ONLY BEEN PRACTICING FOR SIX MONTHS WHEN MOM SAYS . . .
RAINBOW, YOU'RE READY TO BE INDEPENDENT.

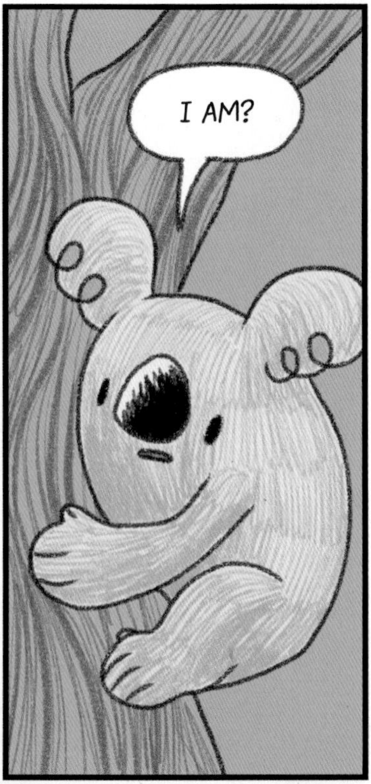
I AM?

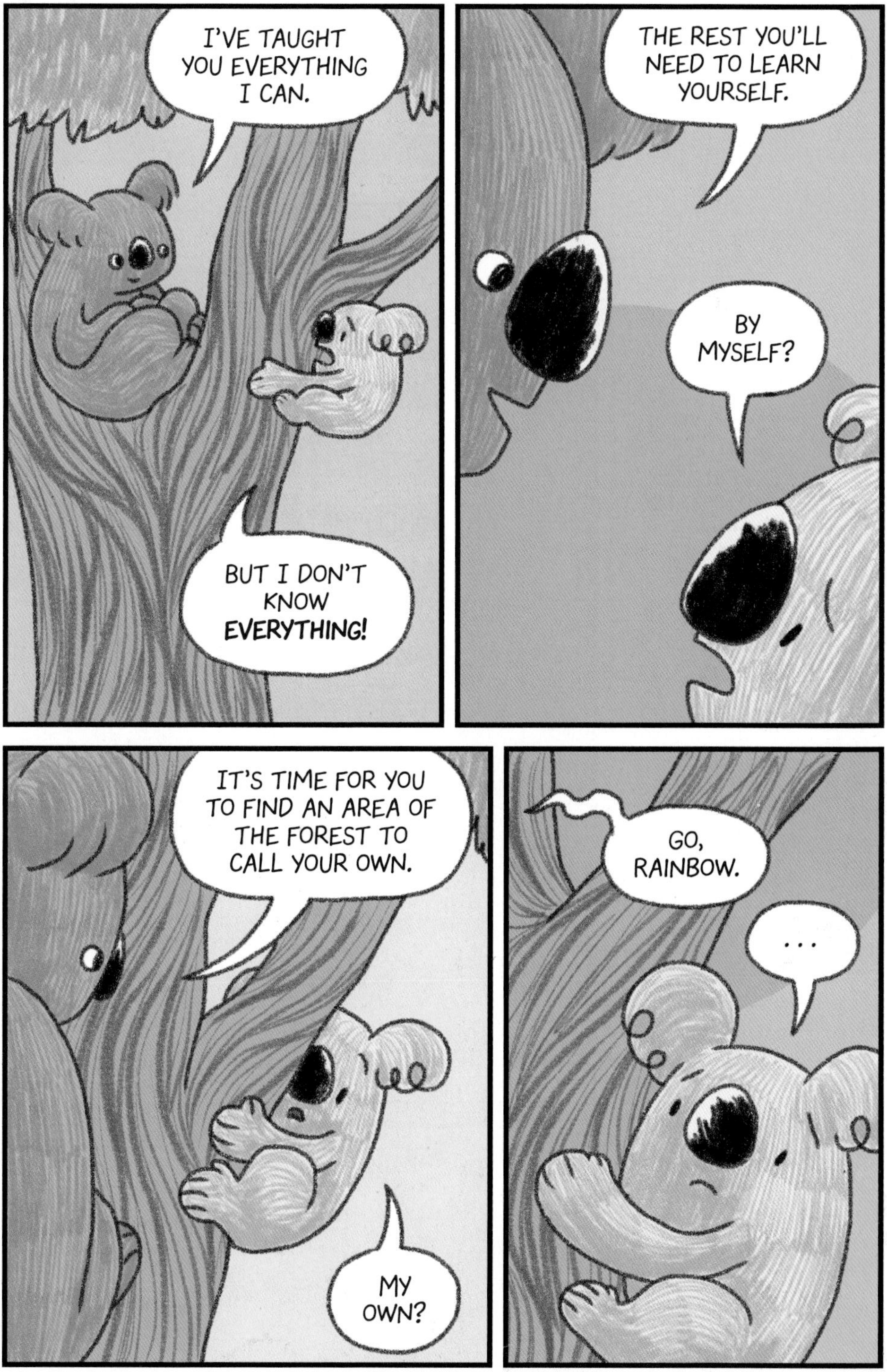
I'VE TAUGHT YOU EVERYTHING I CAN.
BUT I DON'T KNOW **EVERYTHING!**
THE REST YOU'LL NEED TO LEARN YOURSELF.
BY MYSELF?
IT'S TIME FOR YOU TO FIND AN AREA OF THE FOREST TO CALL YOUR OWN.
MY OWN?
GO, RAINBOW.
. . .

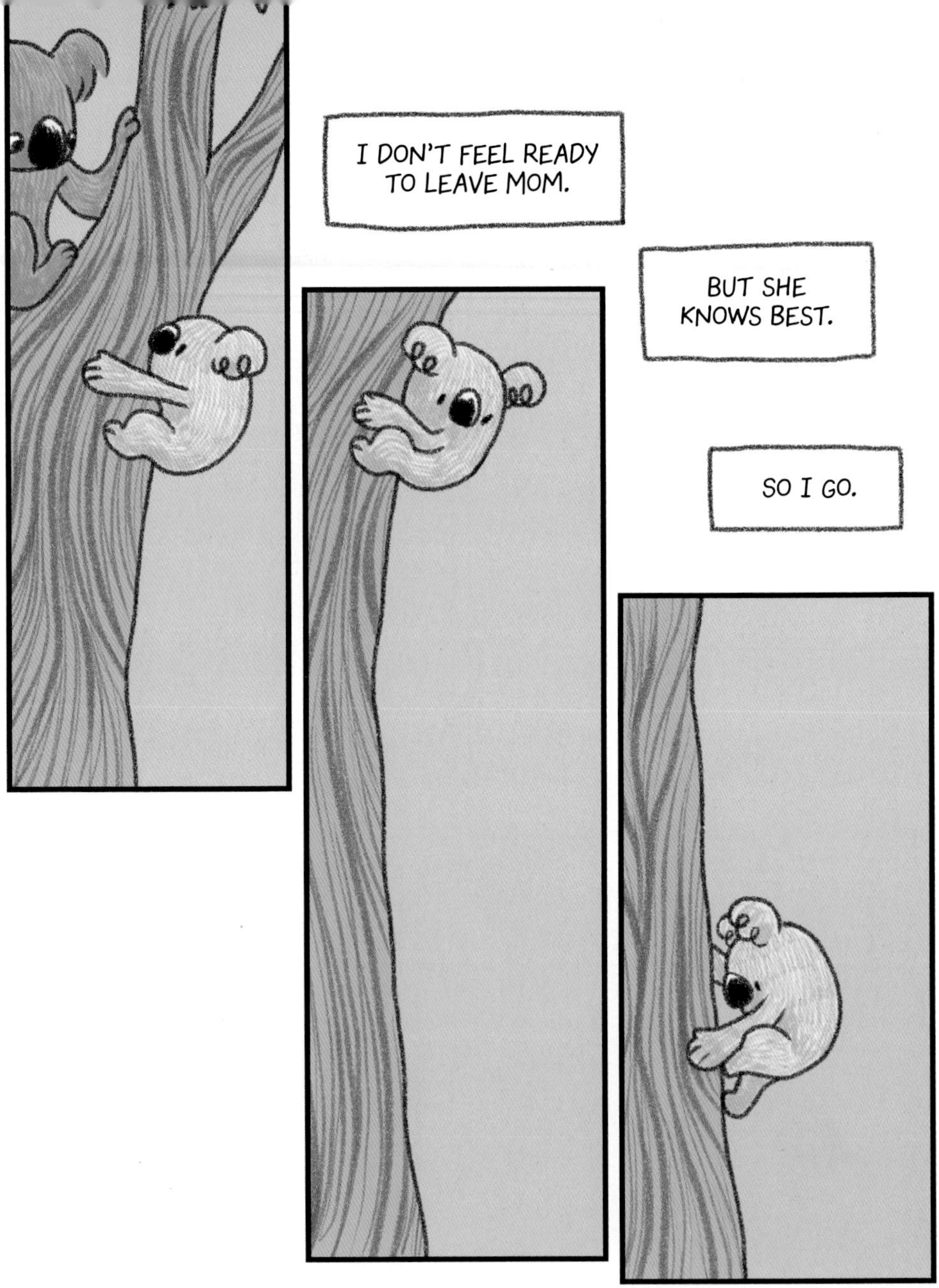
I DON'T FEEL READY TO LEAVE MOM.
BUT SHE KNOWS BEST.
SO I GO.

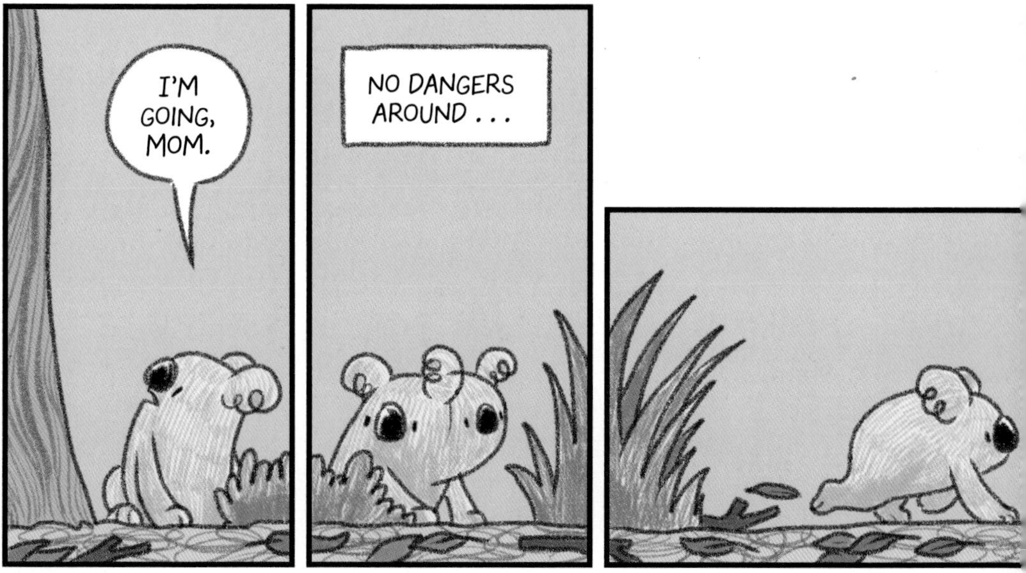
I'M GOING, MOM.
NO DANGERS AROUND . . .

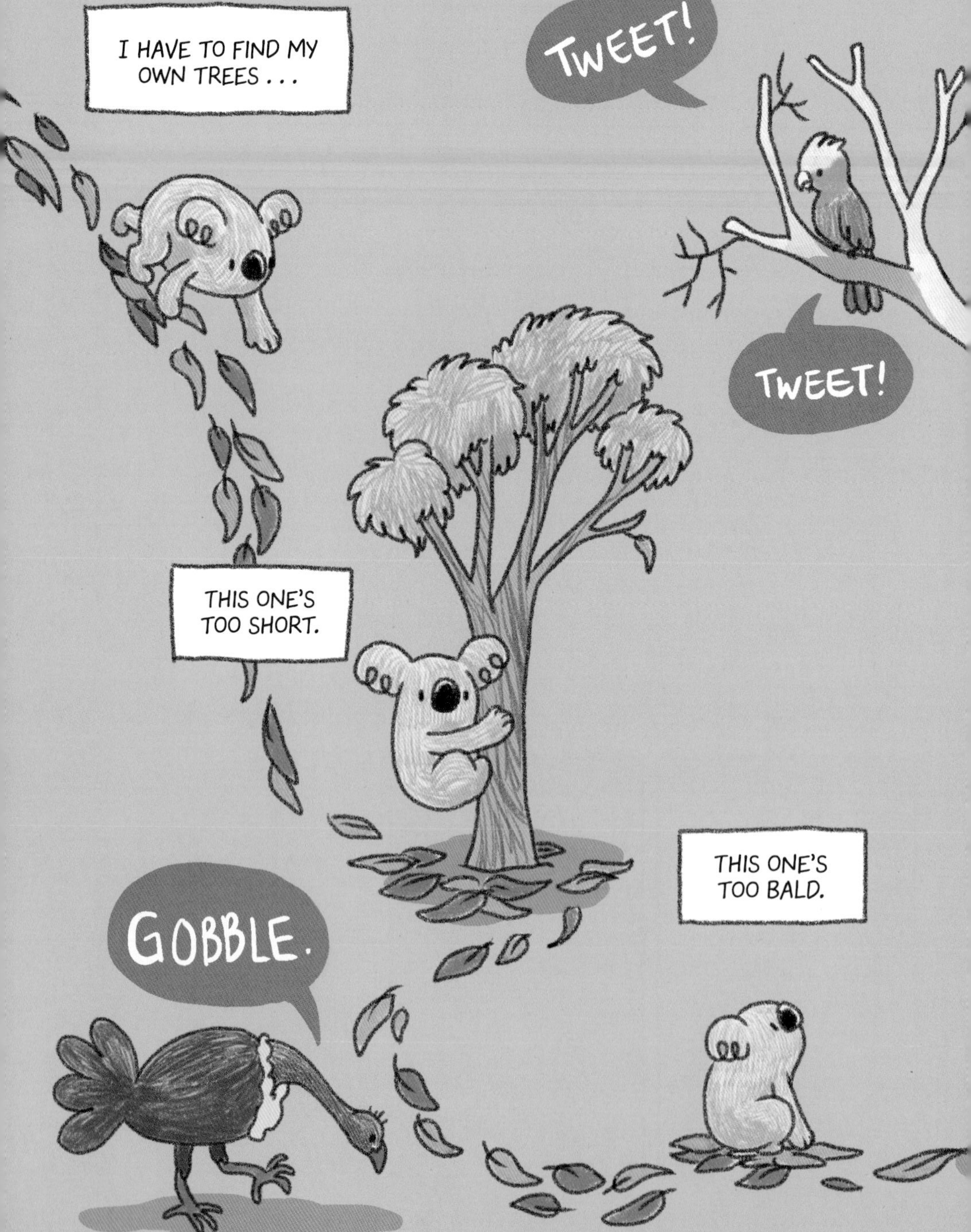
I HAVE TO FIND MY OWN TREES . . .
TWEET!
TWEET!
THIS ONE'S TOO SHORT.
THIS ONE'S TOO BALD.
GOBBLE.

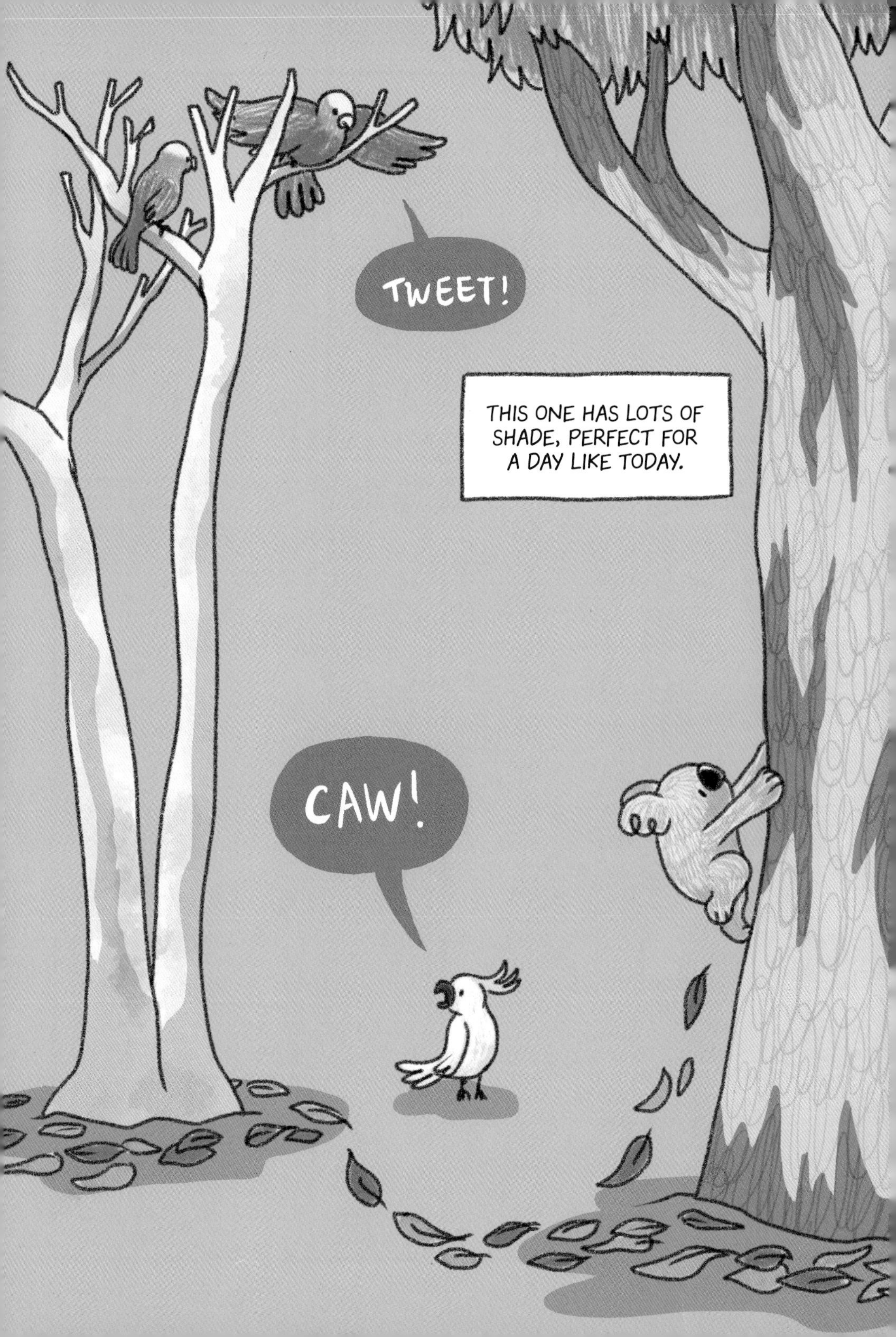
TWEET!
THIS ONE HAS LOTS OF SHADE, PERFECT FOR A DAY LIKE TODAY.
CAW!

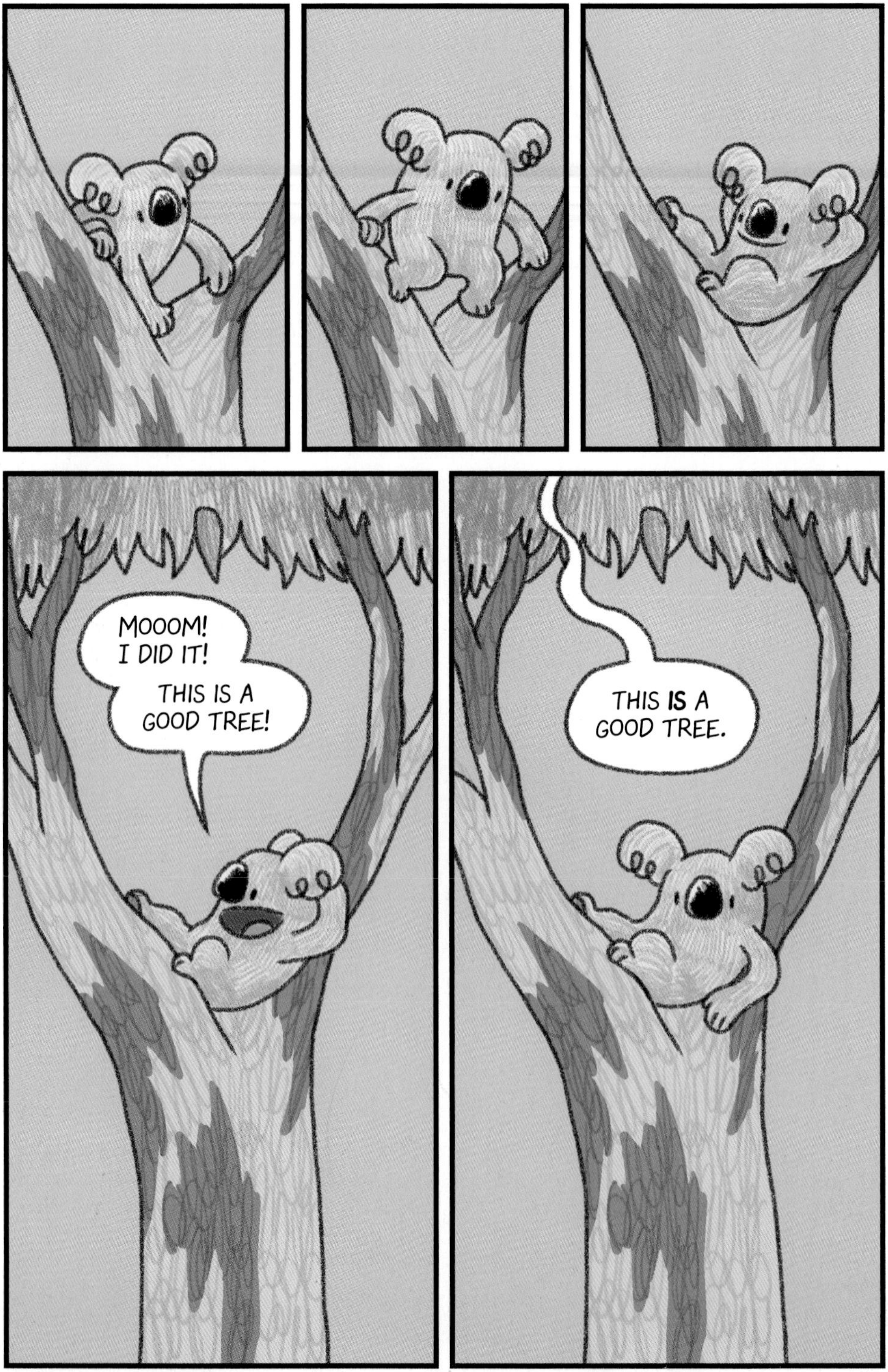
MOOOM! I DID IT!
THIS IS A GOOD TREE!
THIS **IS** A GOOD TREE.

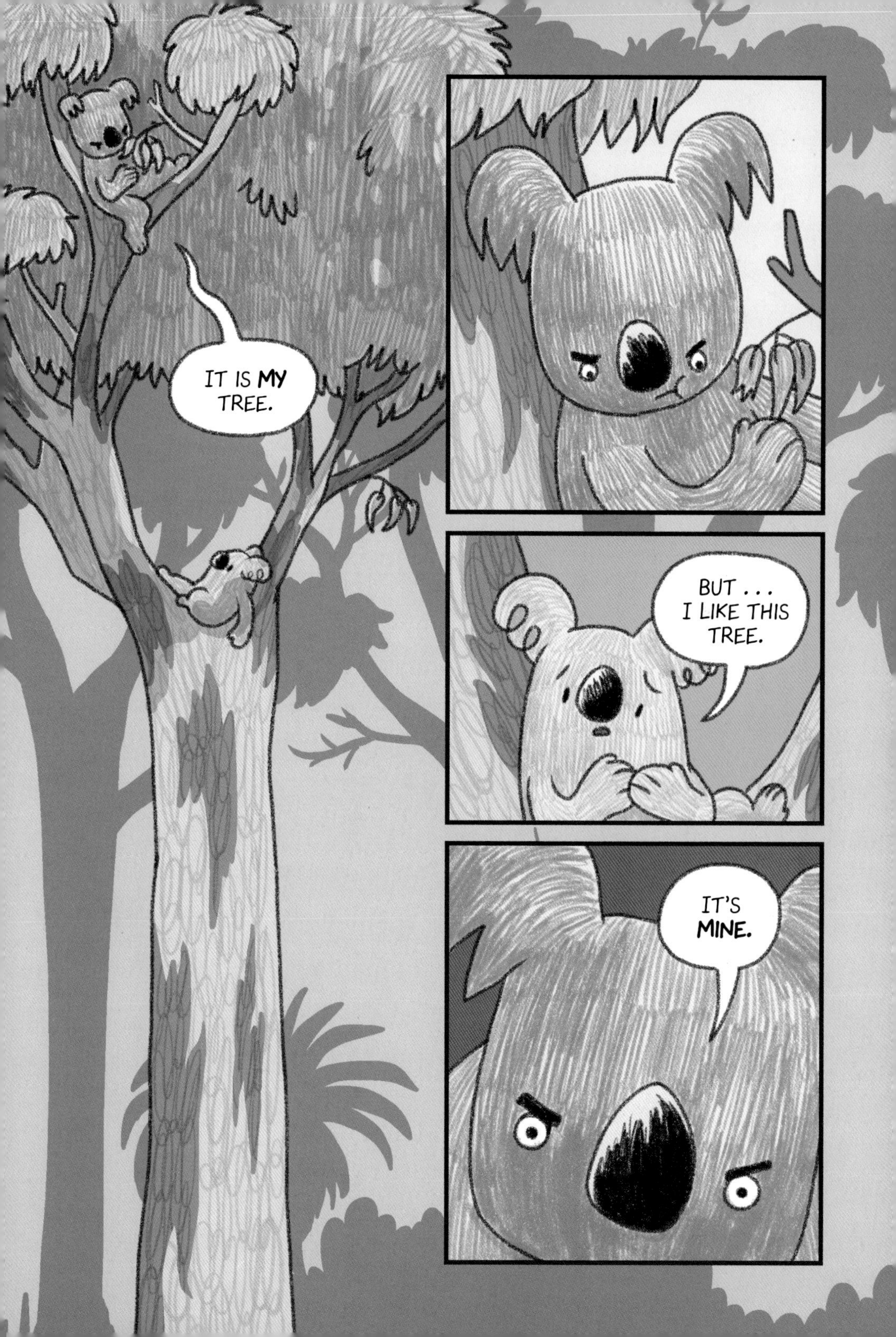
IT IS **MY** TREE.
BUT . . . I LIKE THIS TREE.
IT'S **MINE.**

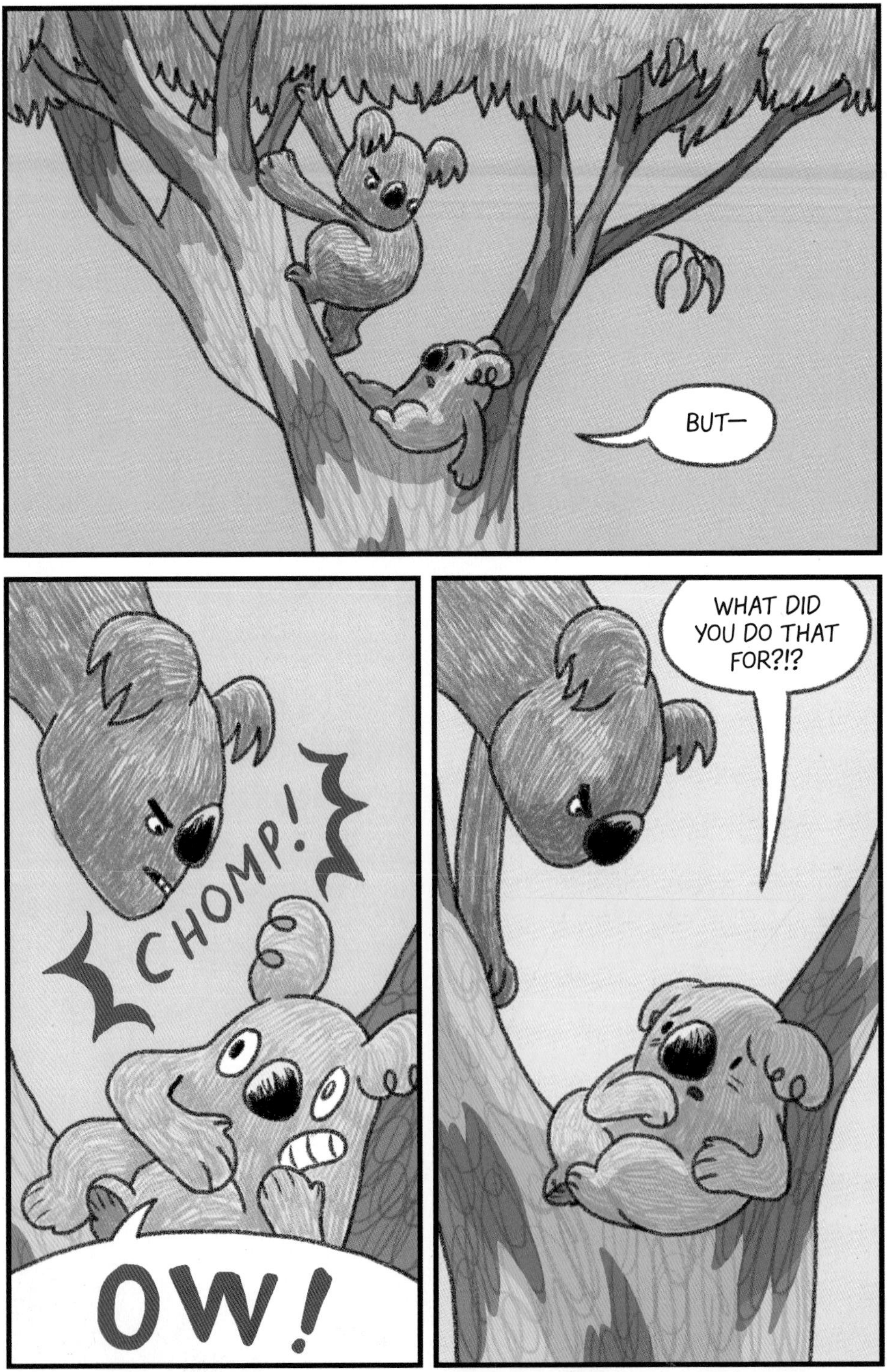
BUT—
CHOMP!
OW!
WHAT DID YOU DO THAT FOR?!?

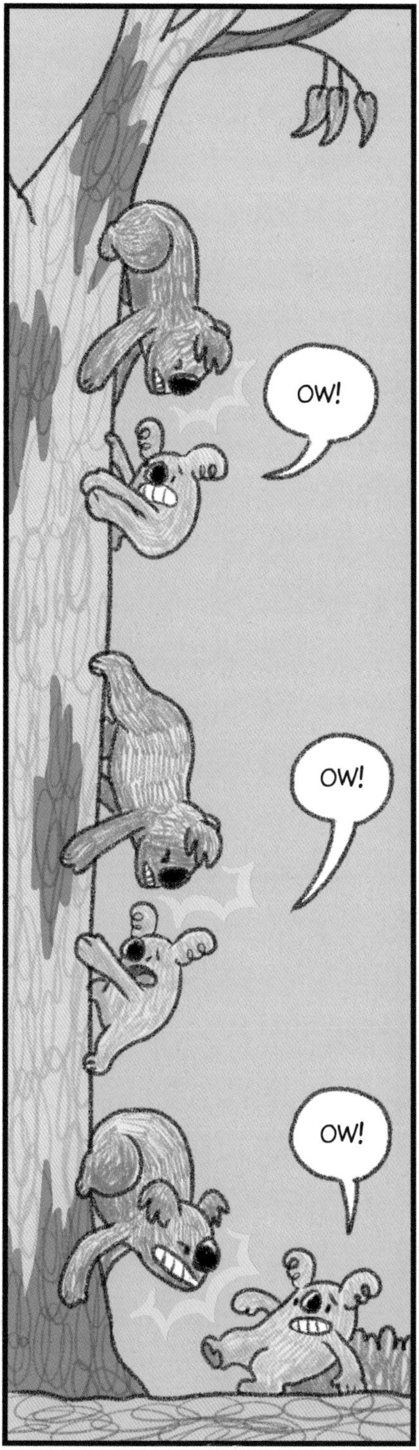
OW!
OW!
OW!

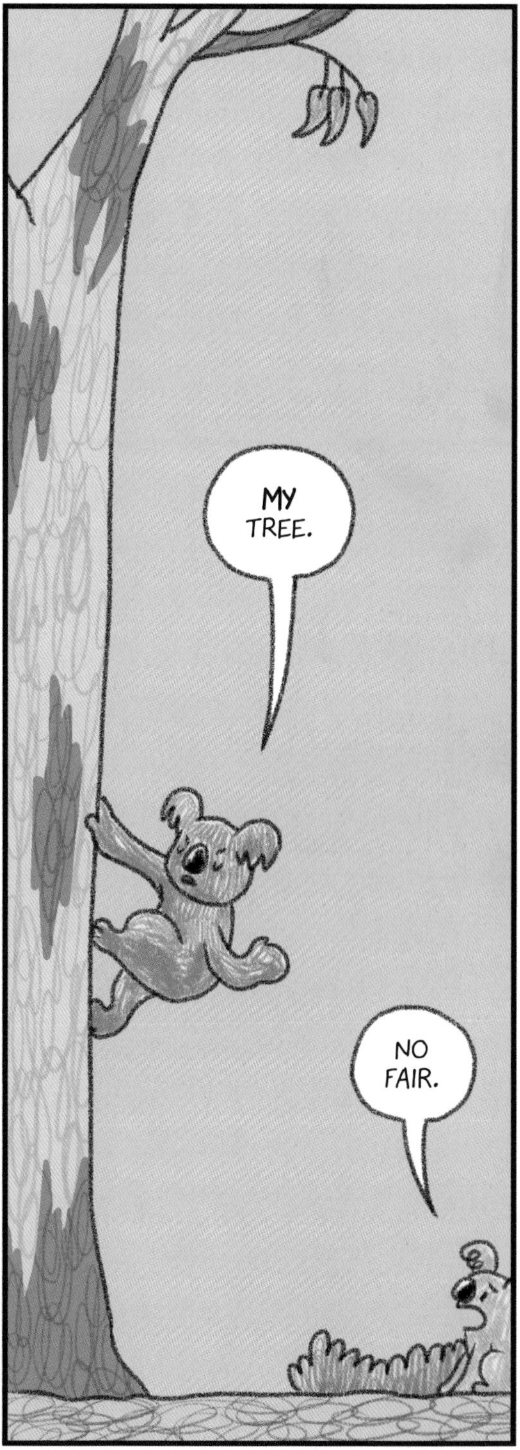
MY TREE.
NO FAIR.

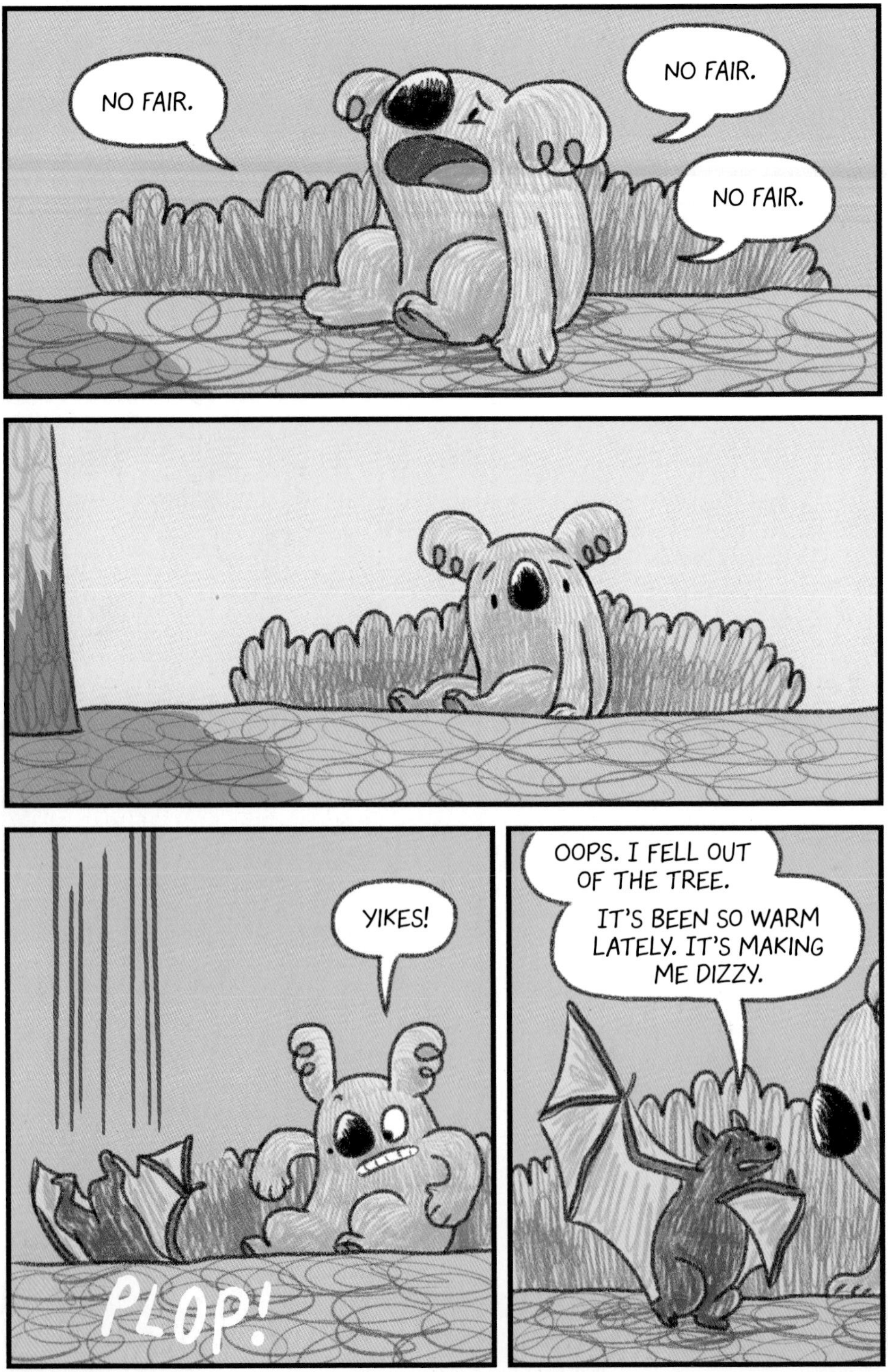
NO FAIR.
NO FAIR.
NO FAIR.
YIKES!
PLOP!
OOPS. I FELL OUT OF THE TREE.
IT'S BEEN SO WARM LATELY. IT'S MAKING ME DIZZY.

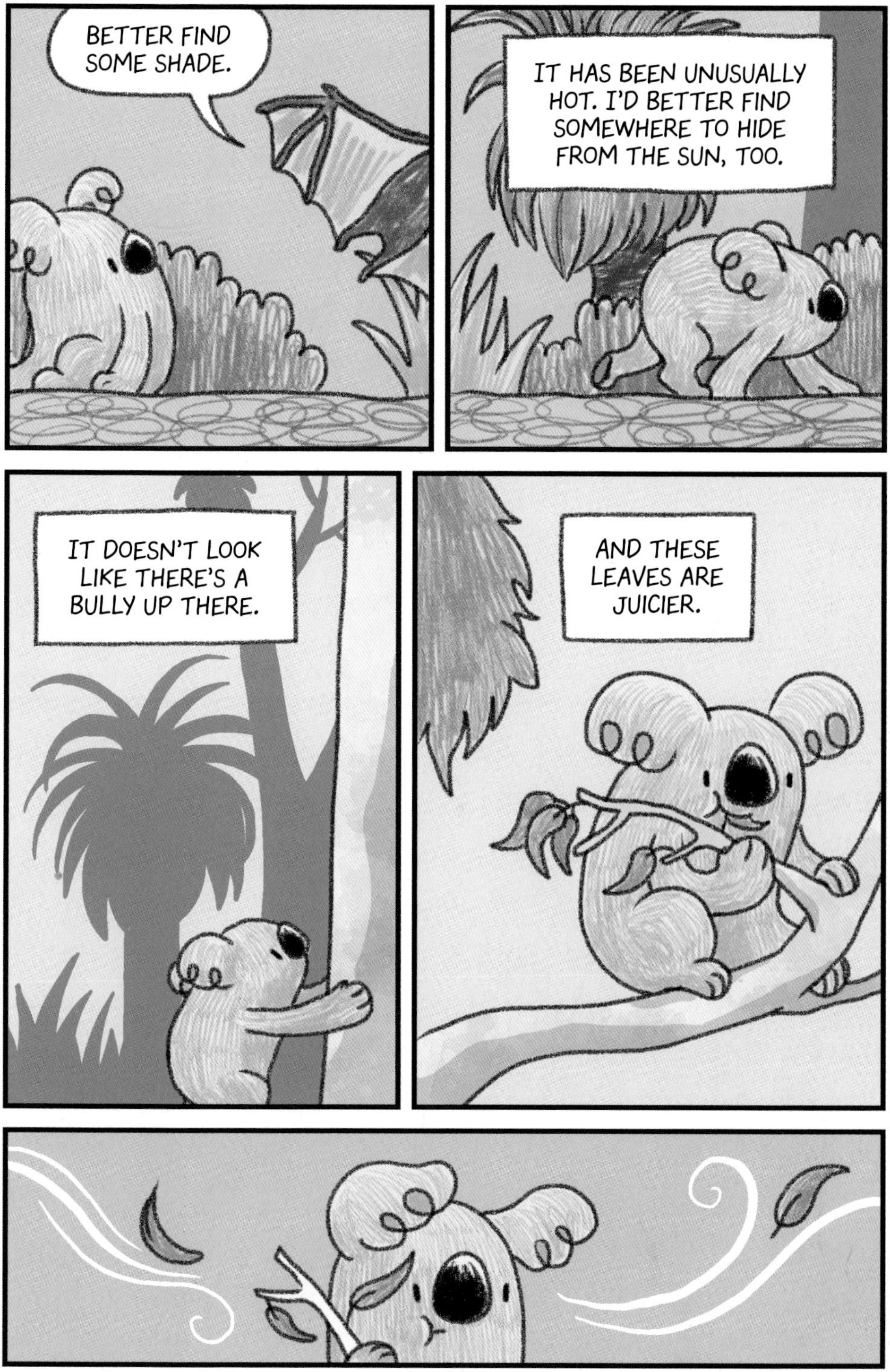
BETTER FIND SOME SHADE.
IT HAS BEEN UNUSUALLY HOT. I'D BETTER FIND SOMEWHERE TO HIDE FROM THE SUN, TOO.
IT DOESN'T LOOK LIKE THERE'S A BULLY UP THERE.
AND THESE LEAVES ARE JUICIER.

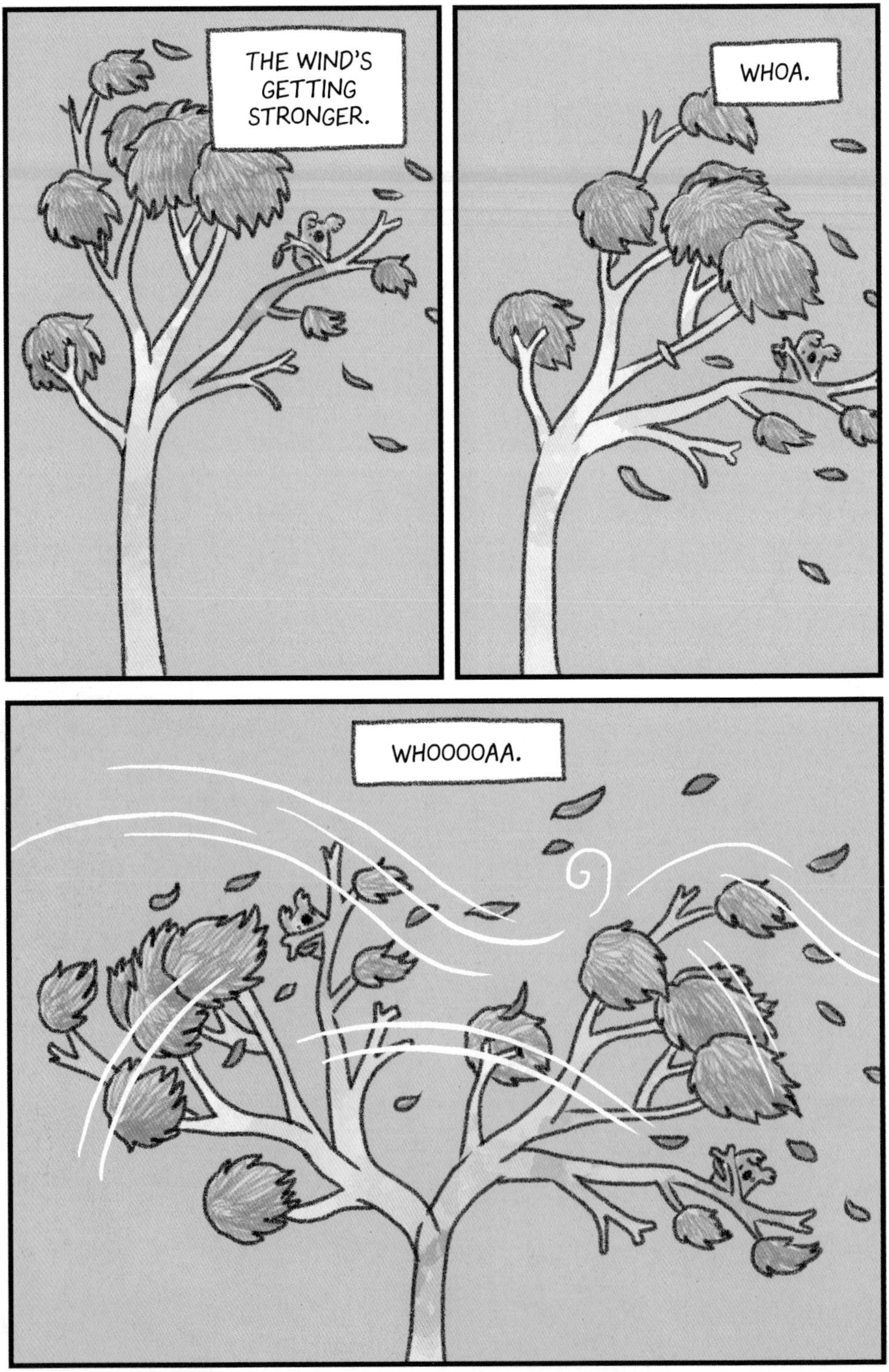
THE WIND'S GETTING STRONGER.
WHOA.
WHOOOOAA.

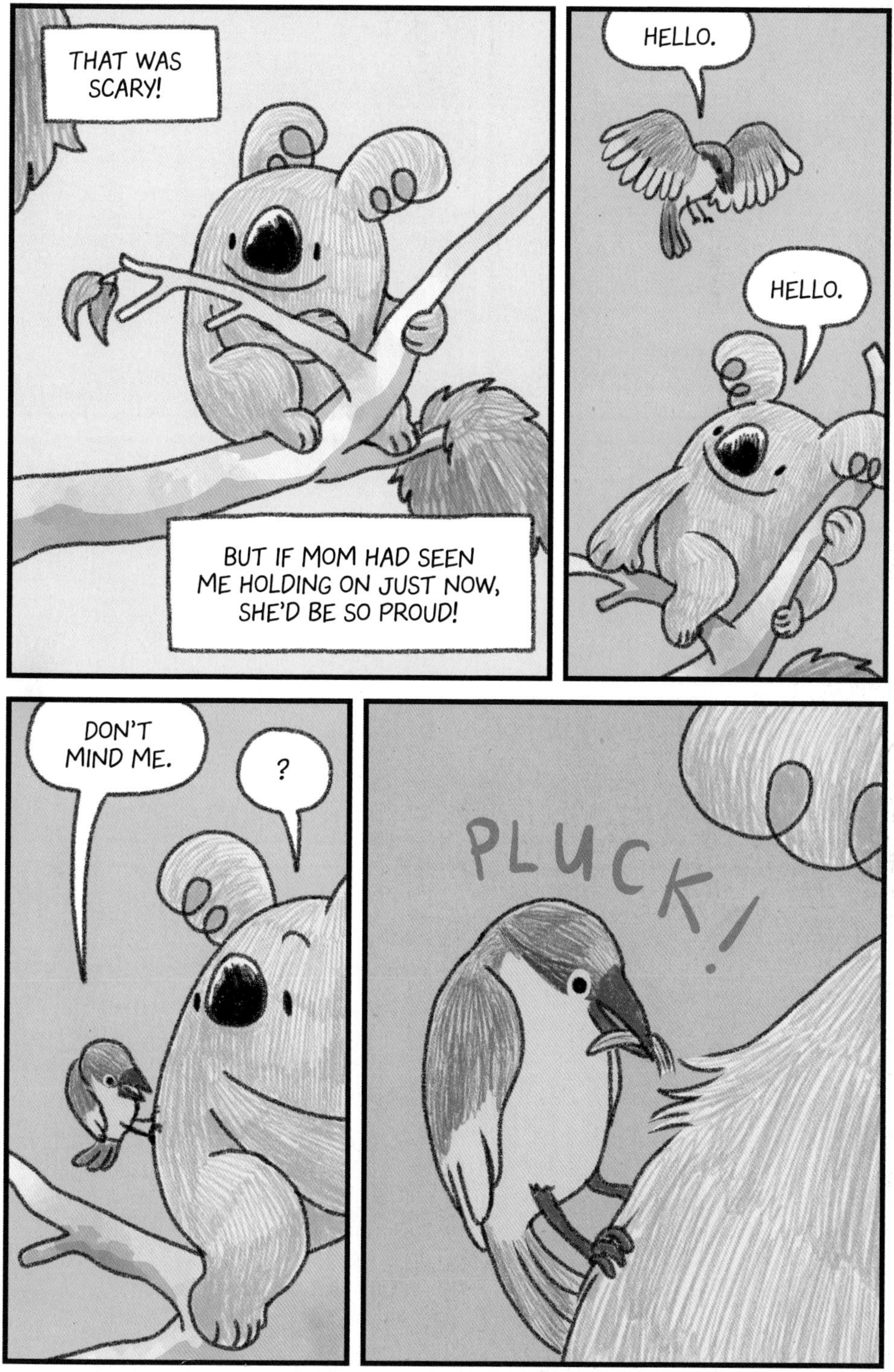
THAT WAS SCARY!
BUT IF MOM HAD SEEN ME HOLDING ON JUST NOW, SHE'D BE SO PROUD!
HELLO.
HELLO.
DON'T MIND ME.
?
PLUCK!

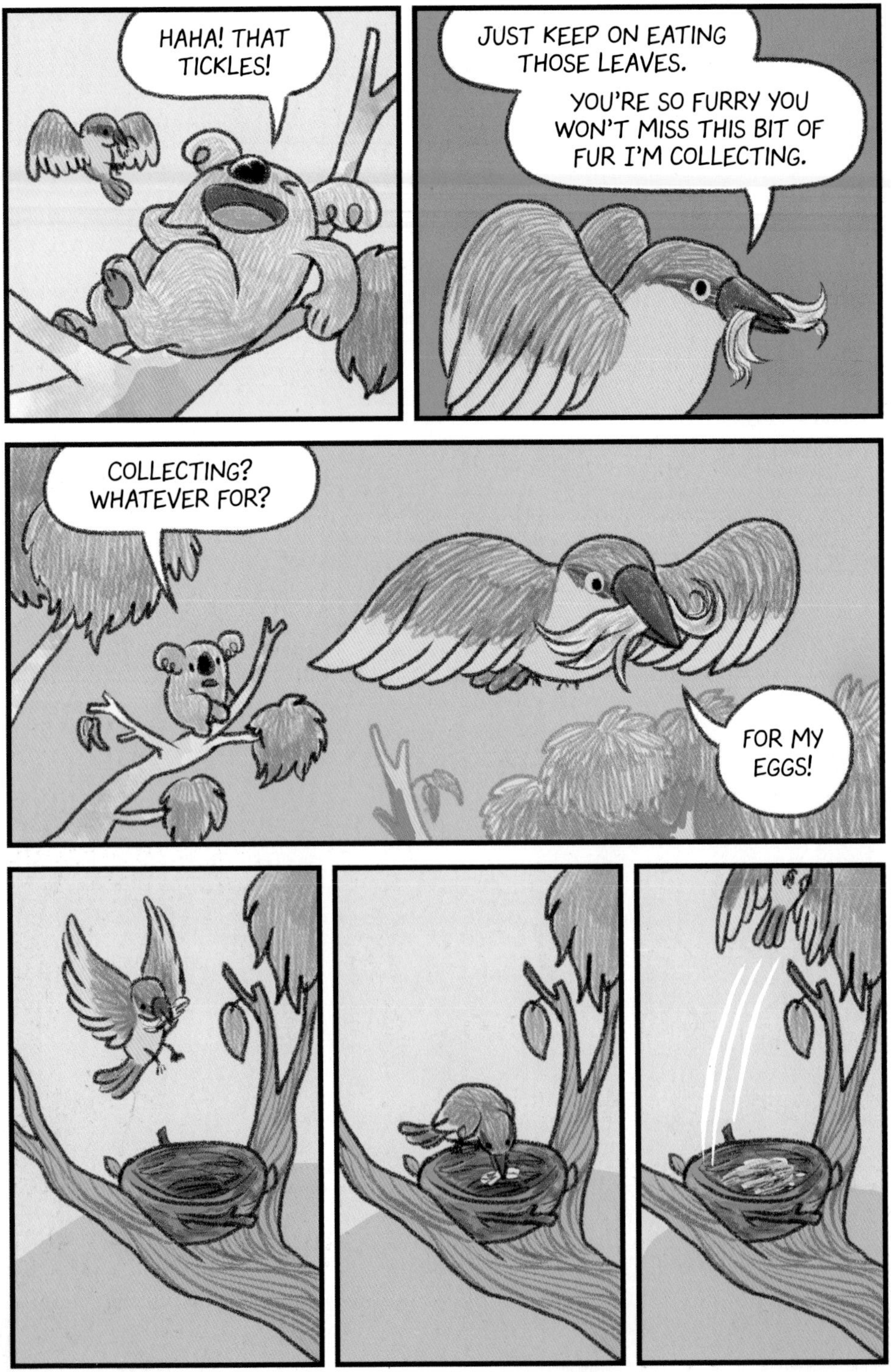
HAHA! THAT TICKLES!
JUST KEEP ON EATING THOSE LEAVES.
YOU'RE SO FURRY YOU WON'T MISS THIS BIT OF FUR I'M COLLECTING.
COLLECTING? WHATEVER FOR?
FOR MY EGGS!

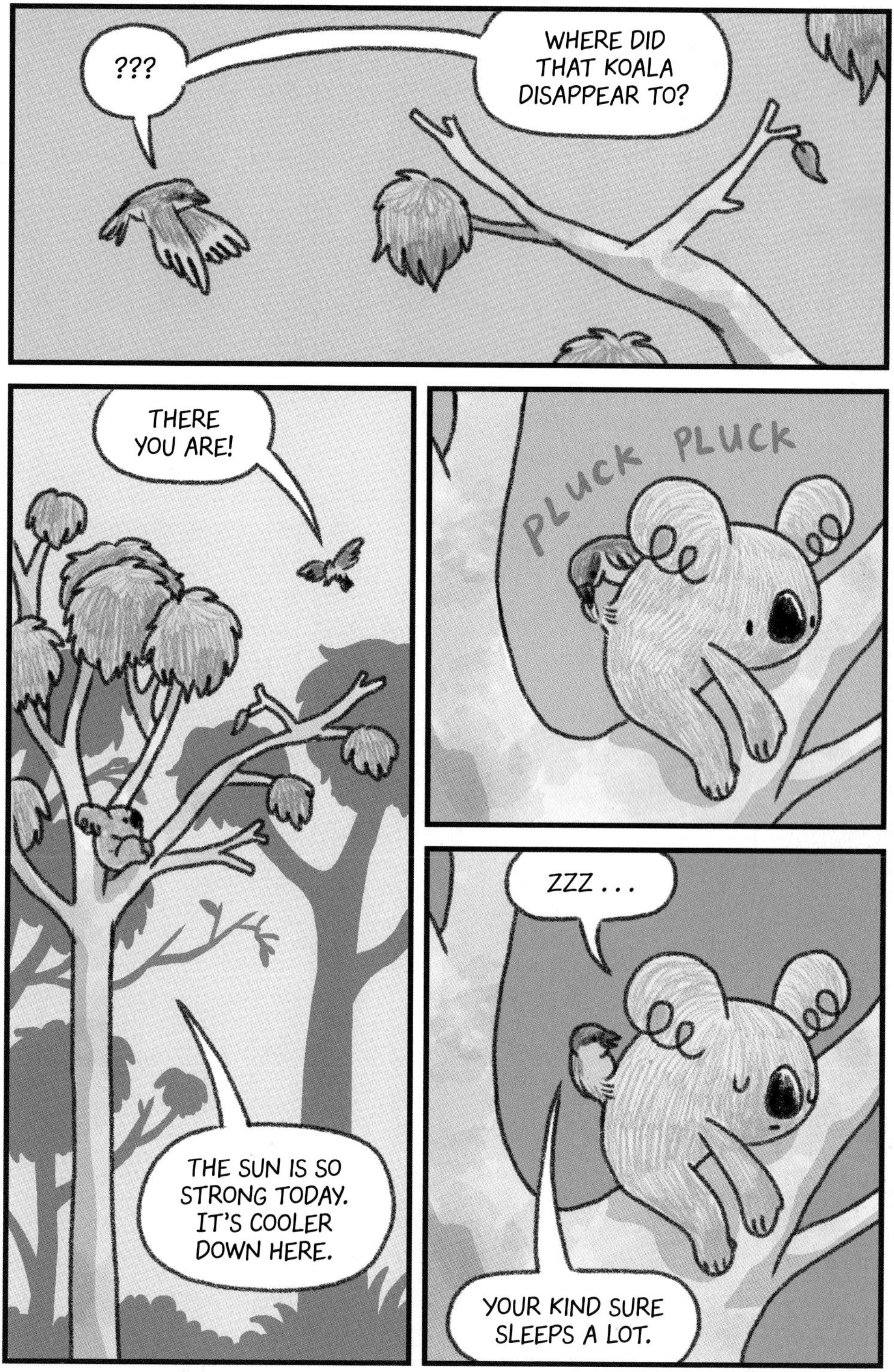
???
WHERE DID THAT KOALA DISAPPEAR TO?
THERE YOU ARE!
THE SUN IS SO STRONG TODAY. IT'S COOLER DOWN HERE.
PLUCK PLUCK
ZZZ . . .
YOUR KIND SURE SLEEPS A LOT.

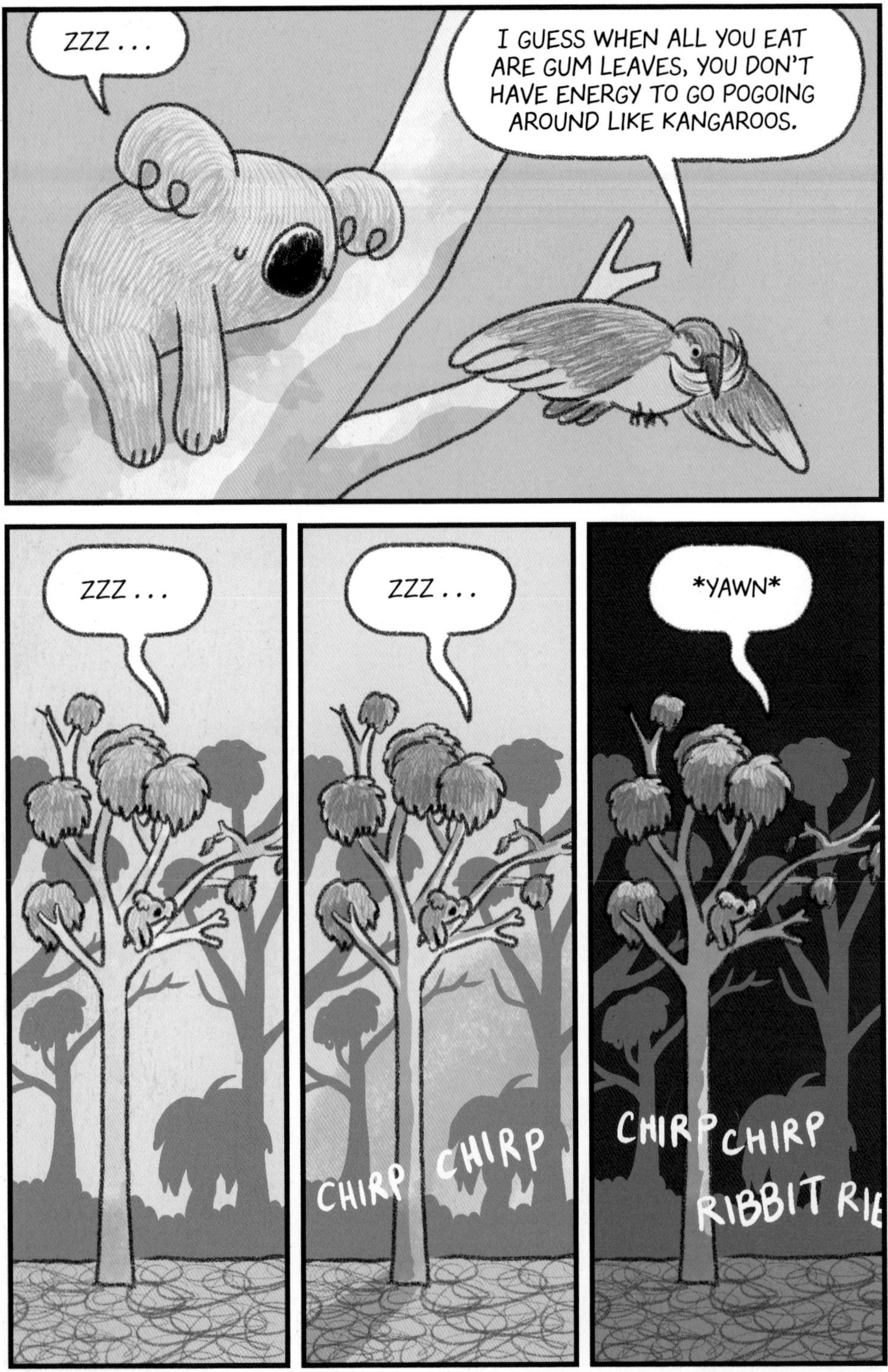
ZZZ . . .
I GUESS WHEN ALL YOU EAT ARE GUM LEAVES, YOU DON'T HAVE ENERGY TO GO POGOING AROUND LIKE KANGAROOS.
ZZZ . . .
ZZZ . . .
CHIRP CHIRP
YAWN
CHIRP CHIRP
RIBBIT

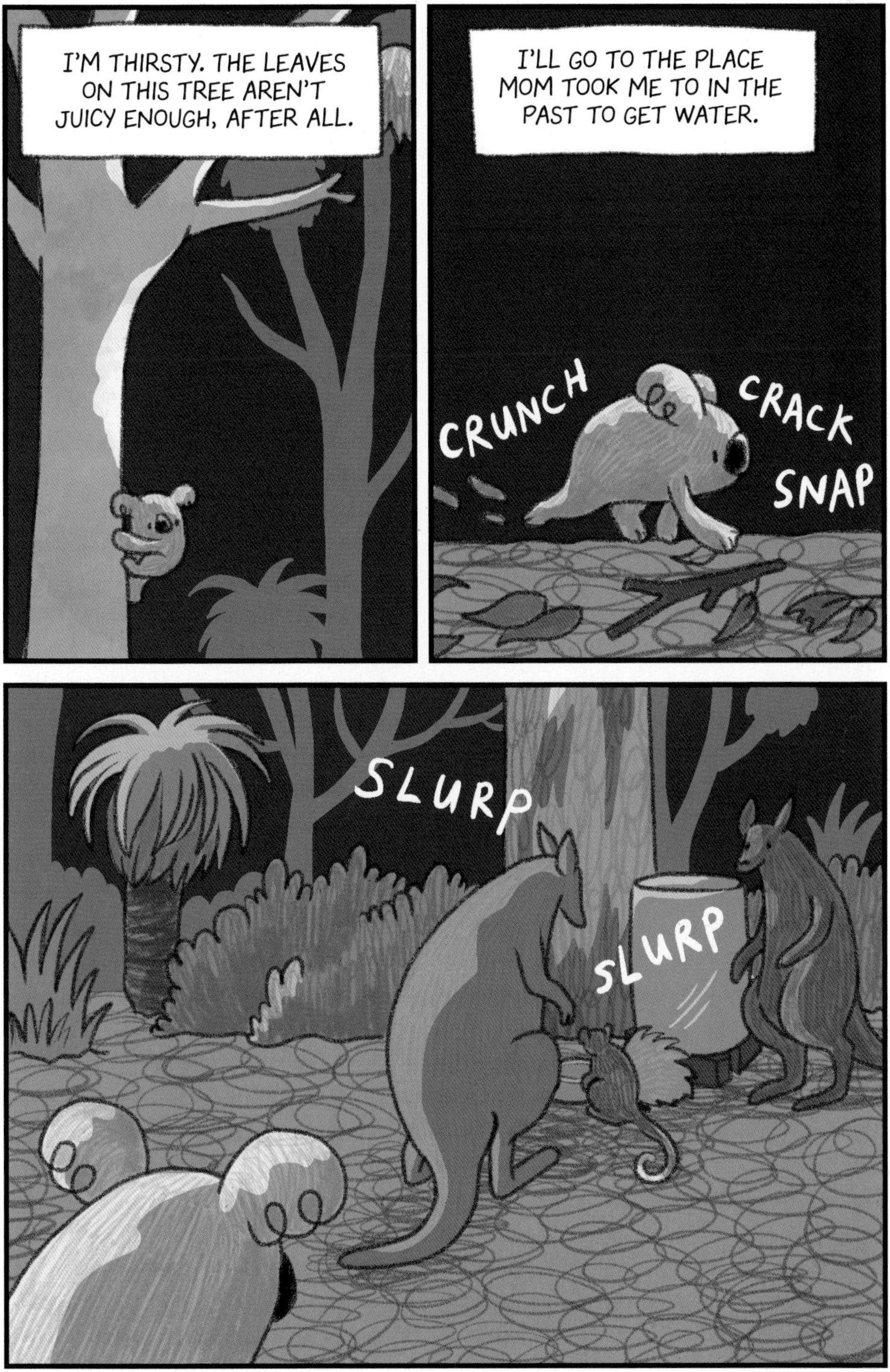
I'M THIRSTY. THE LEAVES ON THIS TREE AREN'T JUICY ENOUGH, AFTER ALL.
I'LL GO TO THE PLACE MOM TOOK ME TO IN THE PAST TO GET WATER.
CRUNCH
CRACK
SNAP
SLURP
SLURP

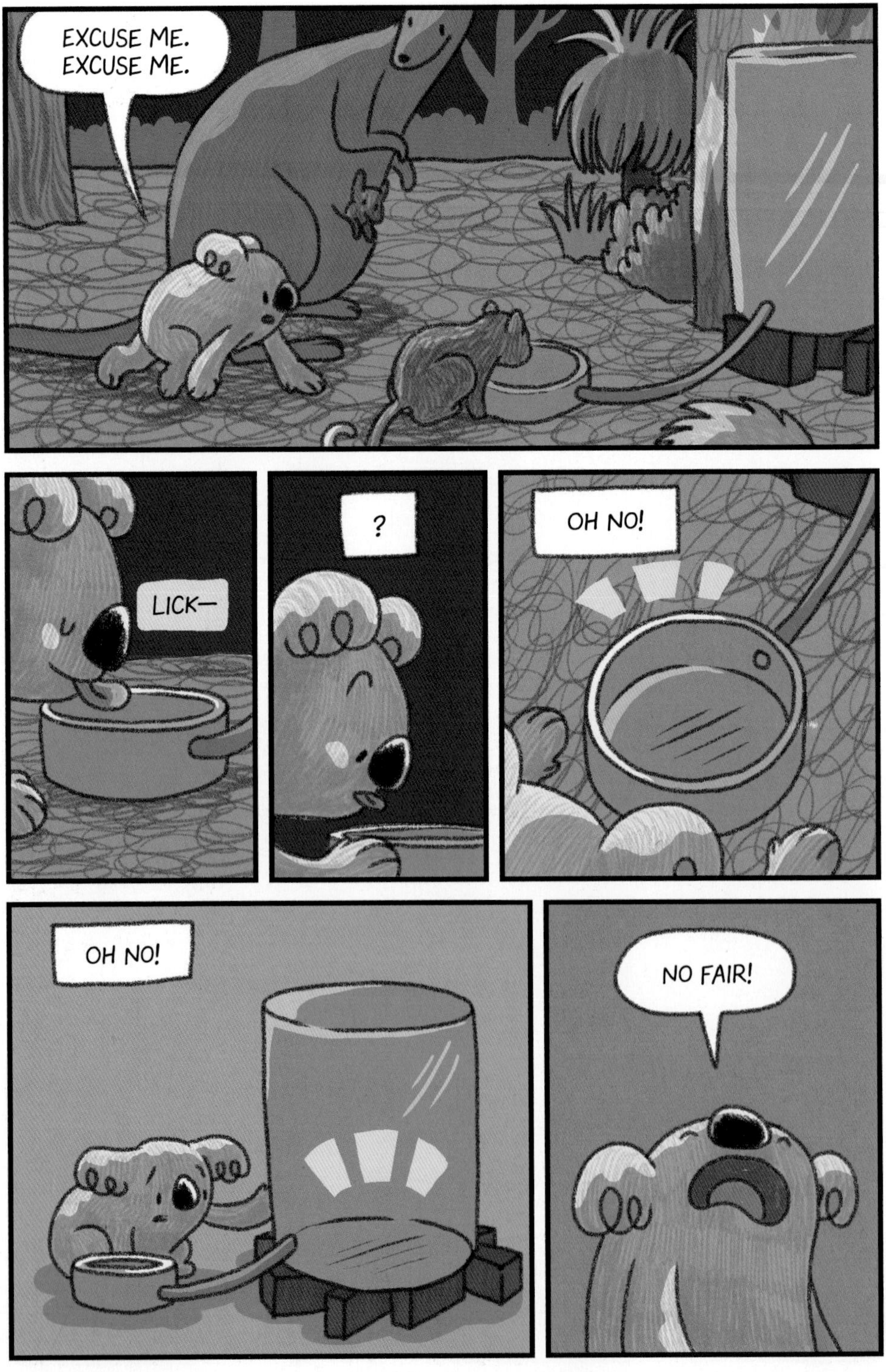
EXCUSE ME.
EXCUSE ME.
LICK—
?
OH NO!
OH NO!
NO FAIR!

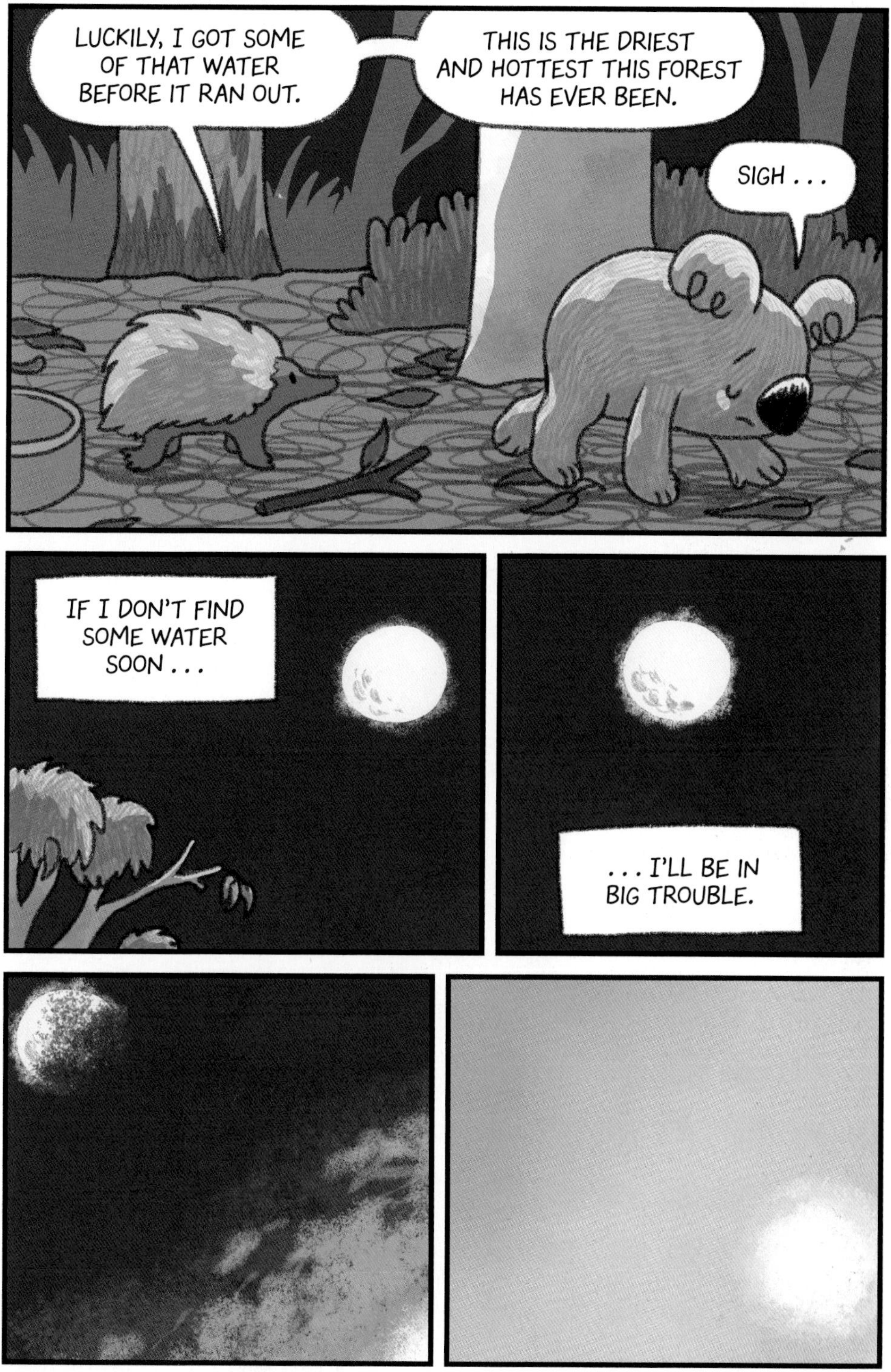
LUCKILY, I GOT SOME OF THAT WATER BEFORE IT RAN OUT.
THIS IS THE DRIEST AND HOTTEST THIS FOREST HAS EVER BEEN.
SIGH . . .
IF I DON'T FIND SOME WATER SOON . . .
. . . I'LL BE IN BIG TROUBLE.

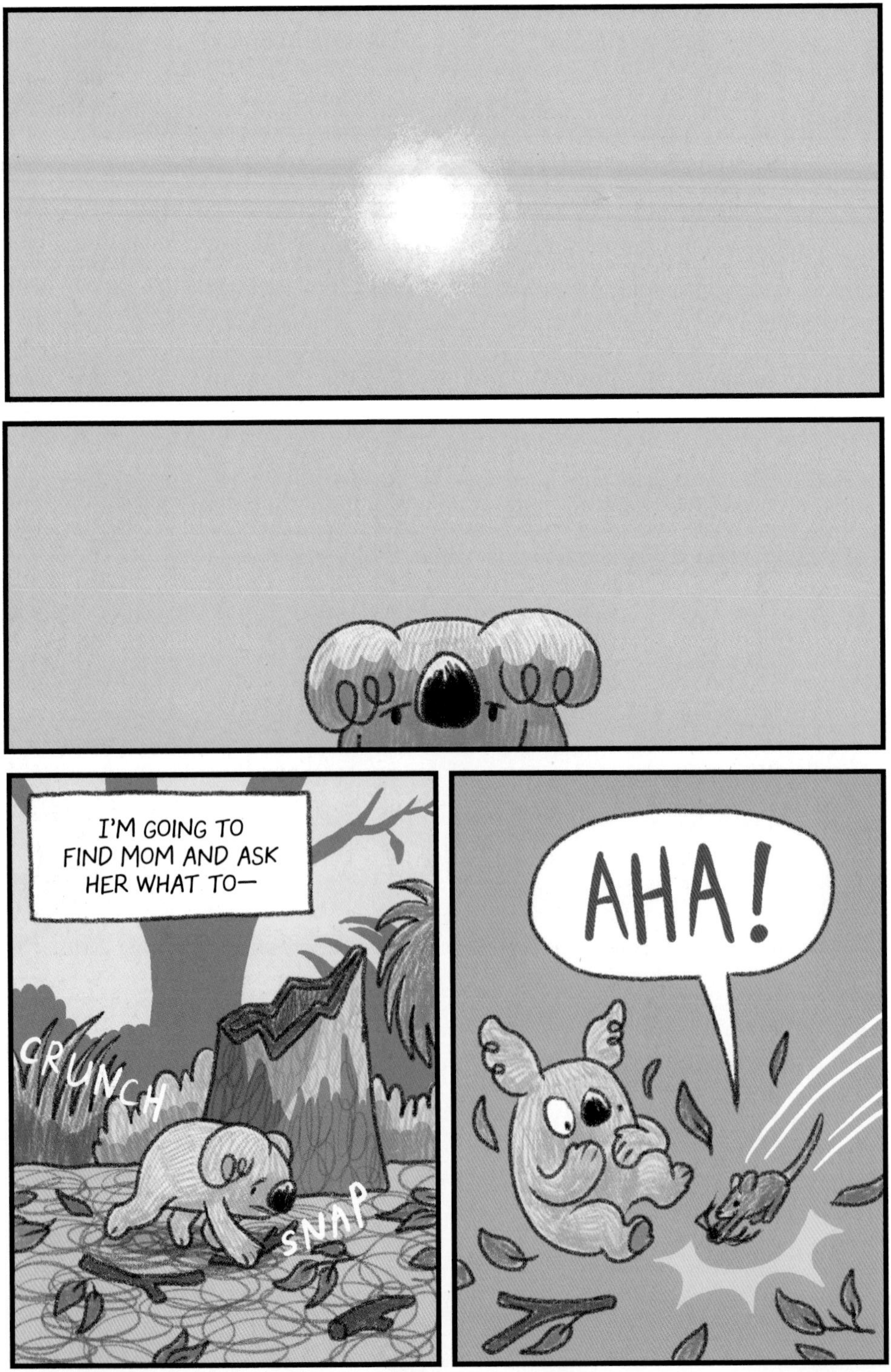
I'M GOING TO FIND MOM AND ASK HER WHAT TO—
CRUNCH
SNAP
AHA!

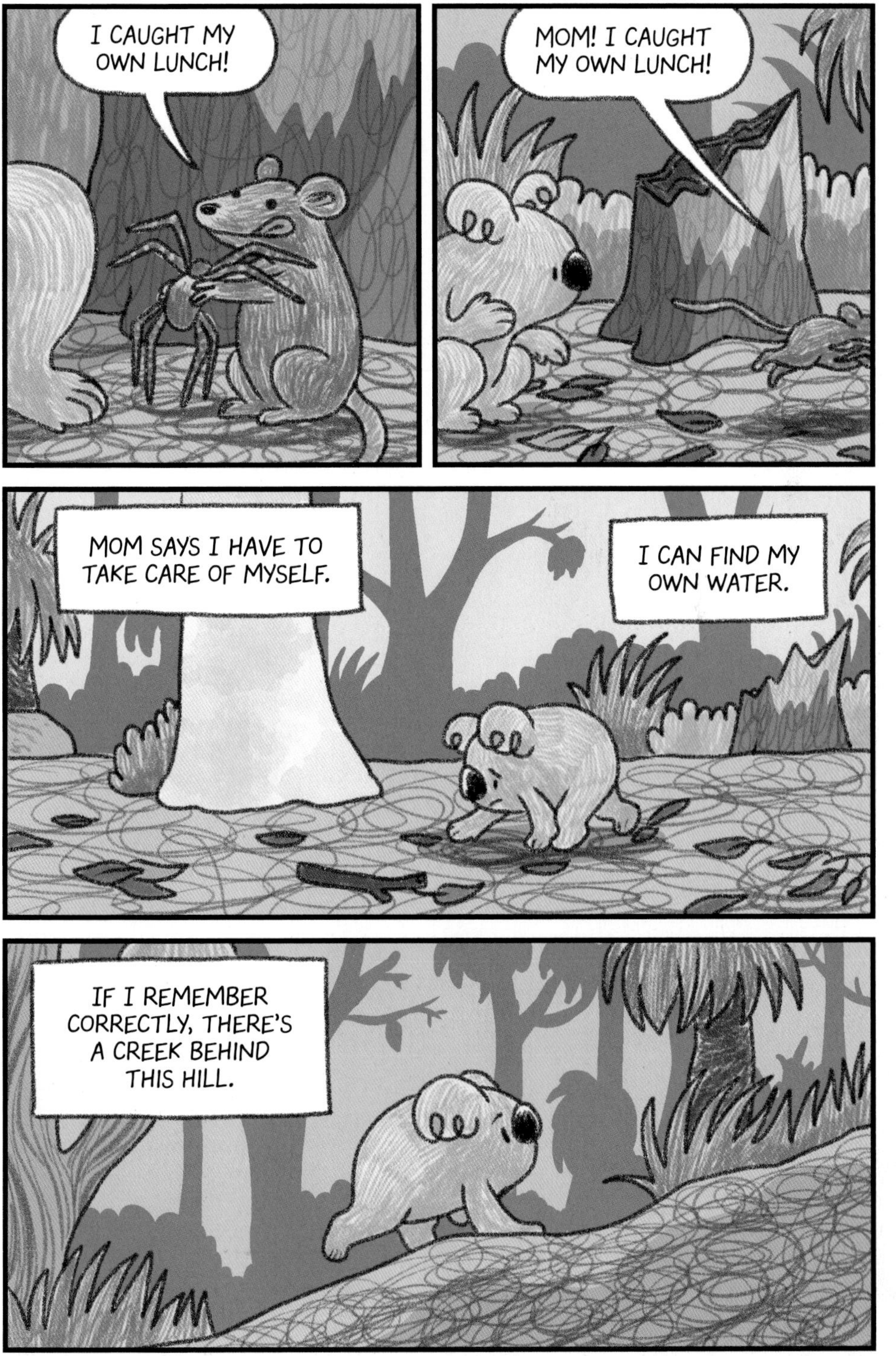
I CAUGHT MY OWN LUNCH!
MOM! I CAUGHT MY OWN LUNCH!
MOM SAYS I HAVE TO TAKE CARE OF MYSELF.
I CAN FIND MY OWN WATER.
IF I REMEMBER CORRECTLY, THERE'S A CREEK BEHIND THIS HILL.

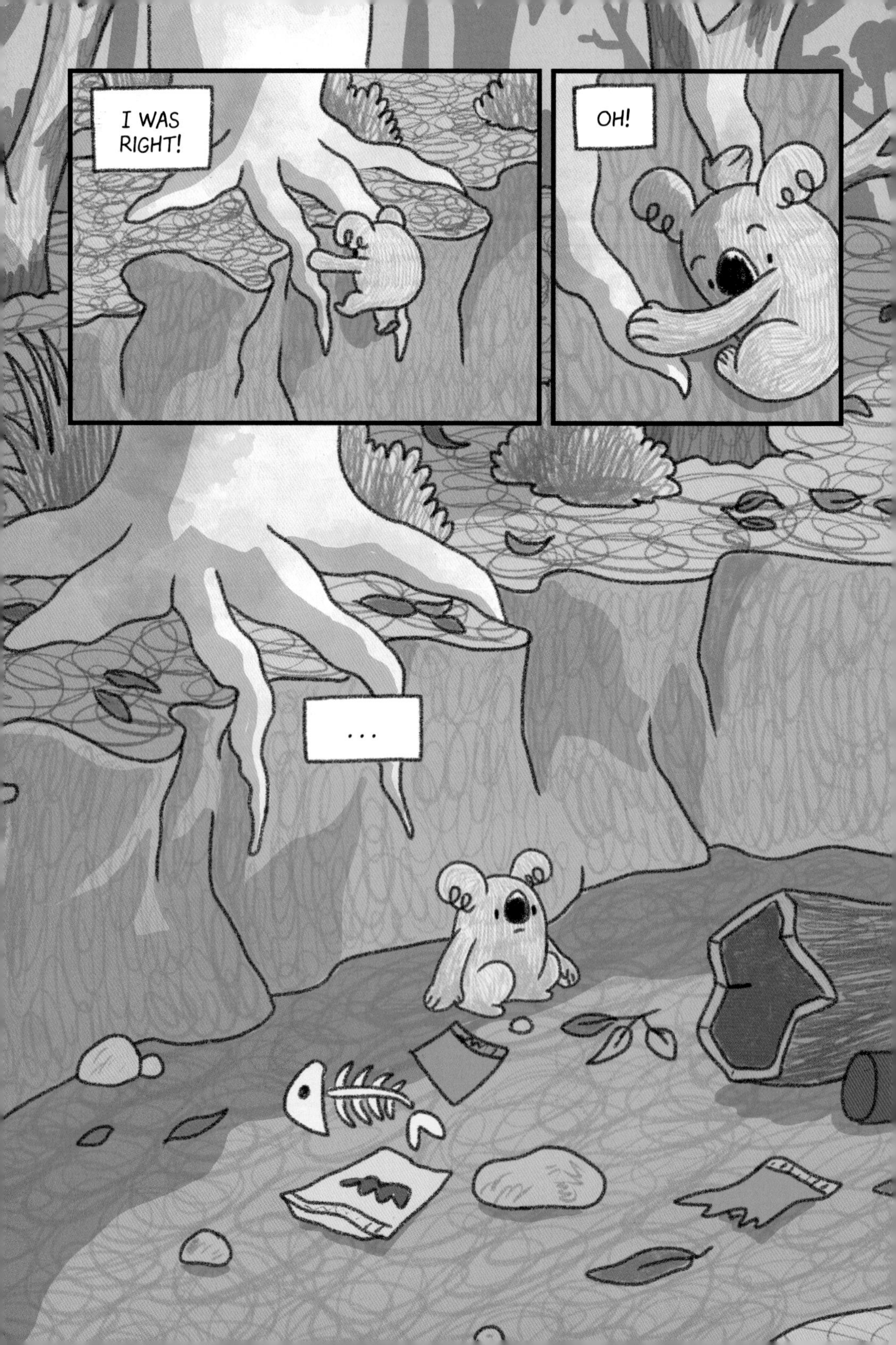
I WAS RIGHT!
OH!
...

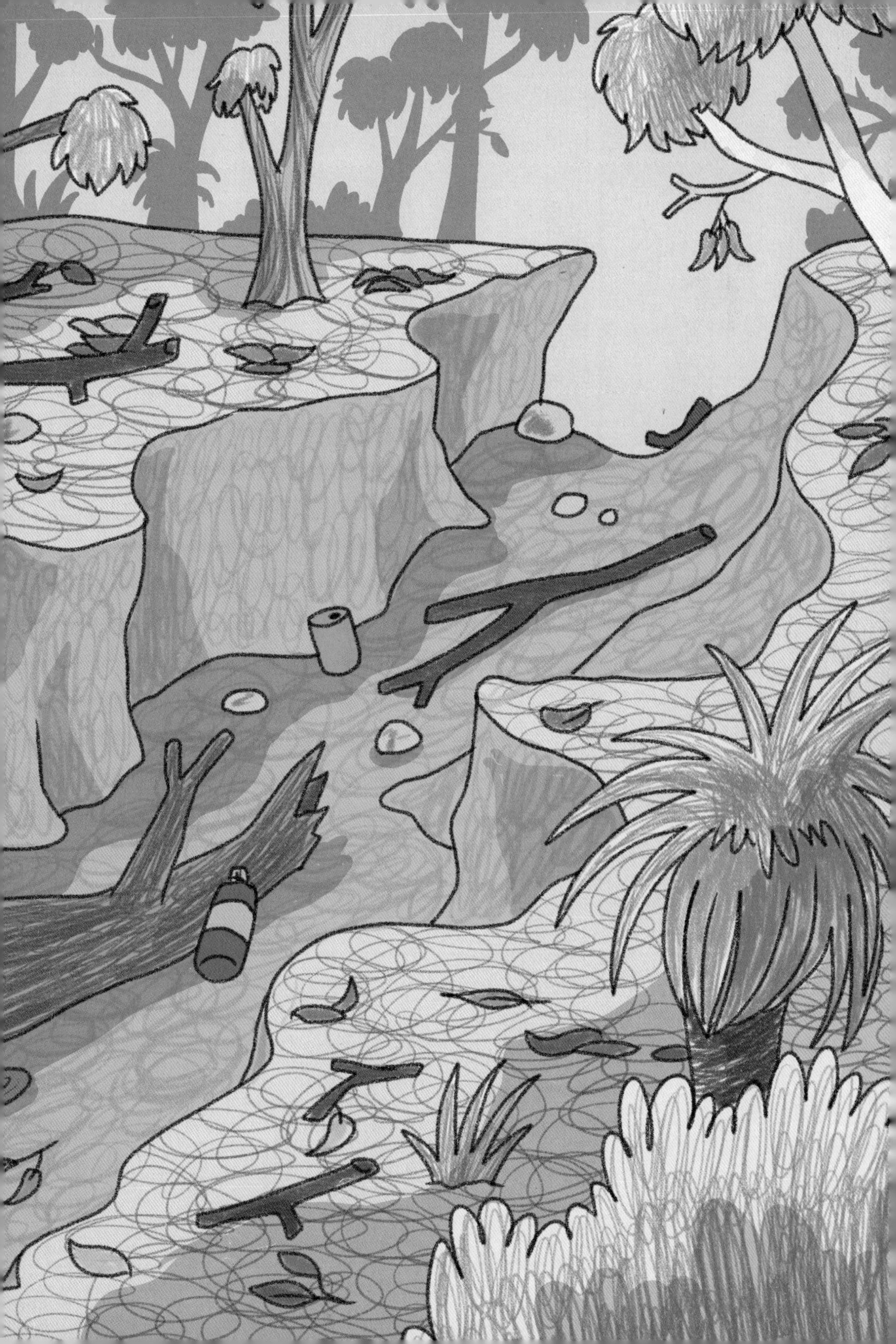

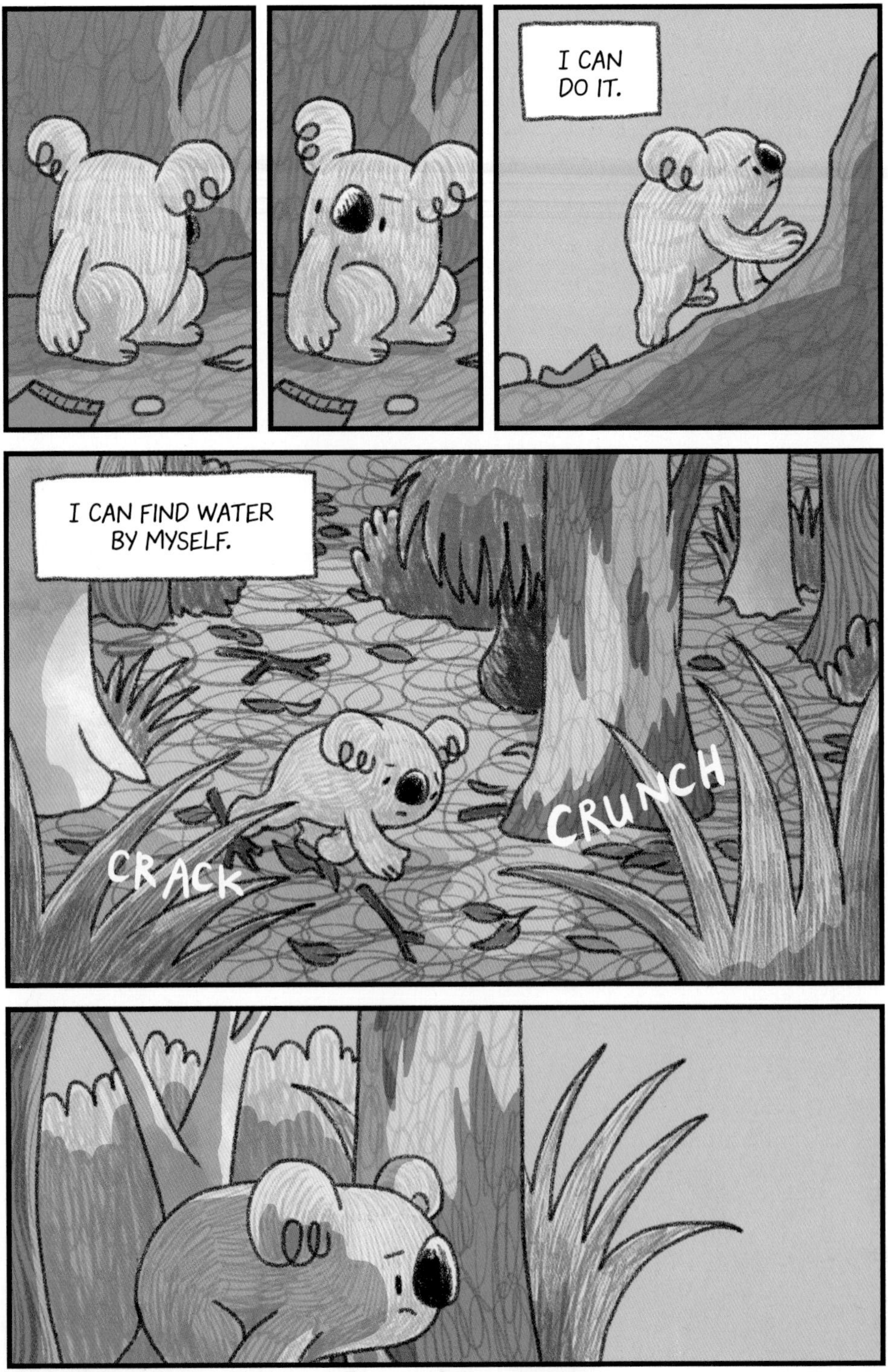
I CAN DO IT.
I CAN FIND WATER BY MYSELF.
CRACK
CRUNCH

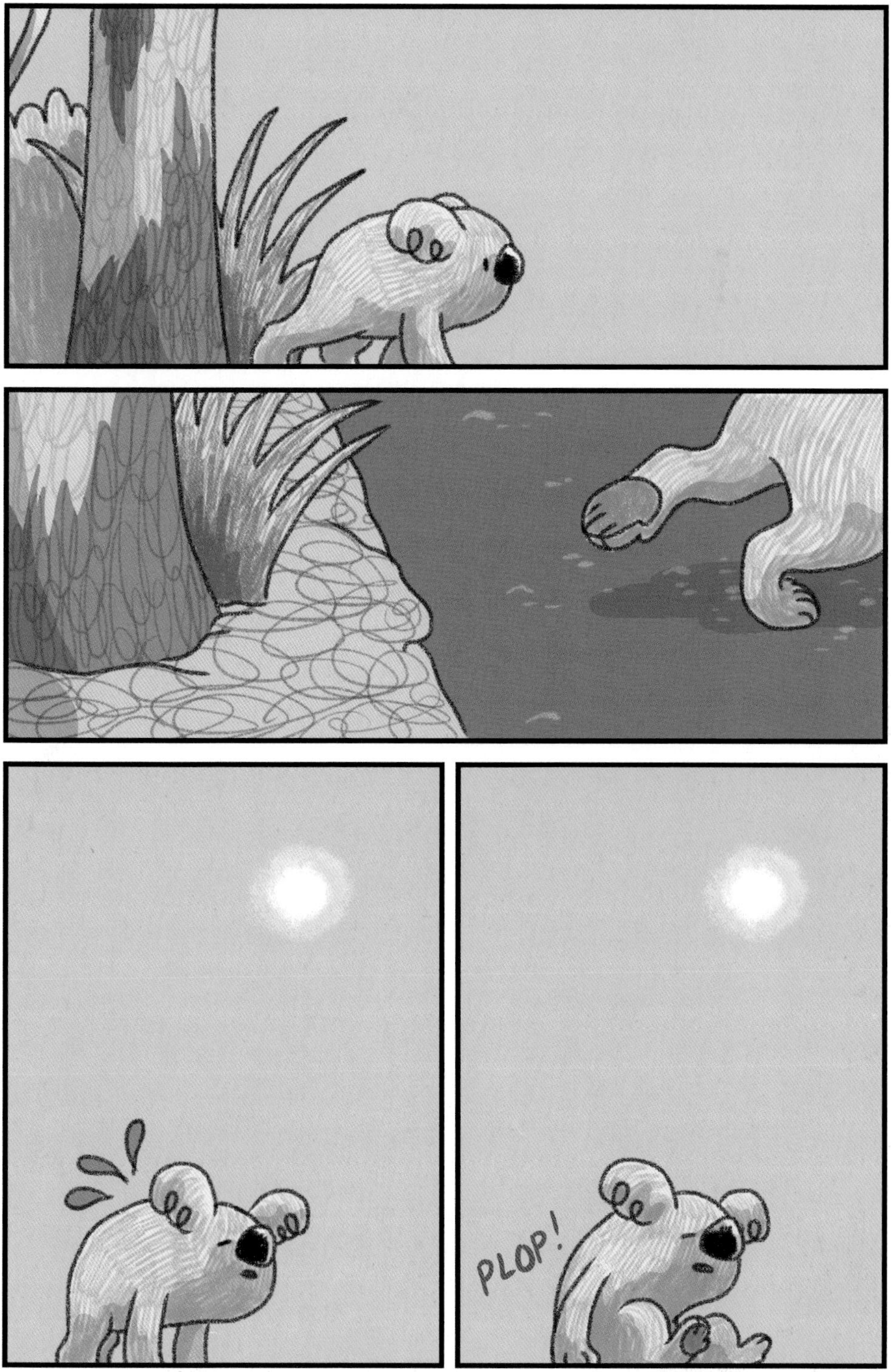
PLOP!

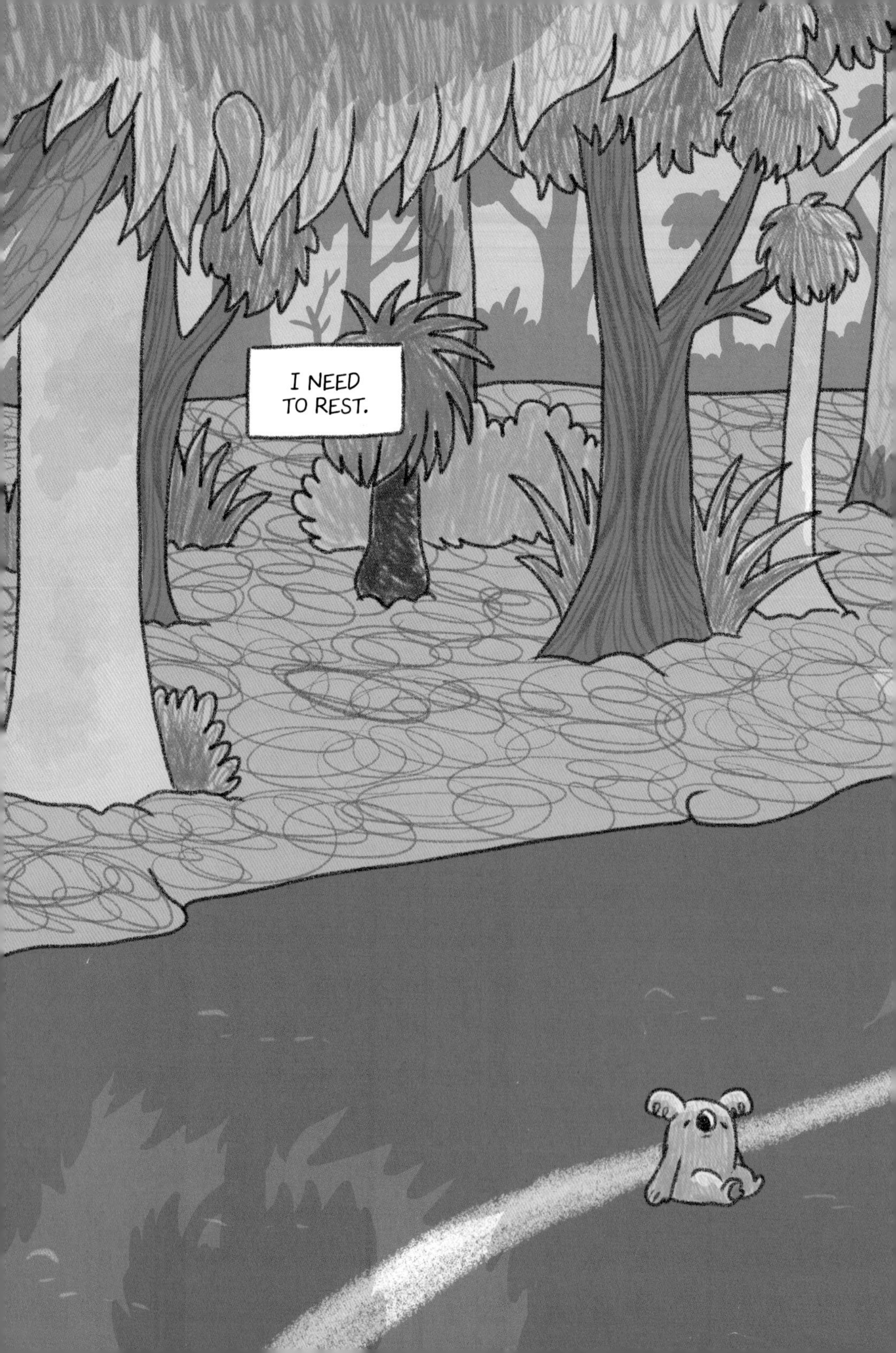
I NEED TO REST.

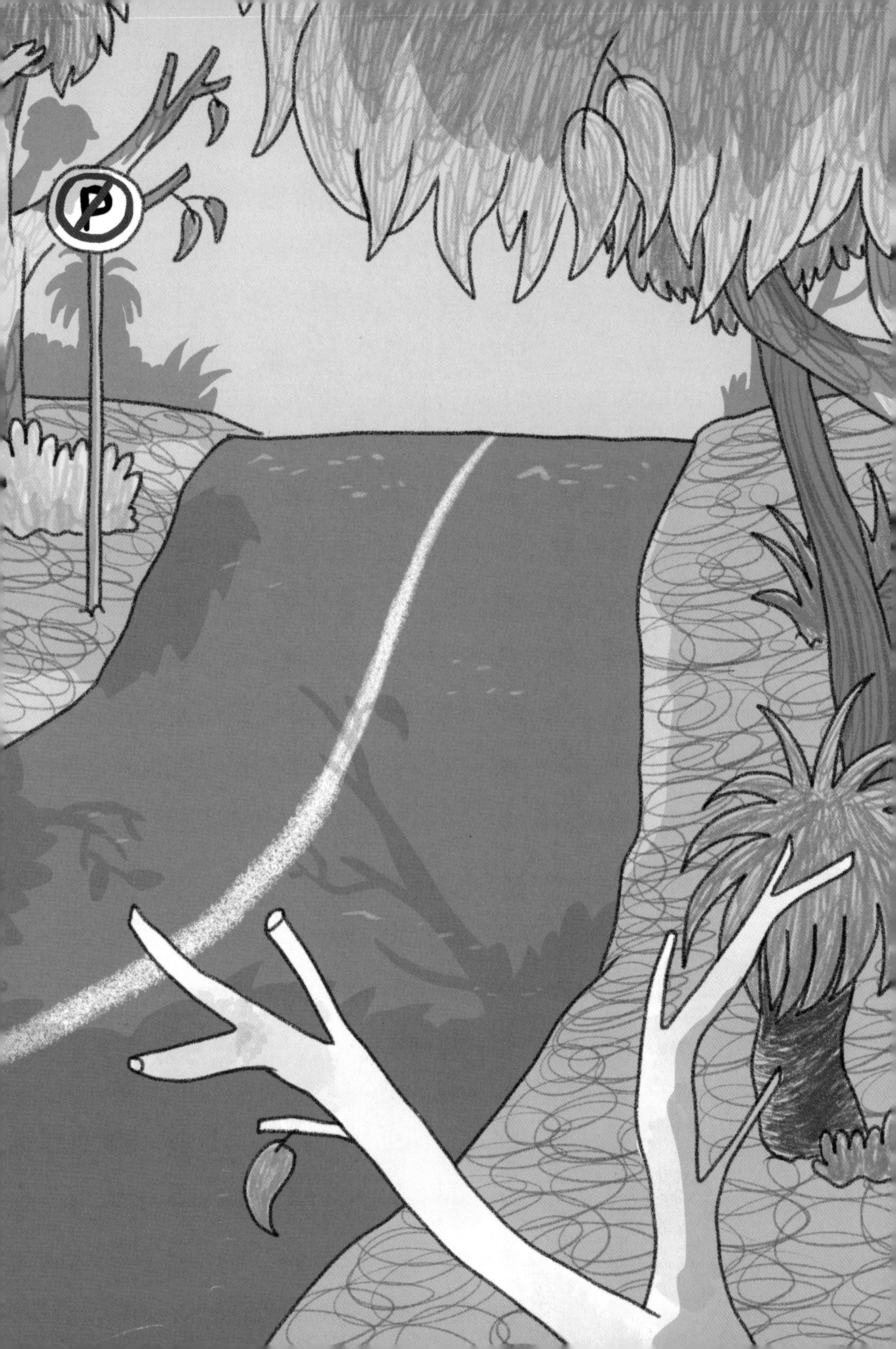

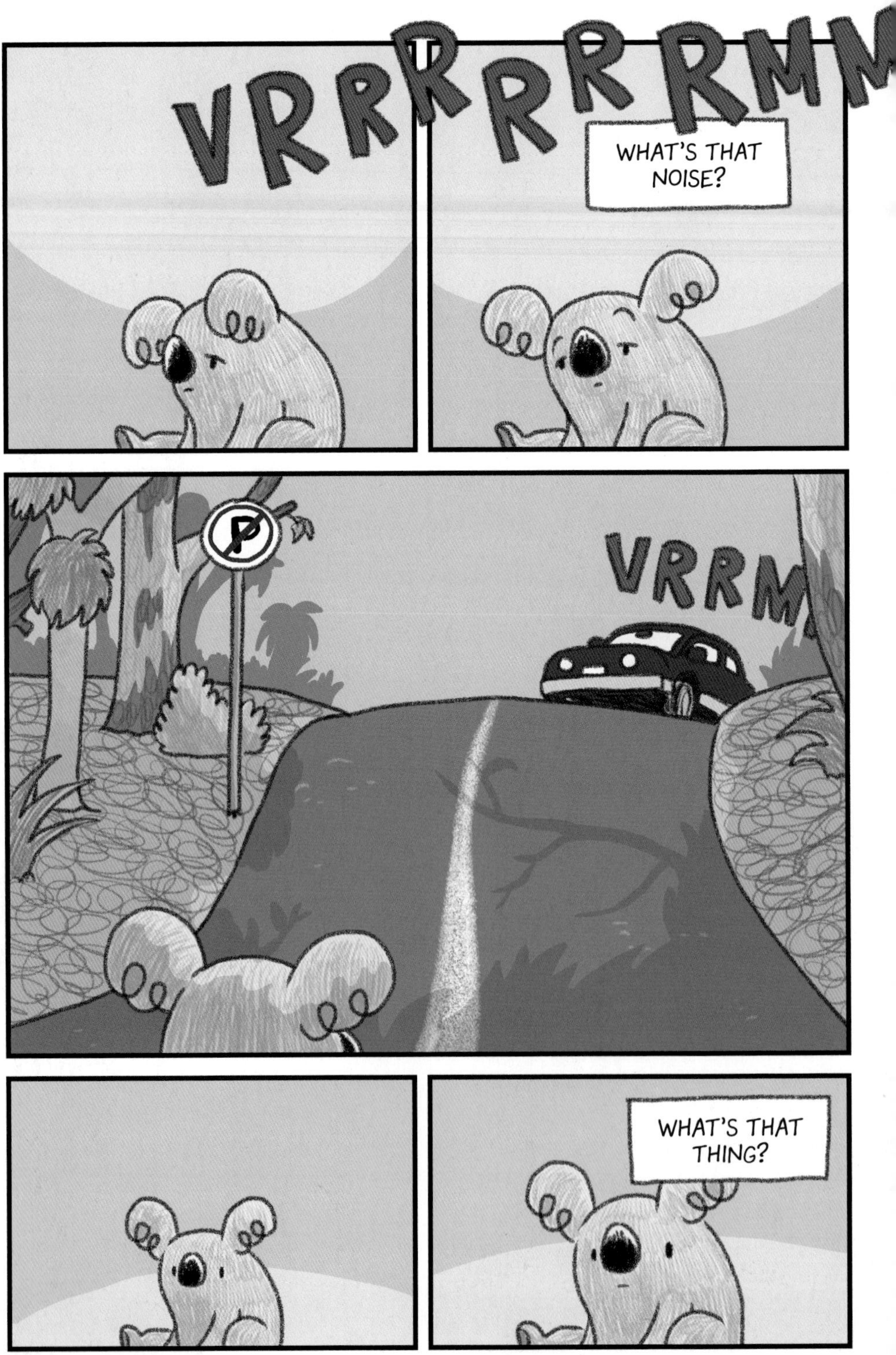
VRRRRRRMM
WHAT'S THAT NOISE?
VRRM
WHAT'S THAT THING?

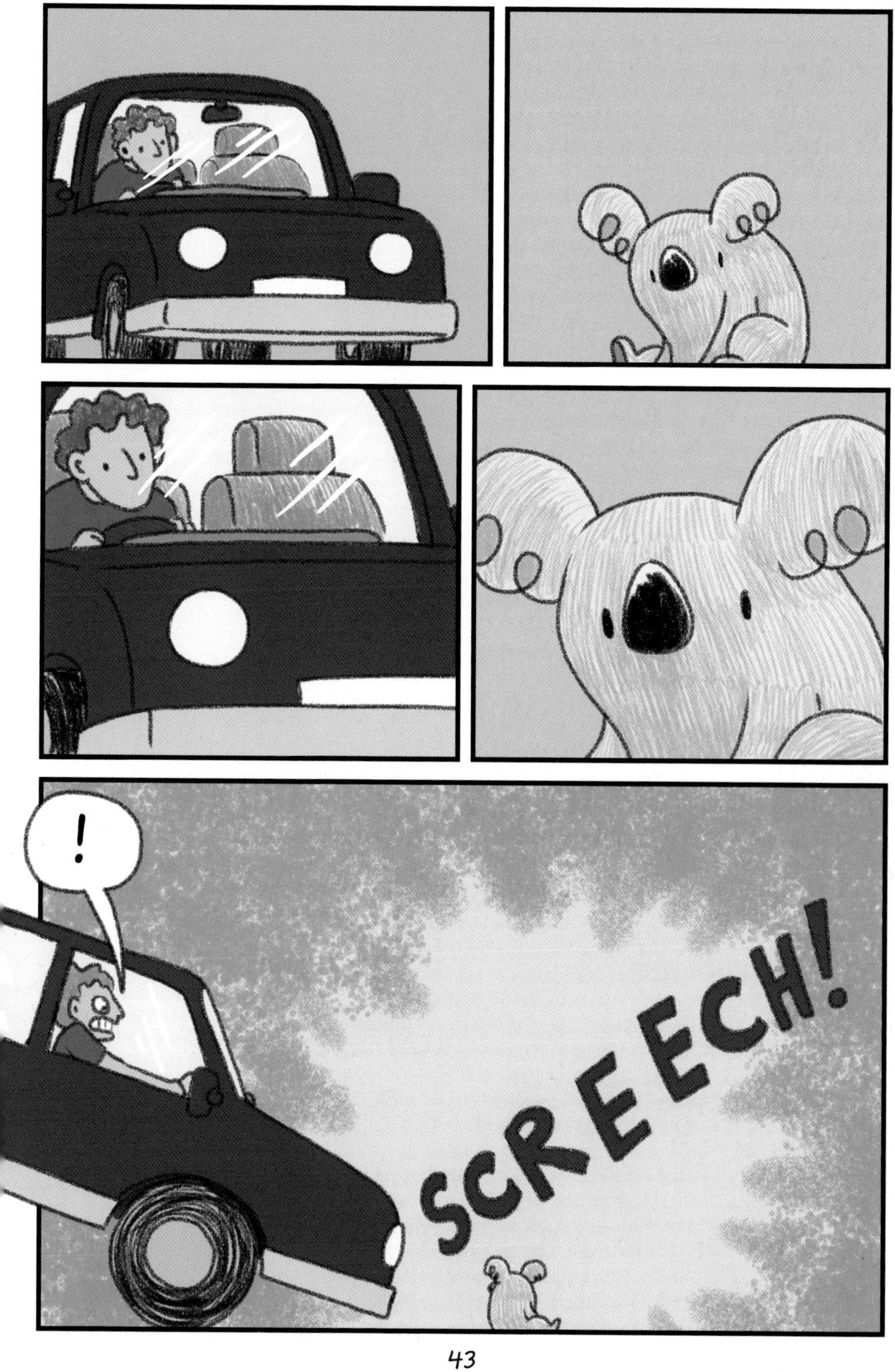
!
SCREECH!

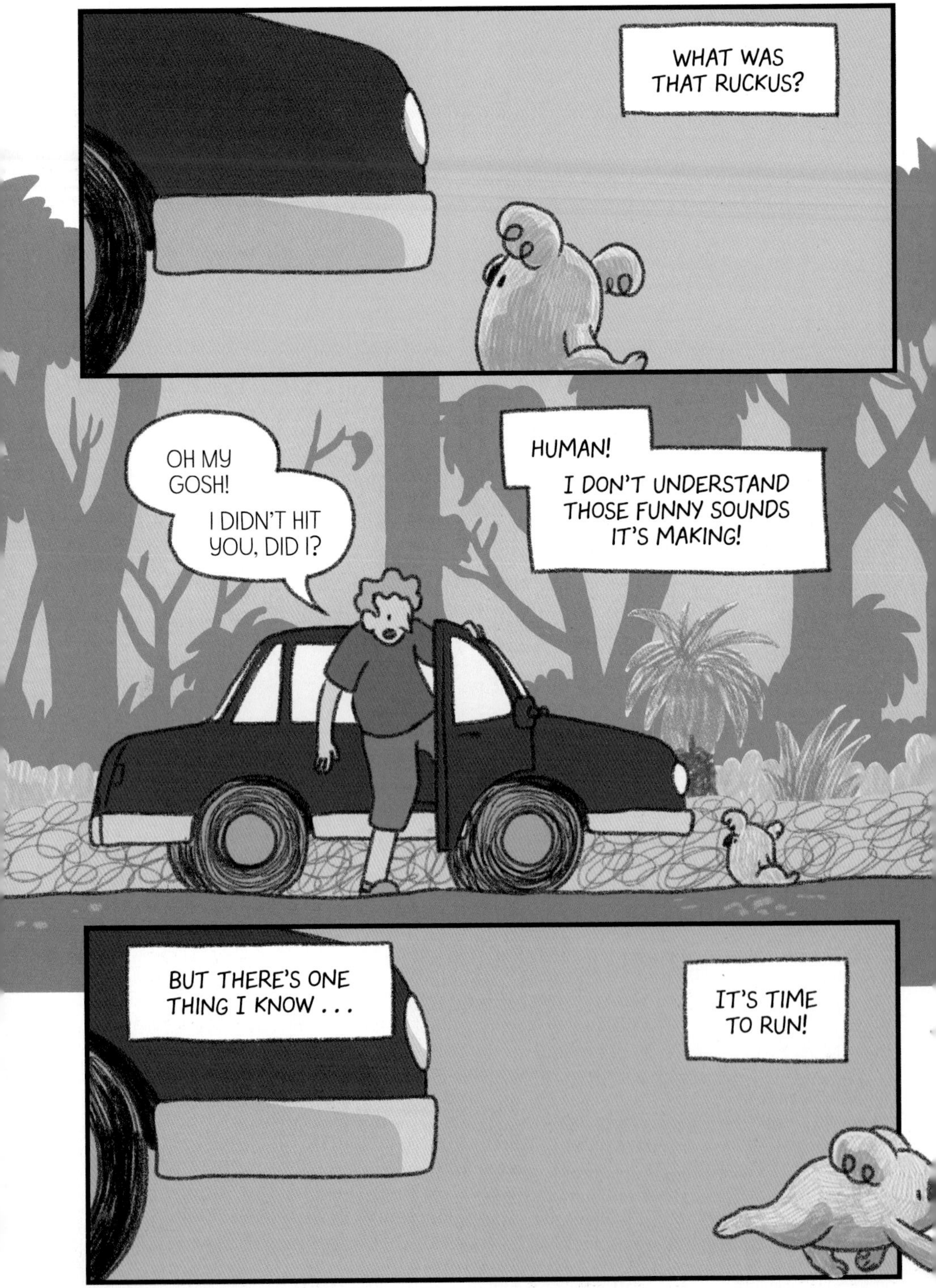
WHAT WAS THAT RUCKUS?
OH MY GOSH!
I DIDN'T HIT YOU, DID I?
HUMAN!
I DON'T UNDERSTAND THOSE FUNNY SOUNDS IT'S MAKING!
BUT THERE'S ONE THING I KNOW . . .
IT'S TIME TO RUN!

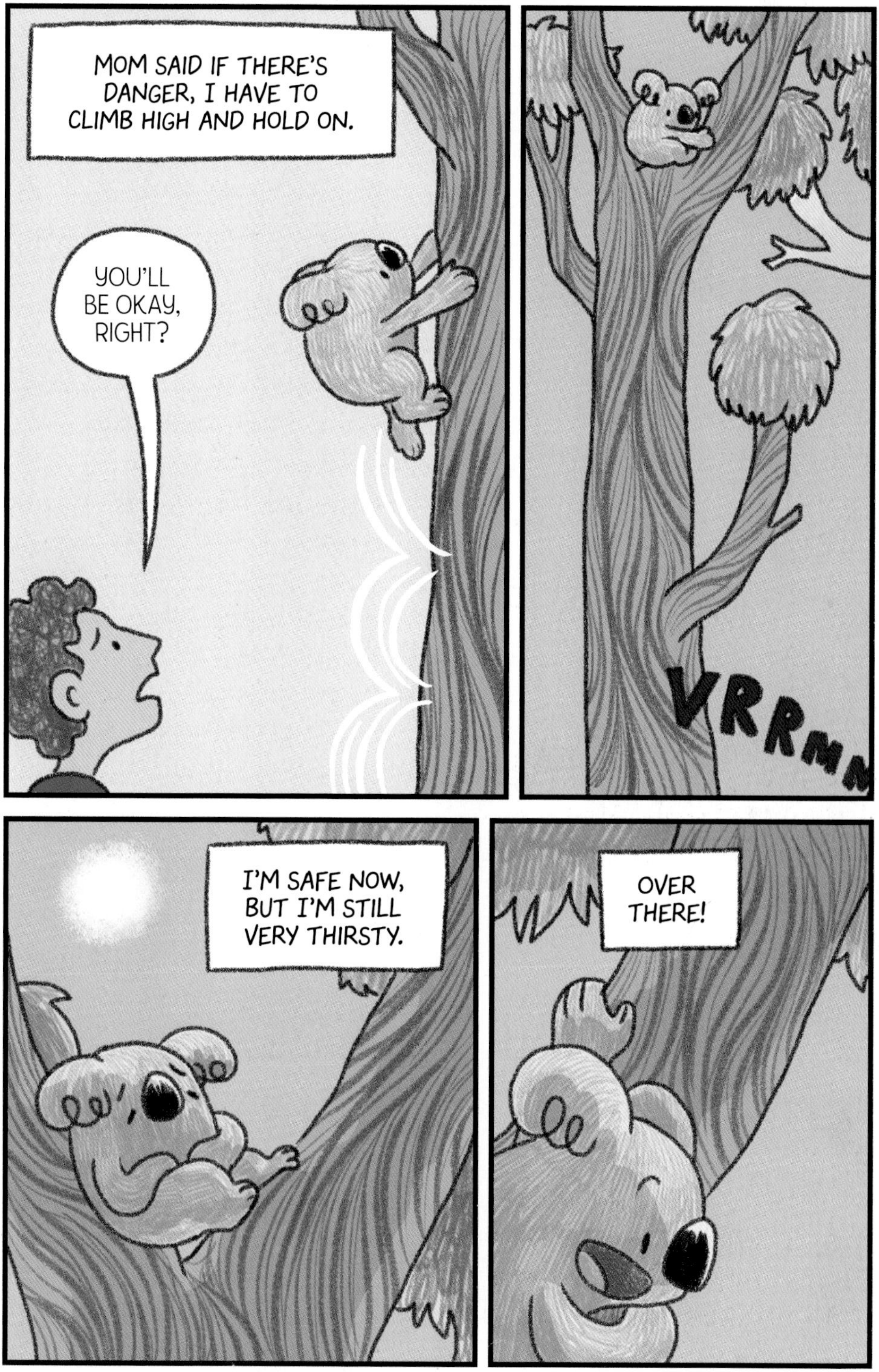

MOM SAID IF THERE'S DANGER, I HAVE TO CLIMB HIGH AND HOLD ON.
YOU'LL BE OKAY, RIGHT?
VRRMM
I'M SAFE NOW, BUT I'M STILL VERY THIRSTY.
OVER THERE!

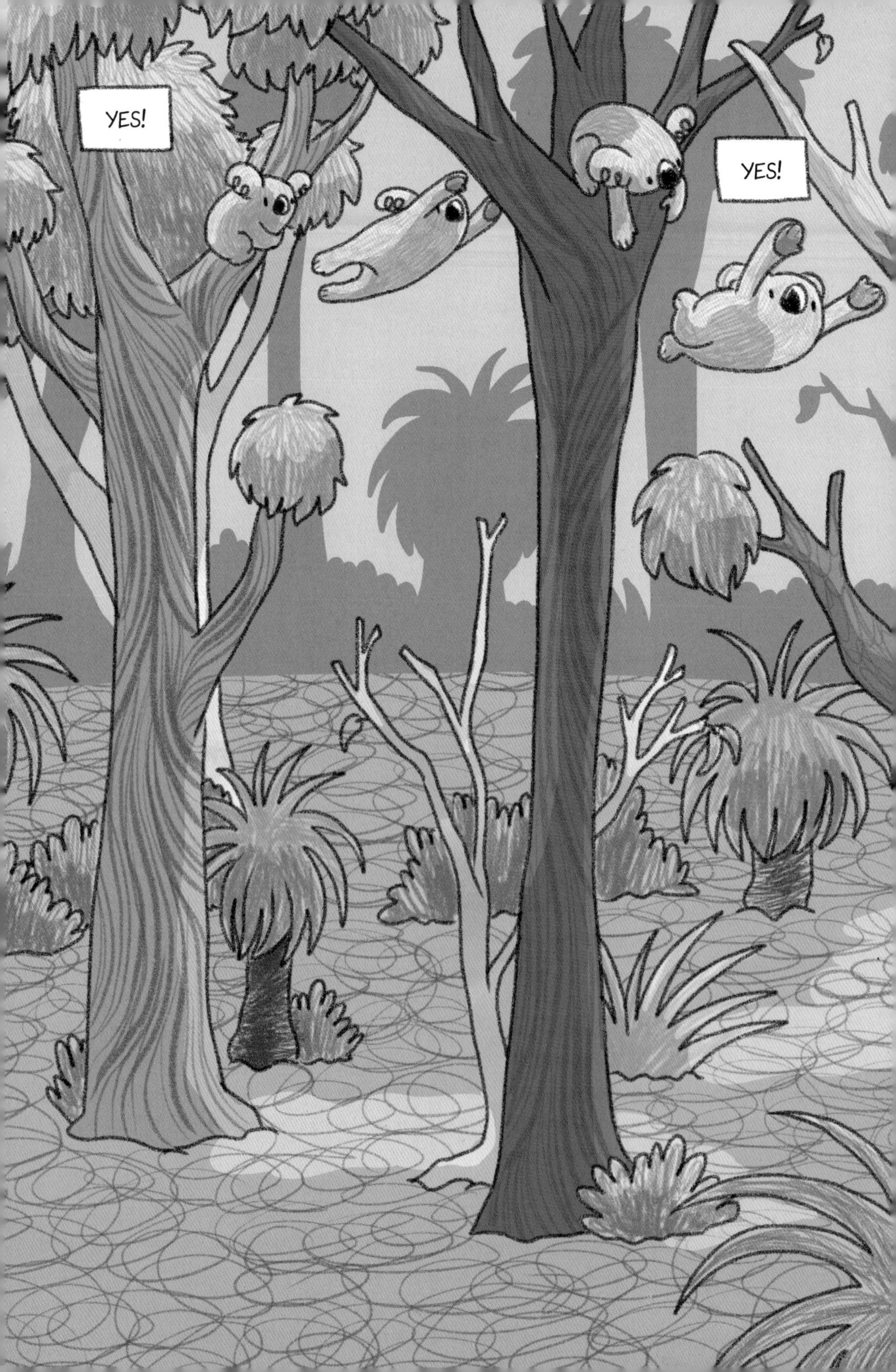
YES!
YES!

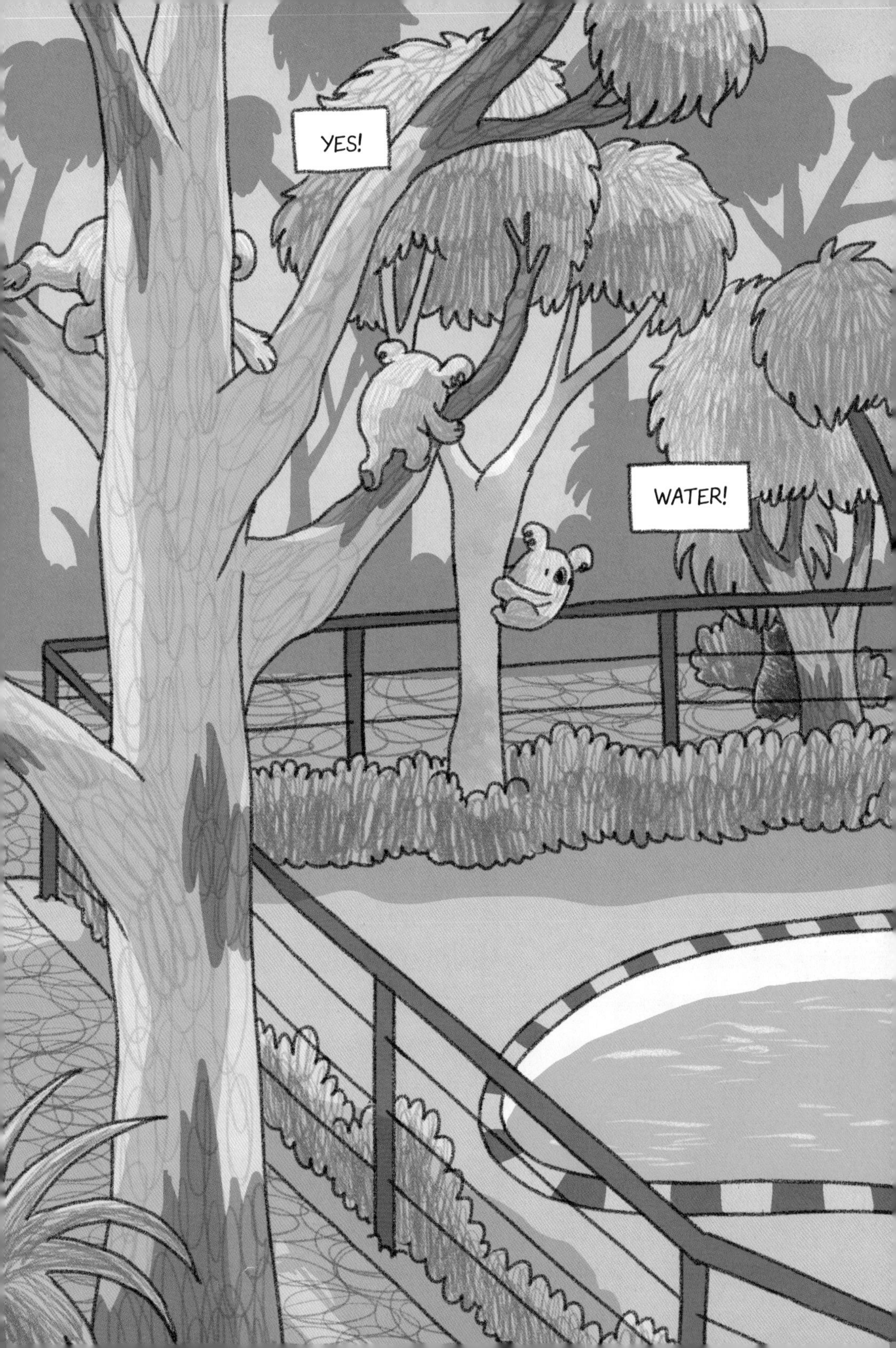
YES!
WATER!

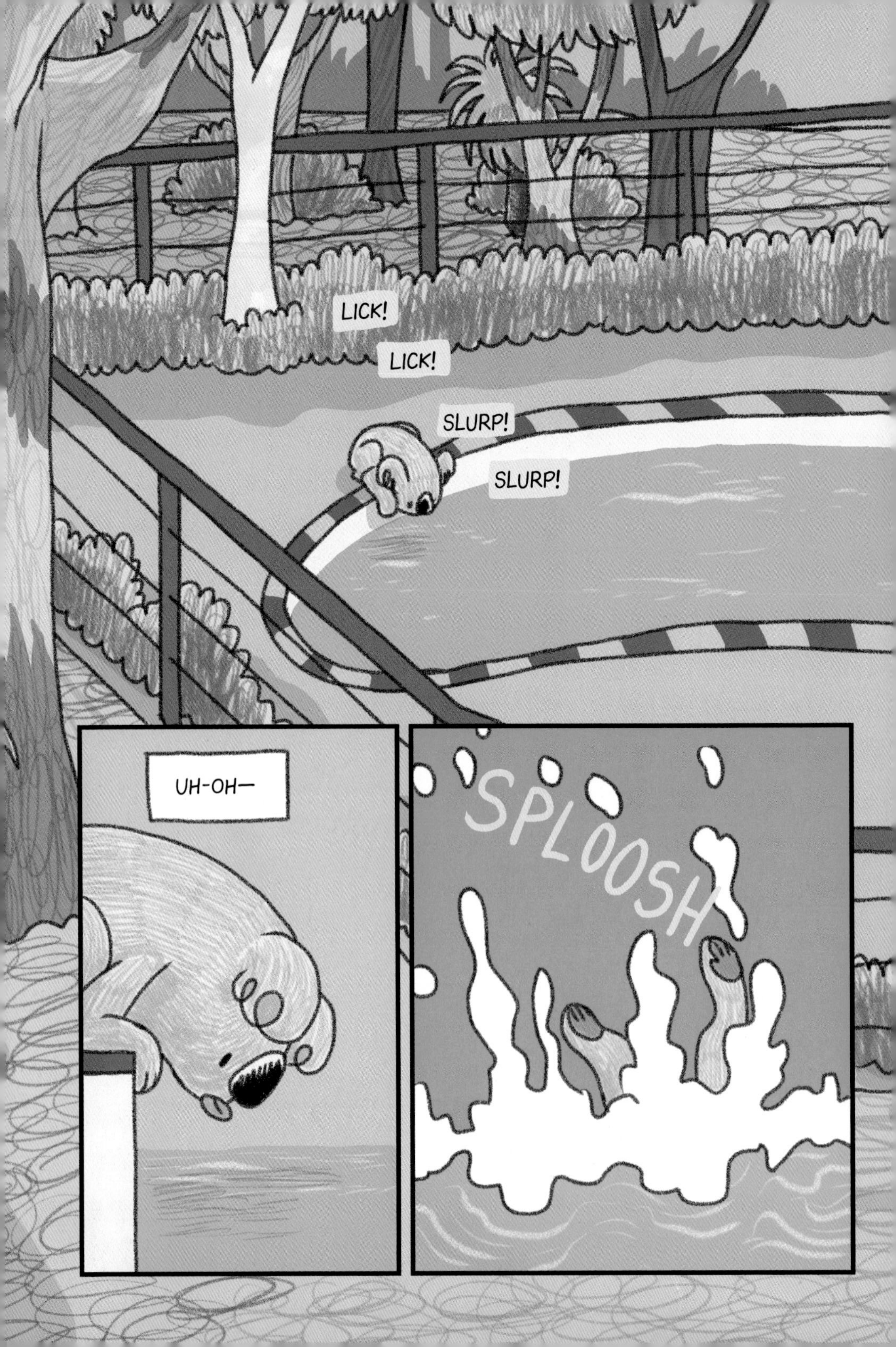
LICK!
LICK!
SLURP!
SLURP!
UH-OH—
SPLOOSH

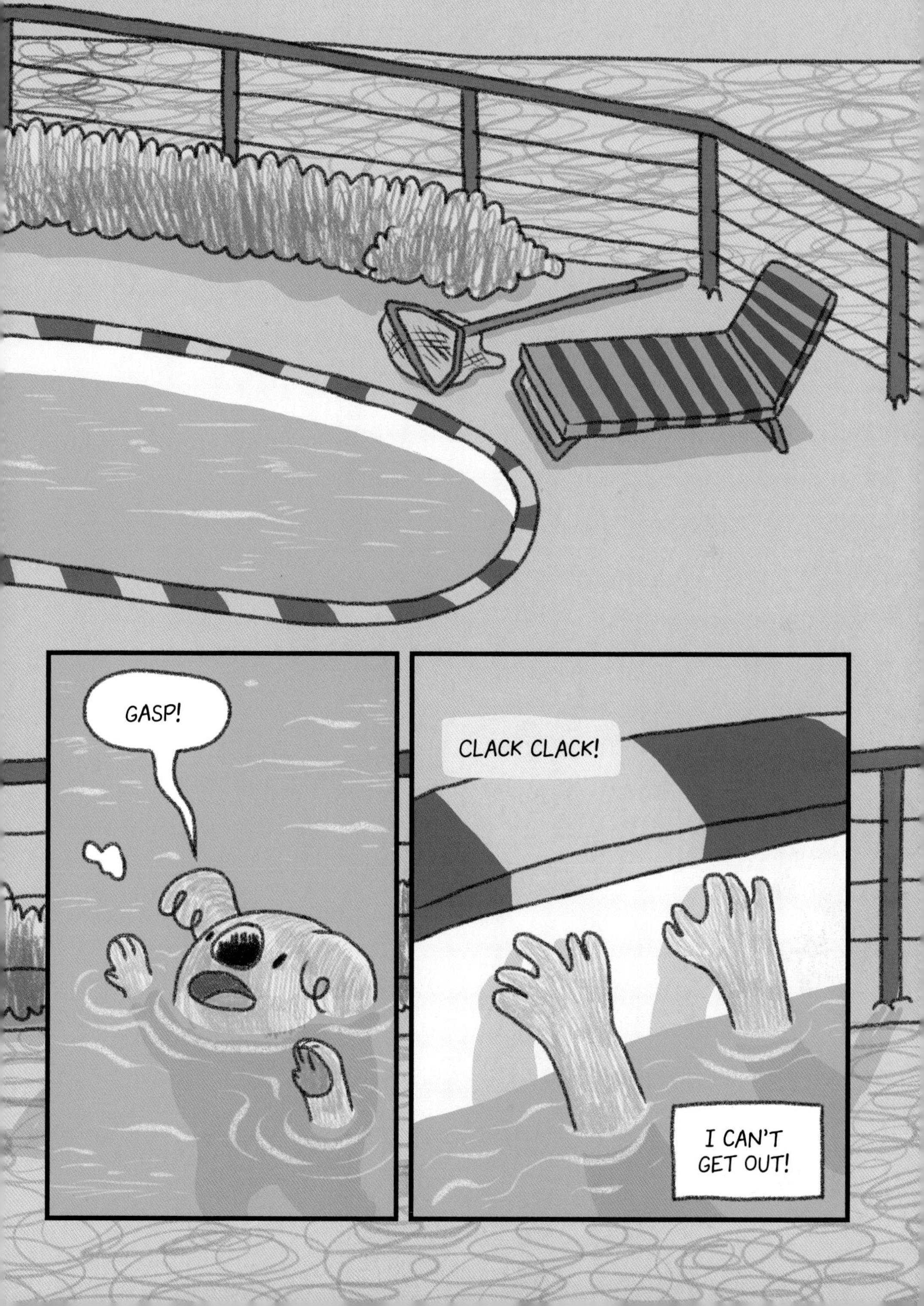
GASP!
CLACK CLACK!
I CAN'T GET OUT!

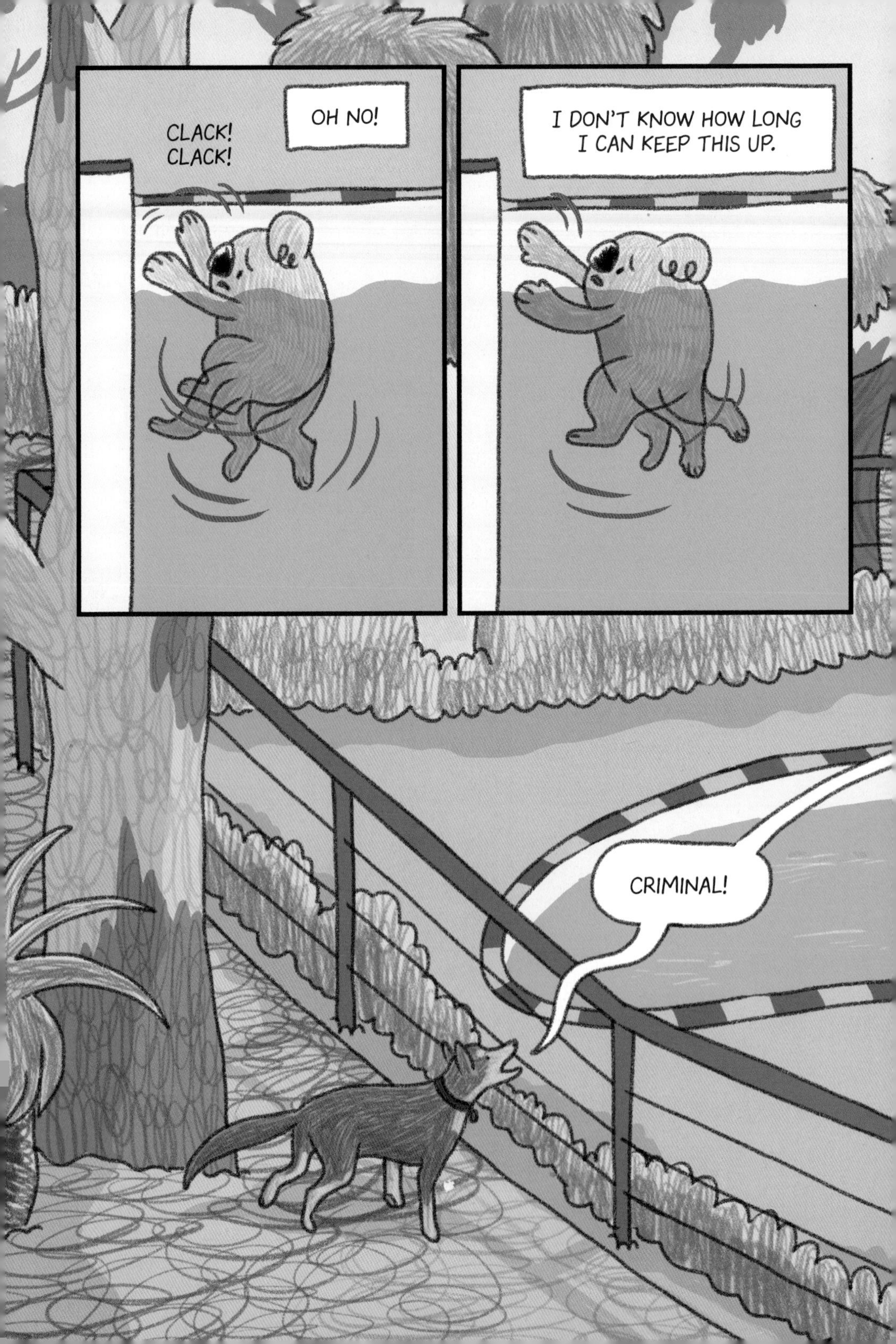
CLACK!
CLACK!
OH NO!
I DON'T KNOW HOW LONG I CAN KEEP THIS UP.
CRIMINAL!

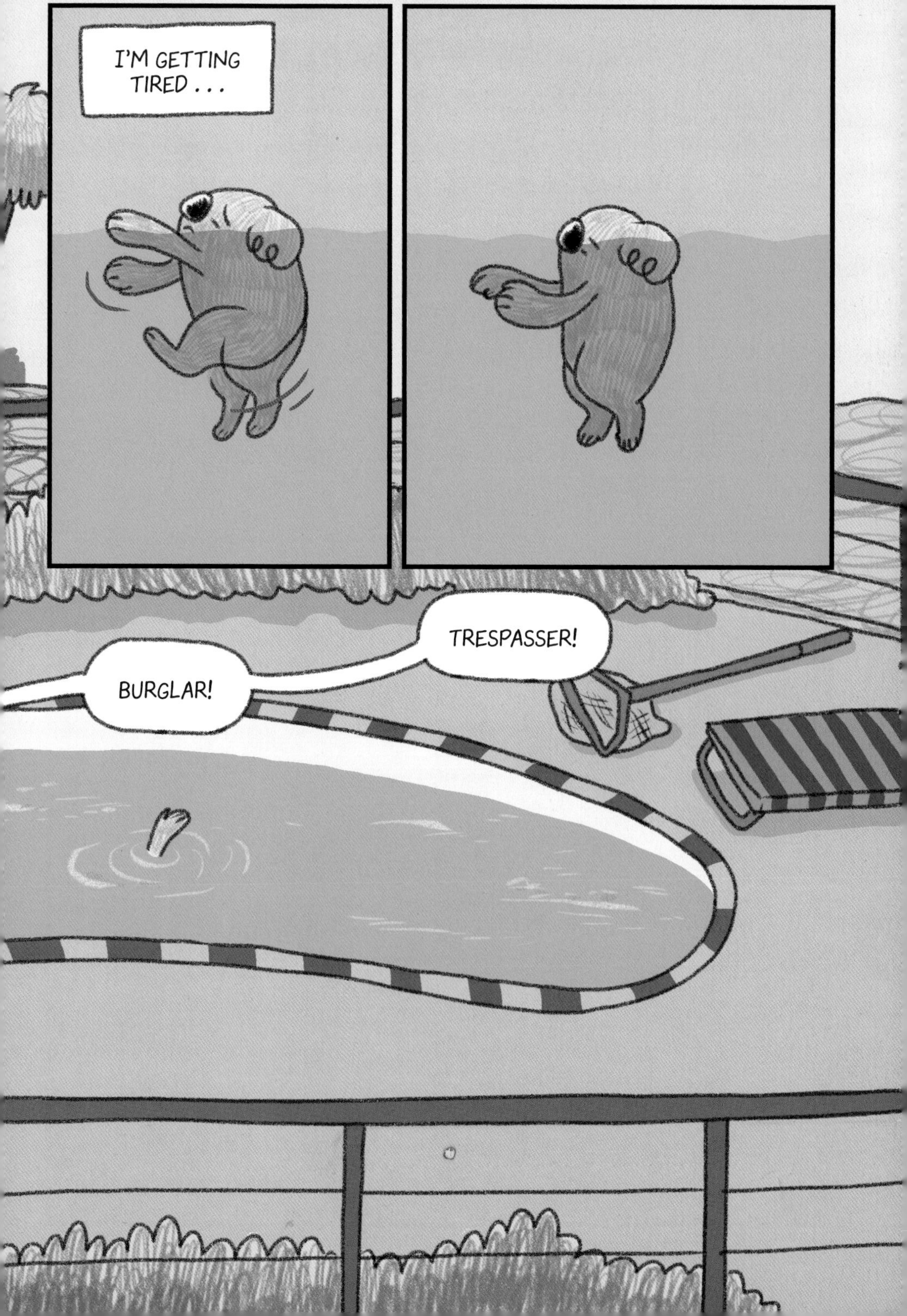
I'M GETTING TIRED . . .
TRESPASSER!
BURGLAR!

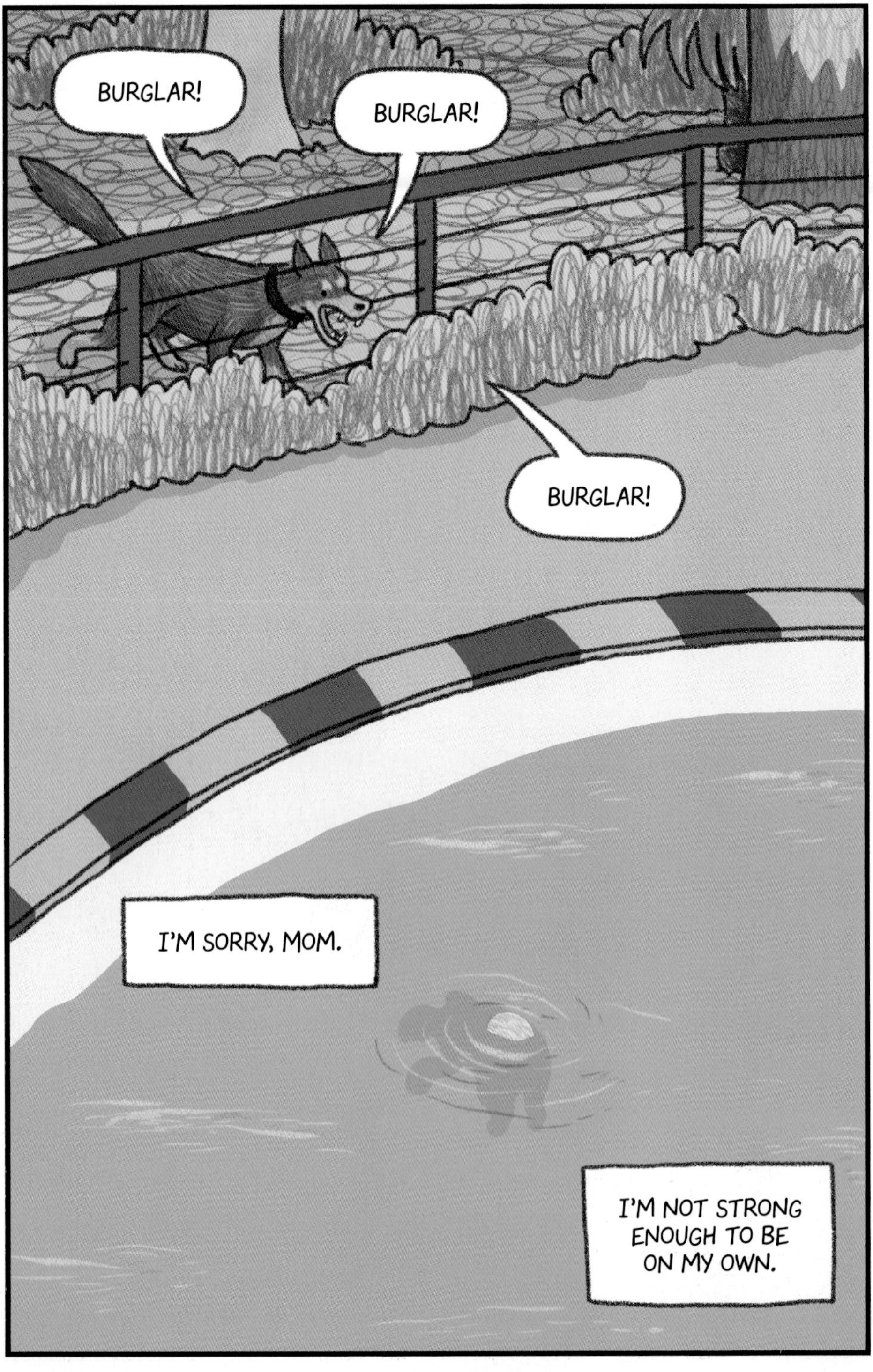
BURGLAR!
BURGLAR!
BURGLAR!
I'M SORRY, MOM.
I'M NOT STRONG ENOUGH TO BE ON MY OWN.

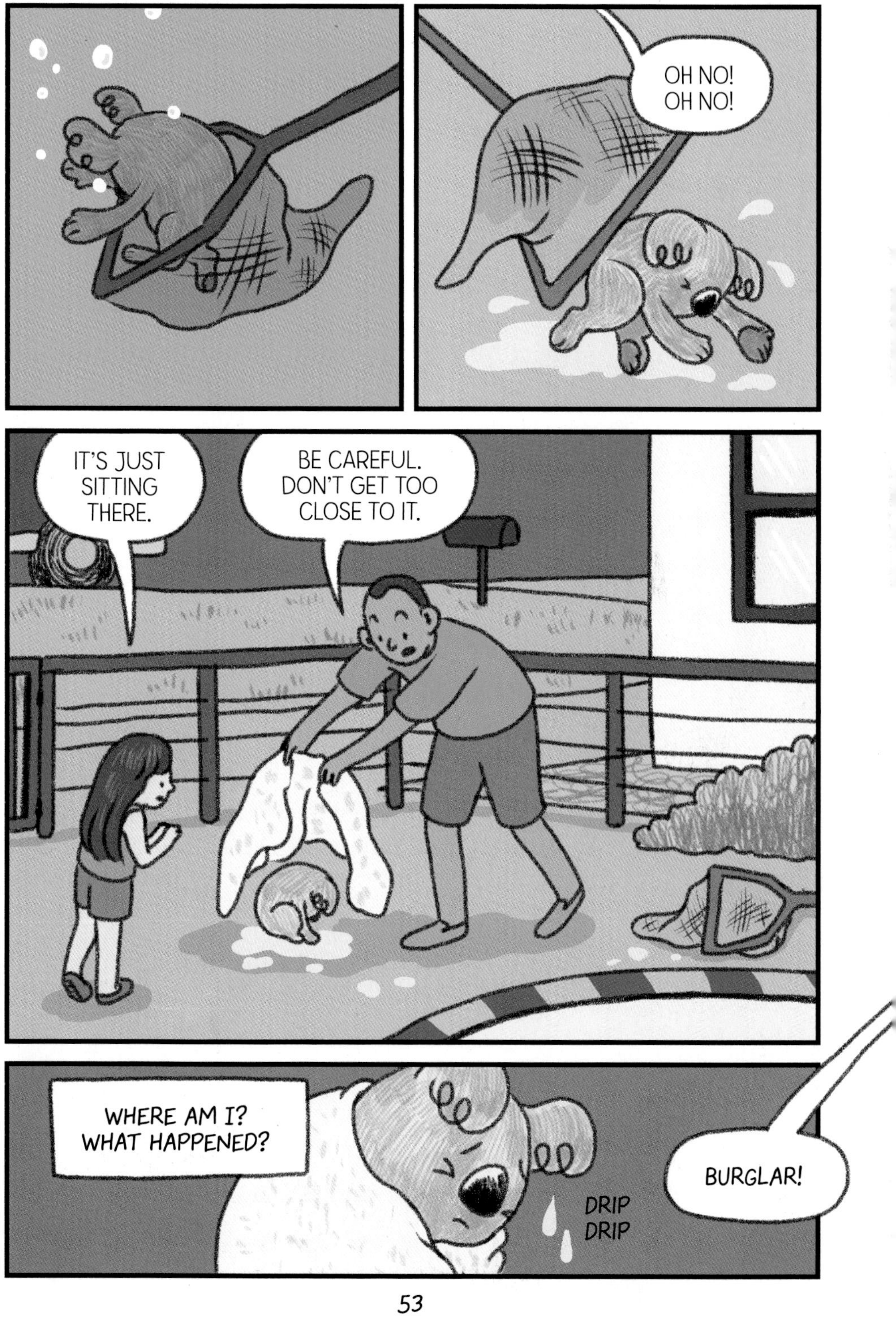
OH NO!
OH NO!
IT'S JUST SITTING THERE.
BE CAREFUL. DON'T GET TOO CLOSE TO IT.
WHERE AM I? WHAT HAPPENED?
DRIP DRIP
BURGLAR!

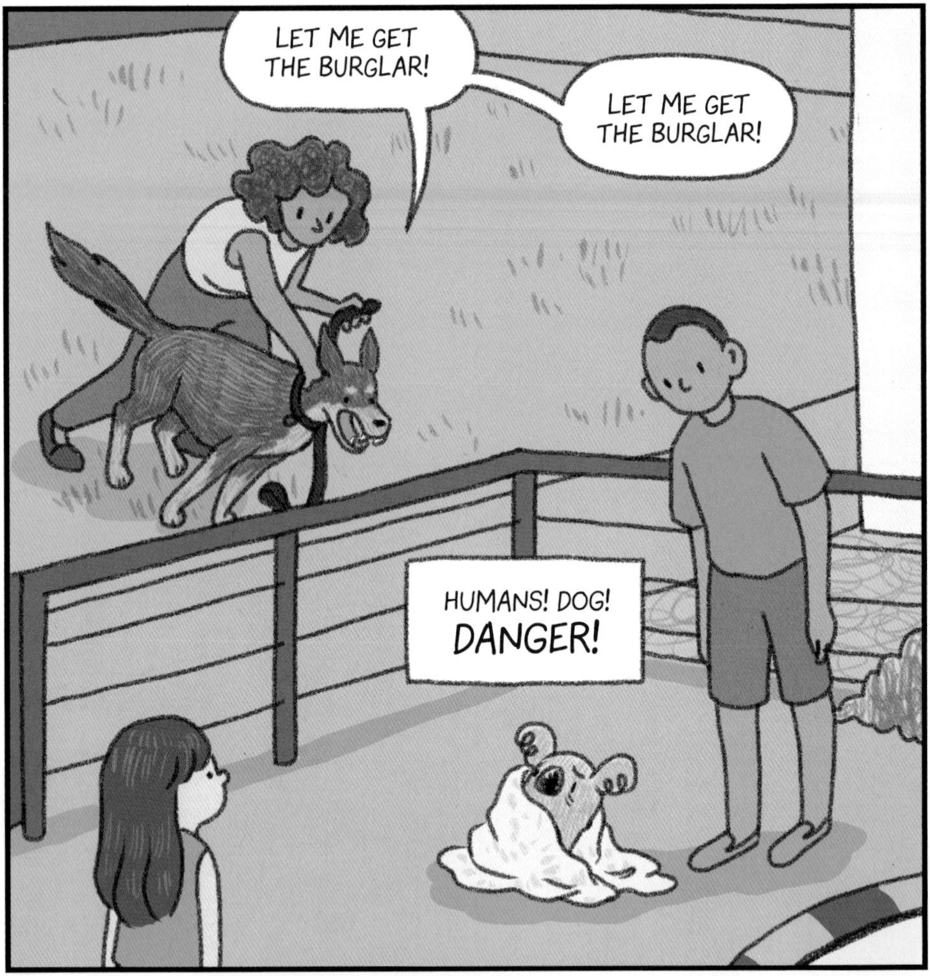
LET ME GET THE BURGLAR!
LET ME GET THE BURGLAR!
HUMANS! DOG! DANGER!

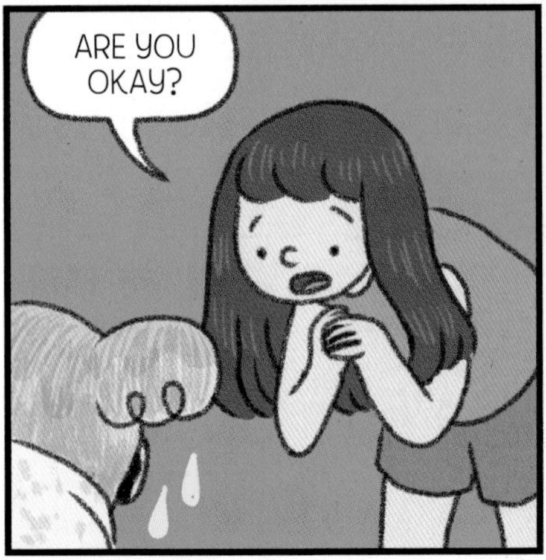
ARE YOU OKAY?

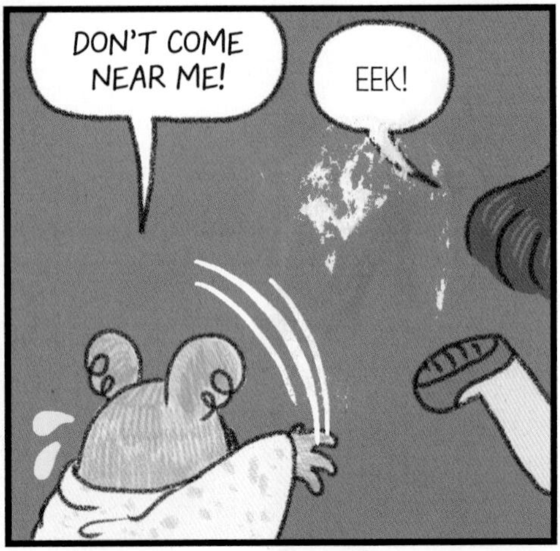
DON'T COME NEAR ME!
EEK!

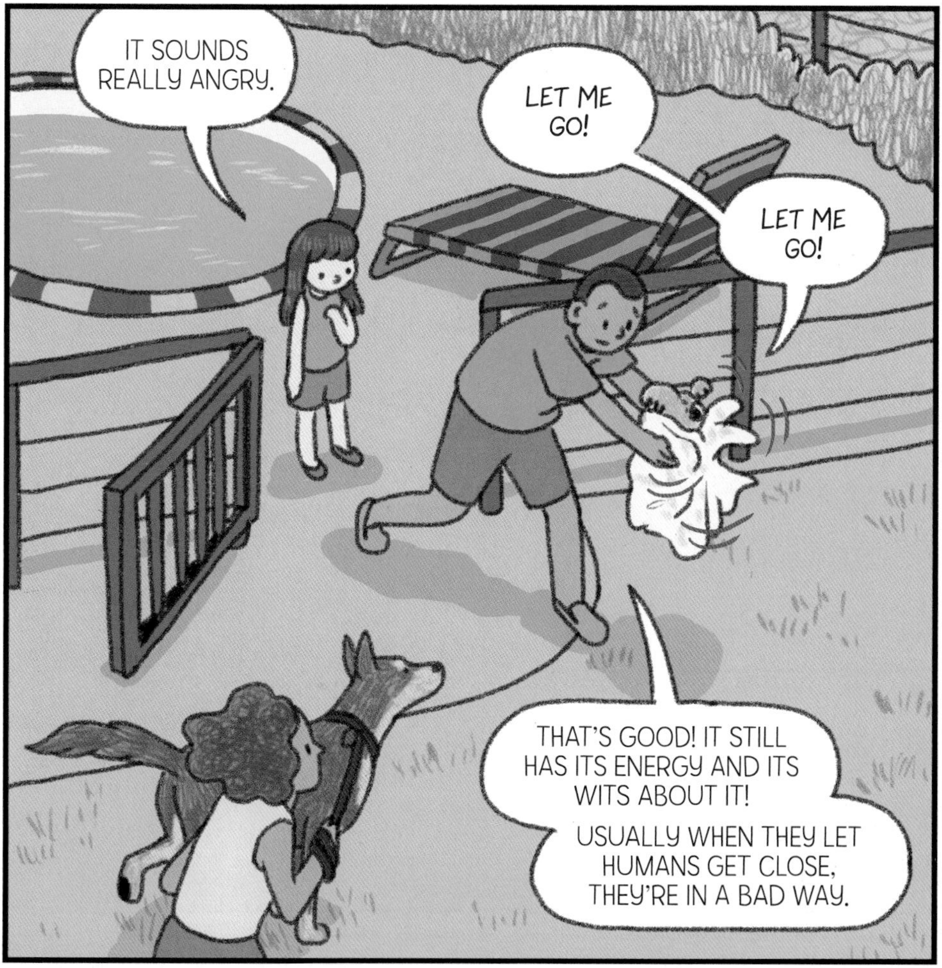
IT SOUNDS REALLY ANGRY.
LET ME GO!
LET ME GO!
THAT'S GOOD! IT STILL HAS ITS ENERGY AND ITS WITS ABOUT IT!
USUALLY WHEN THEY LET HUMANS GET CLOSE, THEY'RE IN A BAD WAY.

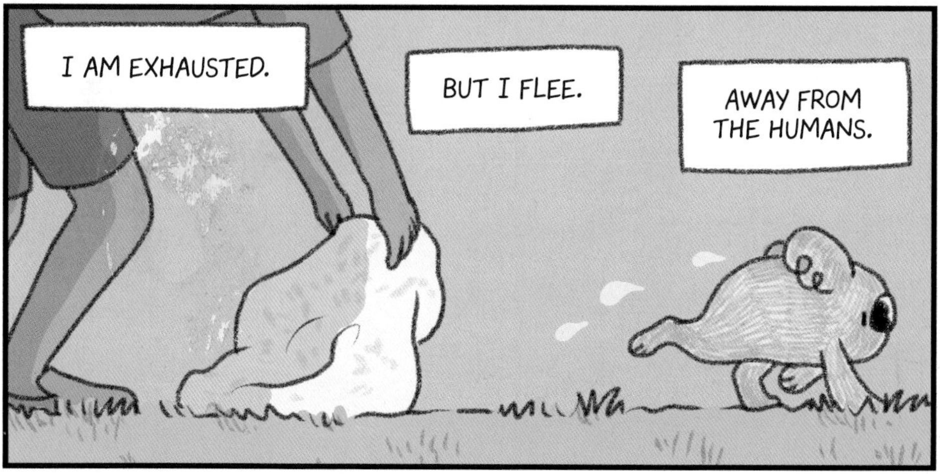
I AM EXHAUSTED.
BUT I FLEE.
AWAY FROM THE HUMANS.

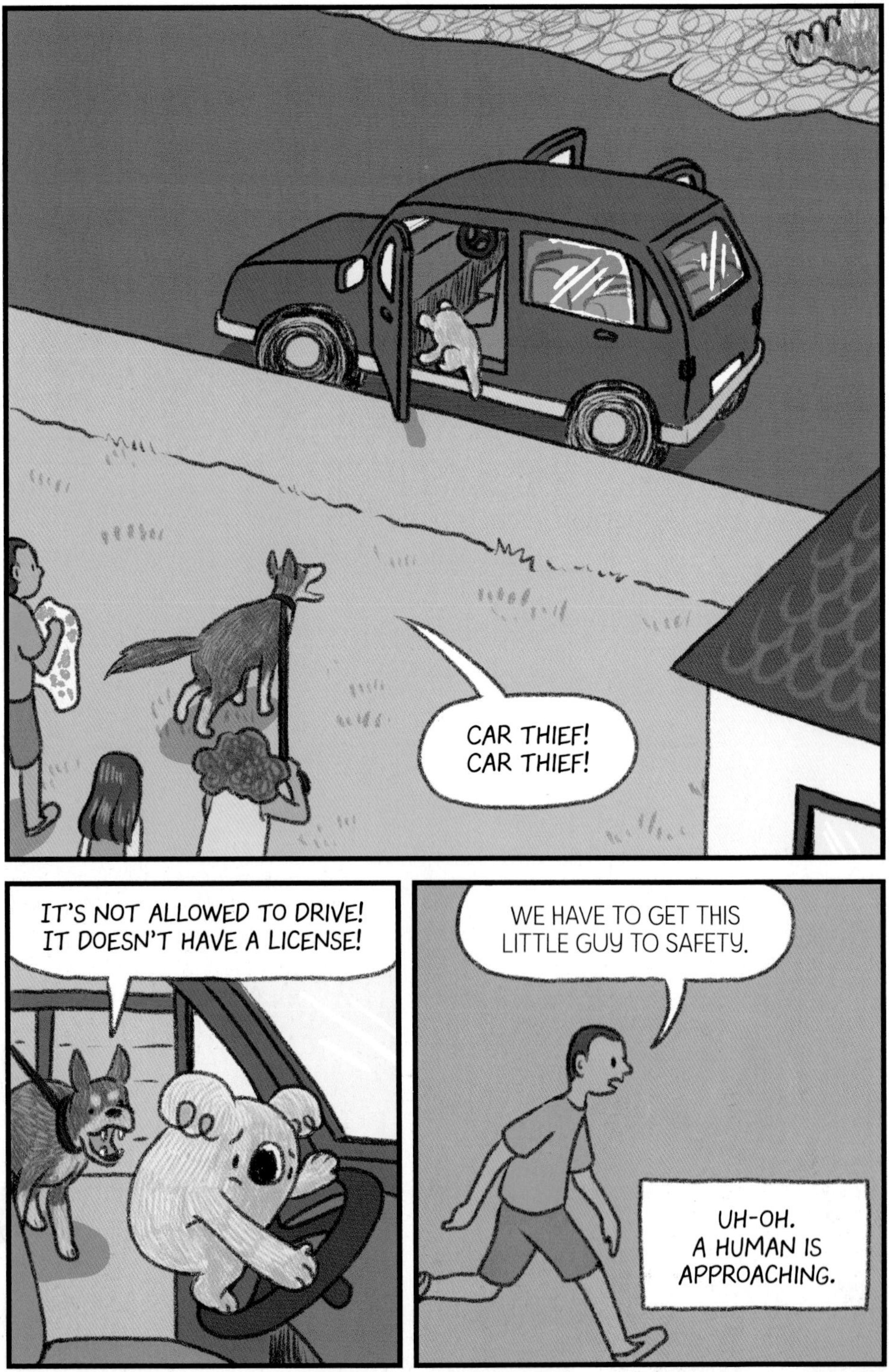
CAR THIEF!
CAR THIEF!
IT'S NOT ALLOWED TO DRIVE!
IT DOESN'T HAVE A LICENSE!
WE HAVE TO GET THIS
LITTLE GUY TO SAFETY.
UH-OH.
A HUMAN IS
APPROACHING.

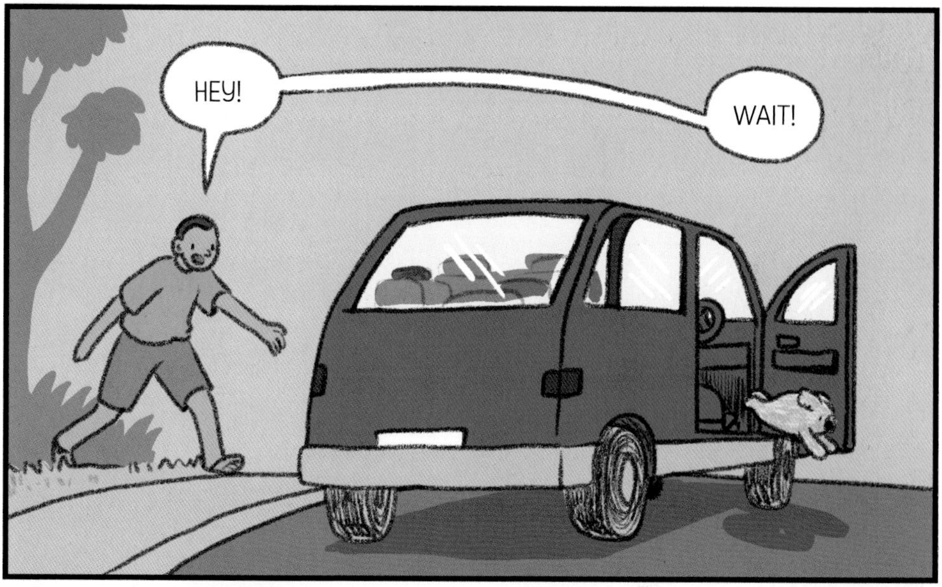
HEY!
WAIT!

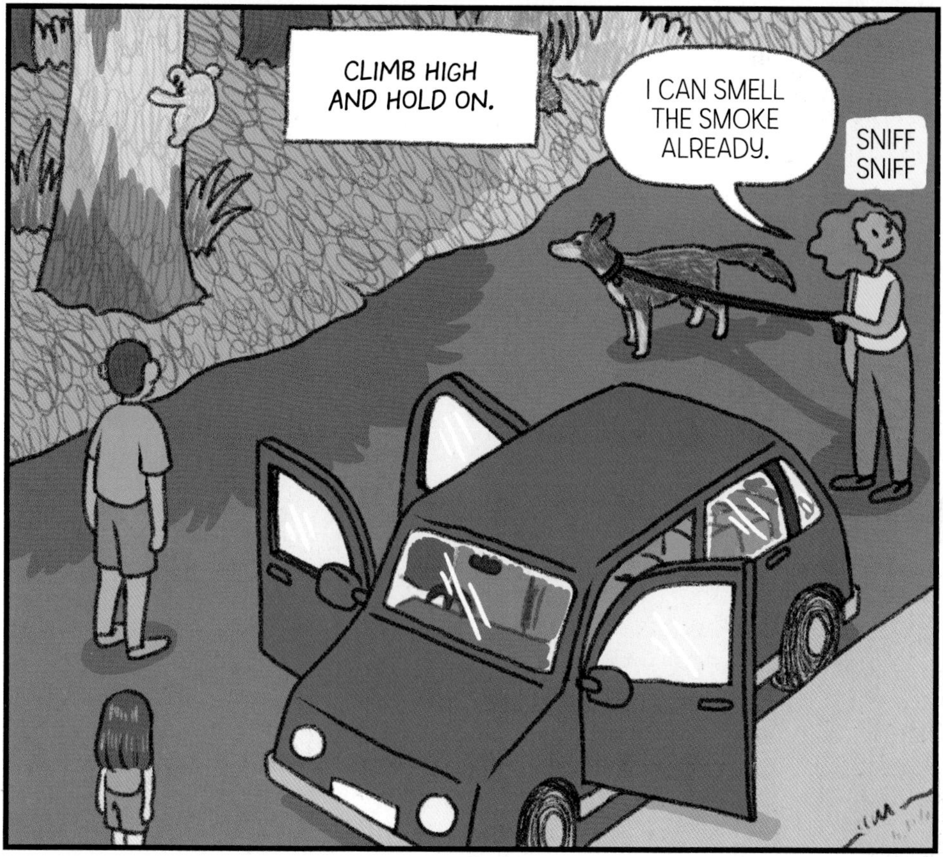
CLIMB HIGH AND HOLD ON.
I CAN SMELL THE SMOKE ALREADY.
SNIFF SNIFF

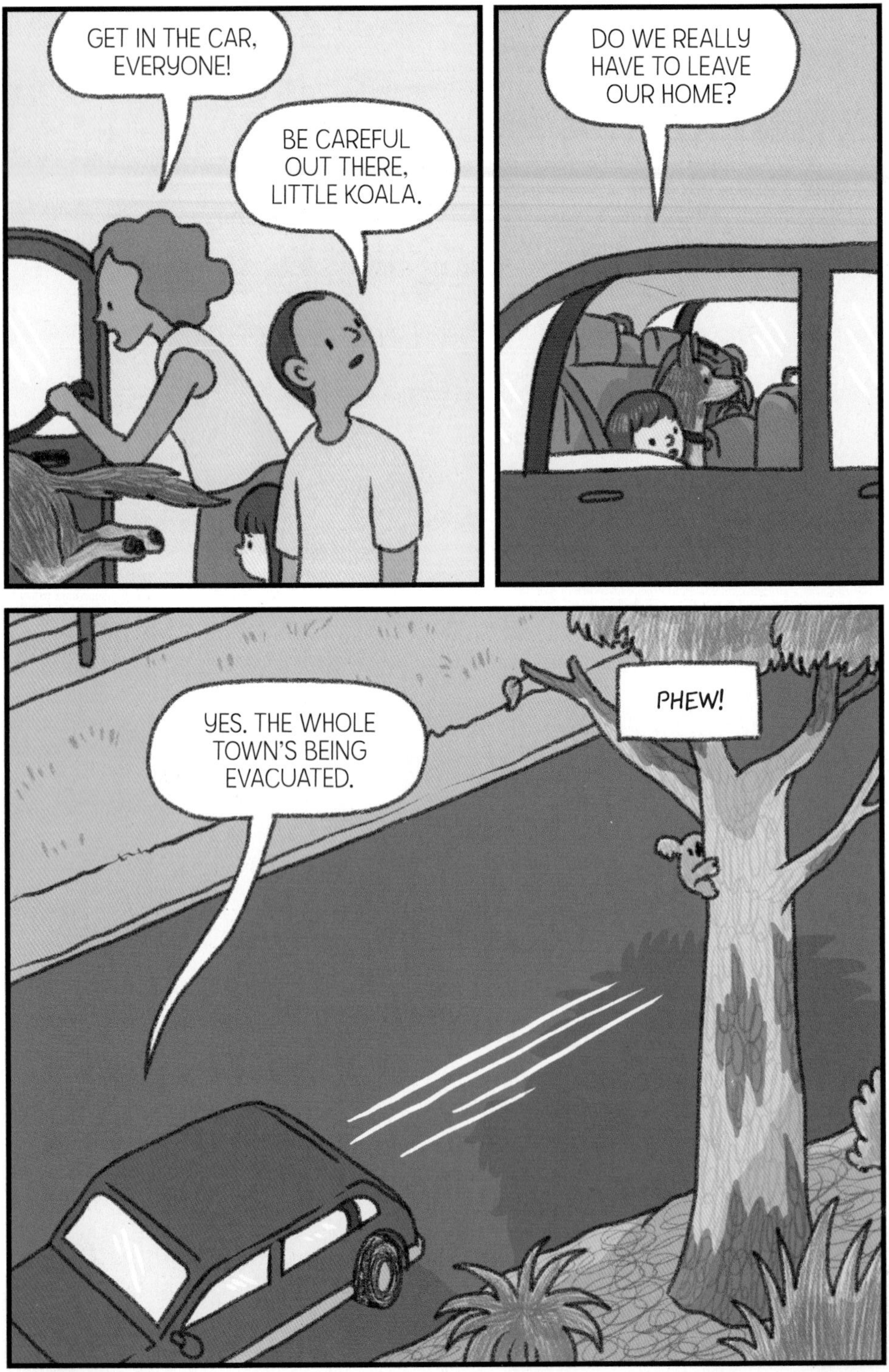
GET IN THE CAR, EVERYONE!
BE CAREFUL OUT THERE, LITTLE KOALA.
DO WE REALLY HAVE TO LEAVE OUR HOME?
YES. THE WHOLE TOWN'S BEING EVACUATED.
PHEW!

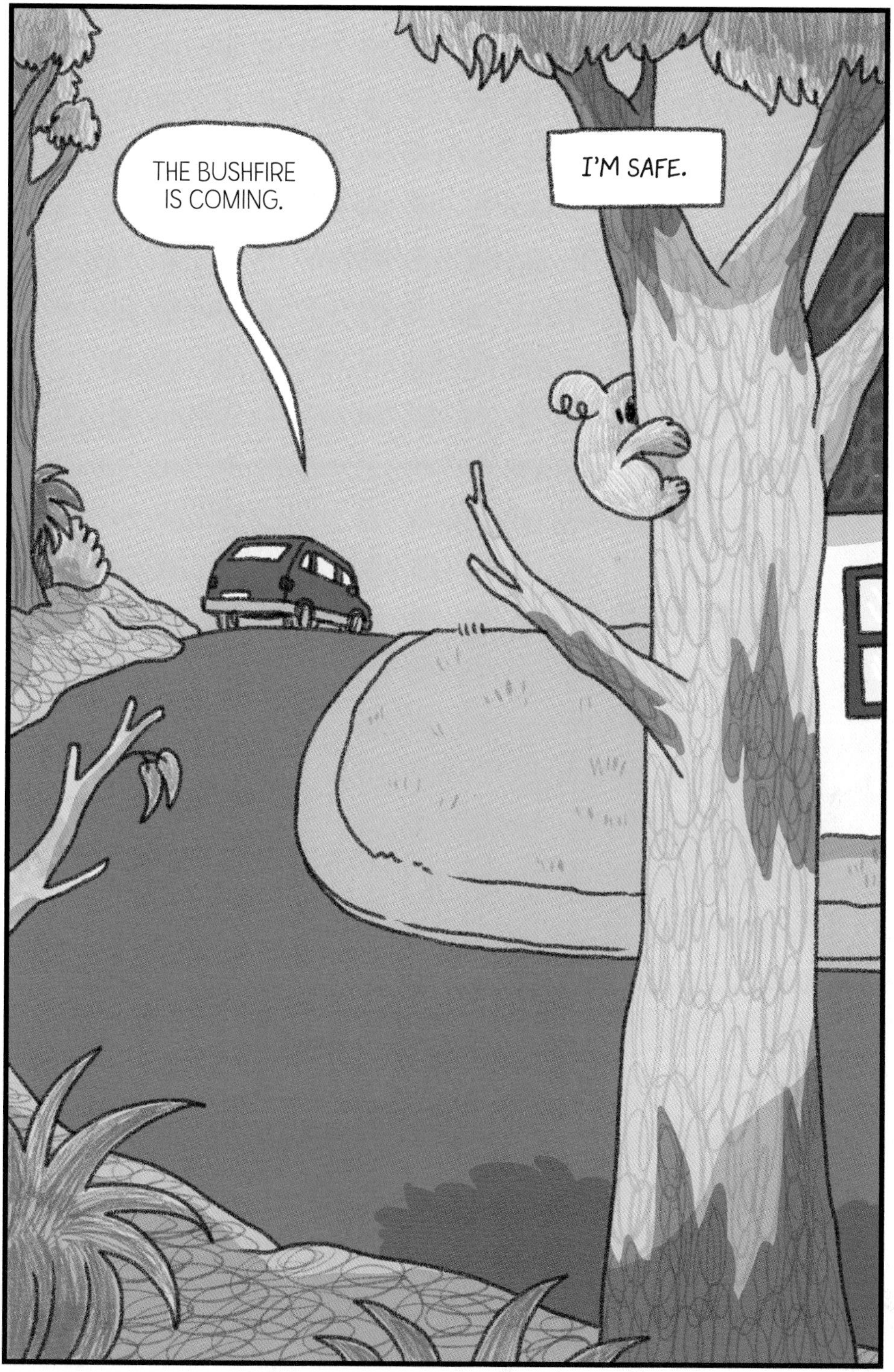
THE BUSHFIRE IS COMING.
I'M SAFE.

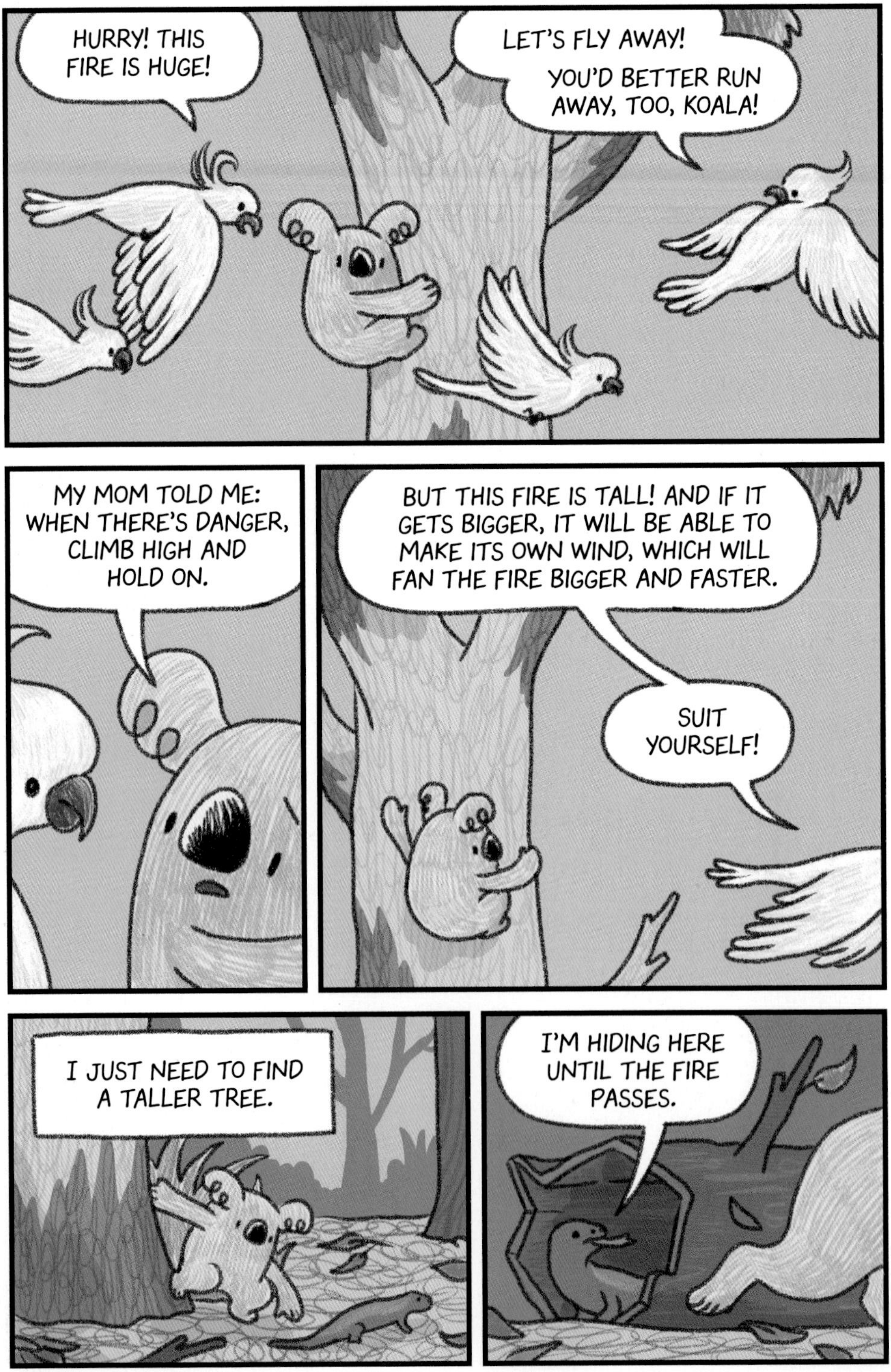
HURRY! THIS FIRE IS HUGE!
LET'S FLY AWAY!
YOU'D BETTER RUN AWAY, TOO, KOALA!
MY MOM TOLD ME: WHEN THERE'S DANGER, CLIMB HIGH AND HOLD ON.
BUT THIS FIRE IS TALL! AND IF IT GETS BIGGER, IT WILL BE ABLE TO MAKE ITS OWN WIND, WHICH WILL FAN THE FIRE BIGGER AND FASTER.
SUIT YOURSELF!
I JUST NEED TO FIND A TALLER TREE.
I'M HIDING HERE UNTIL THE FIRE PASSES.

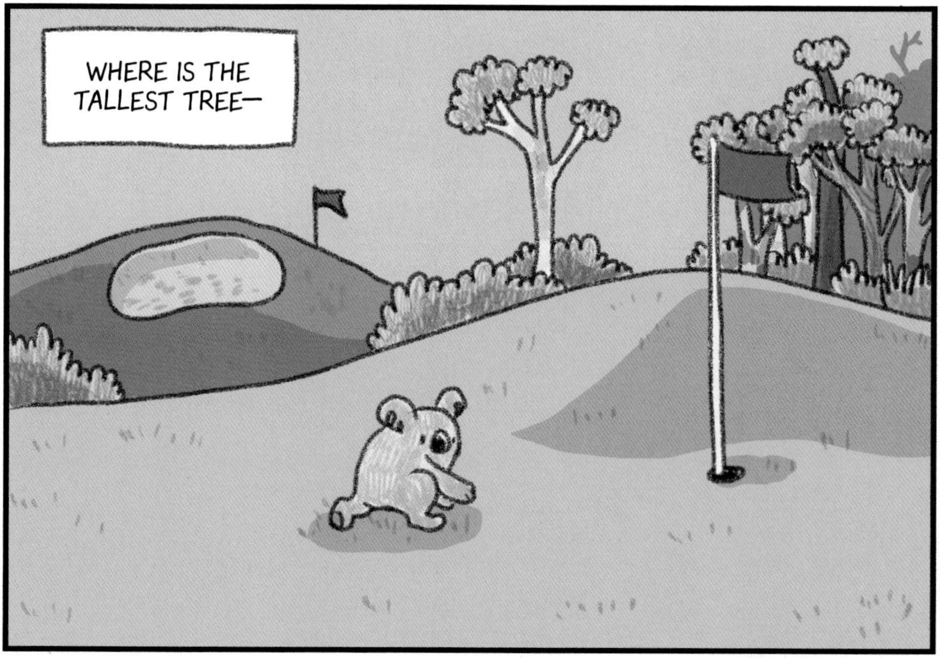
WHERE IS THE TALLEST TREE—

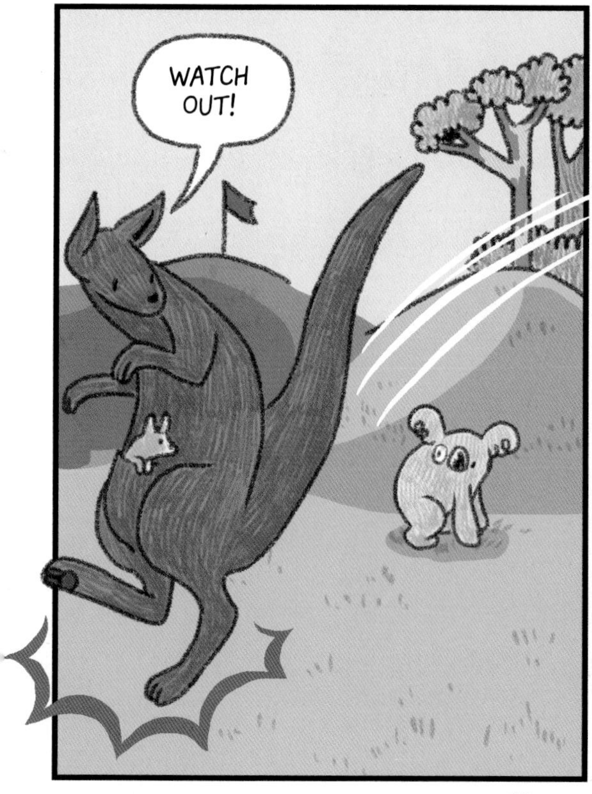
WATCH OUT!

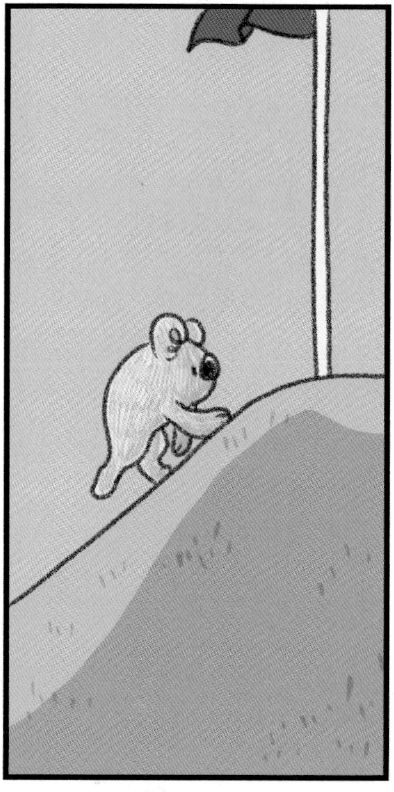

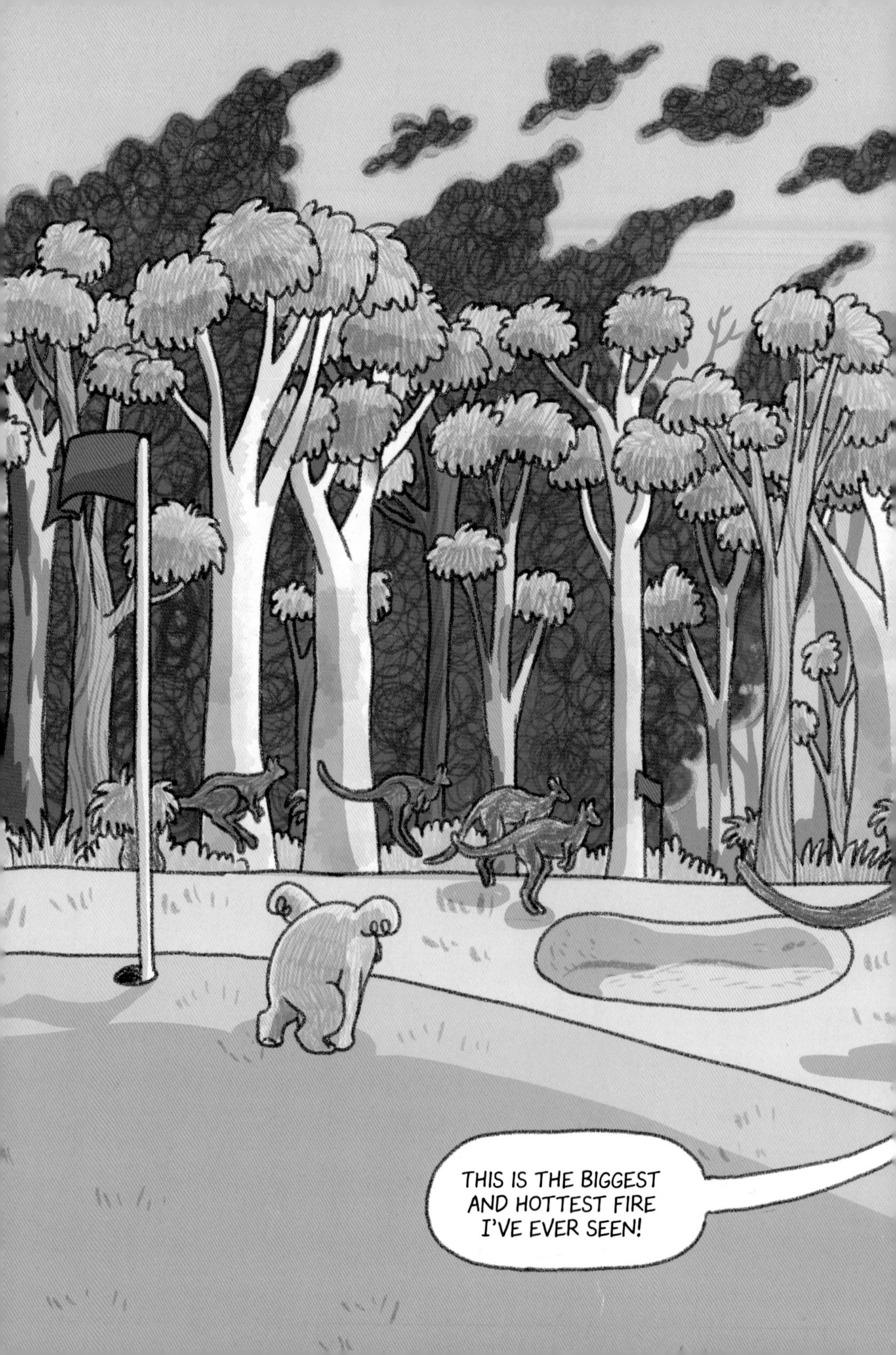
THIS IS THE BIGGEST AND HOTTEST FIRE I'VE EVER SEEN!

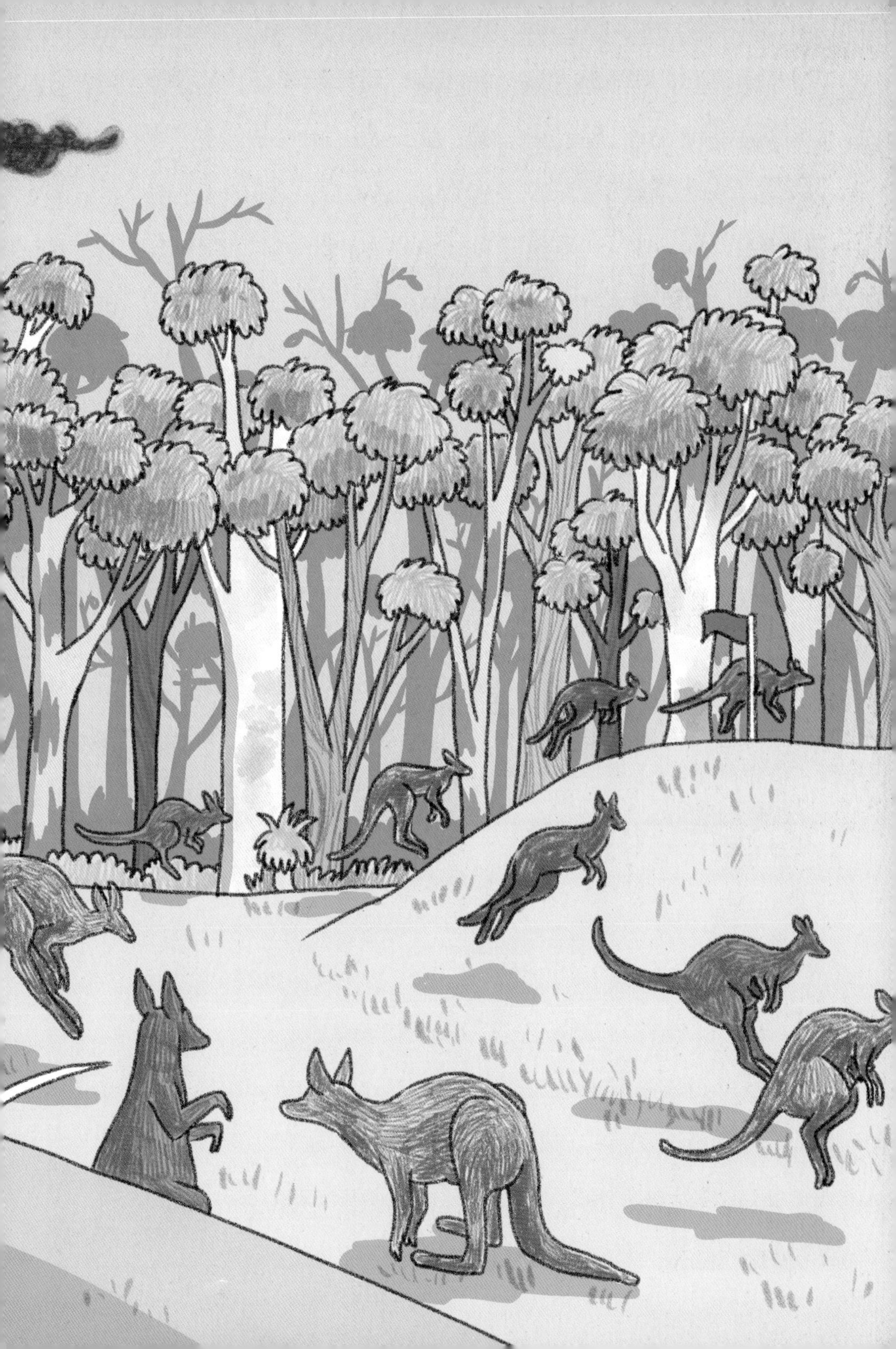

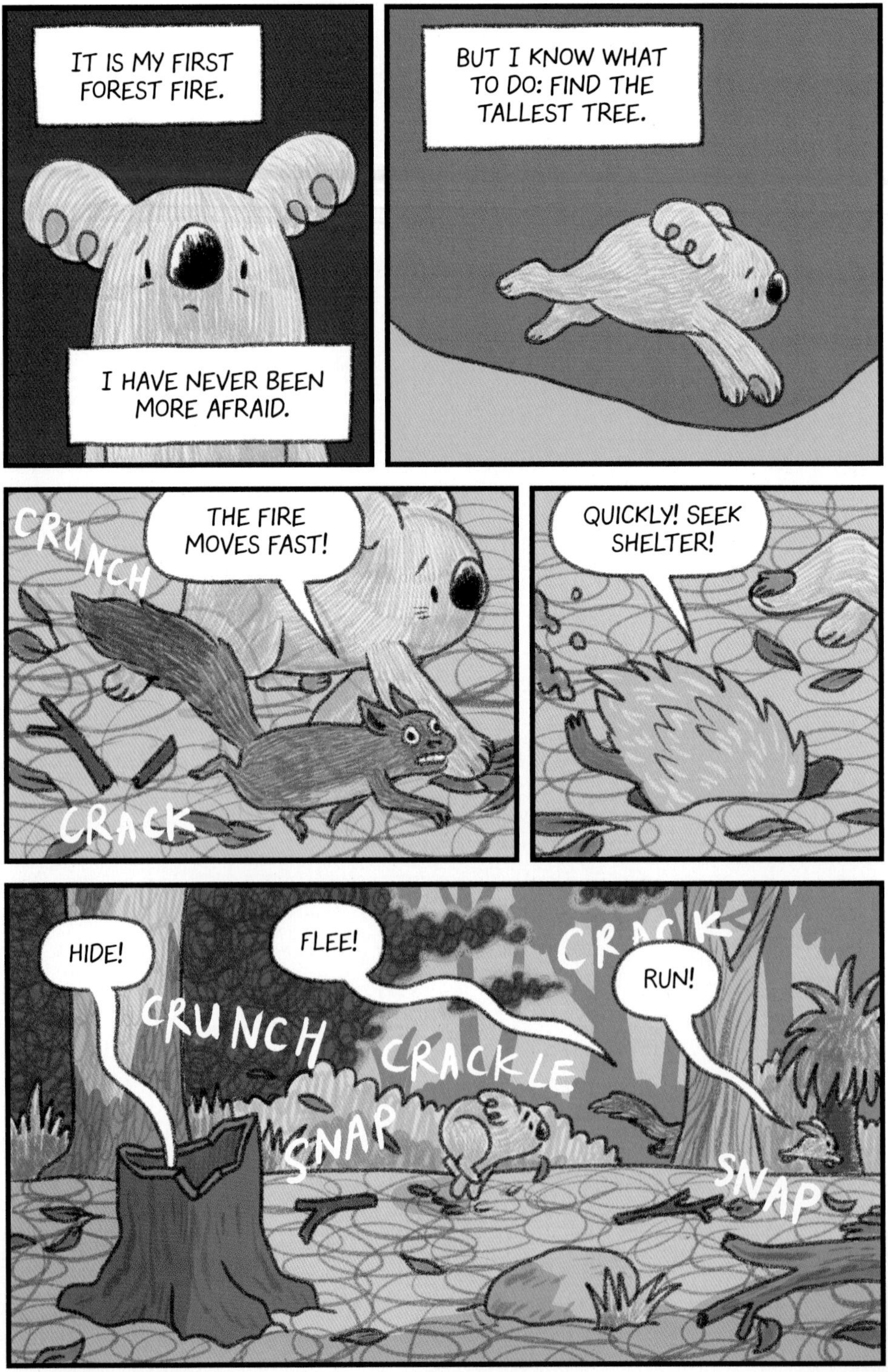
IT IS MY FIRST FOREST FIRE.
I HAVE NEVER BEEN MORE AFRAID.
BUT I KNOW WHAT TO DO: FIND THE TALLEST TREE.
CRUNCH
THE FIRE MOVES FAST!
CRACK
QUICKLY! SEEK SHELTER!
HIDE!
CRUNCH
FLEE!
CRACKLE
SNAP
CRACK
RUN!
SNAP

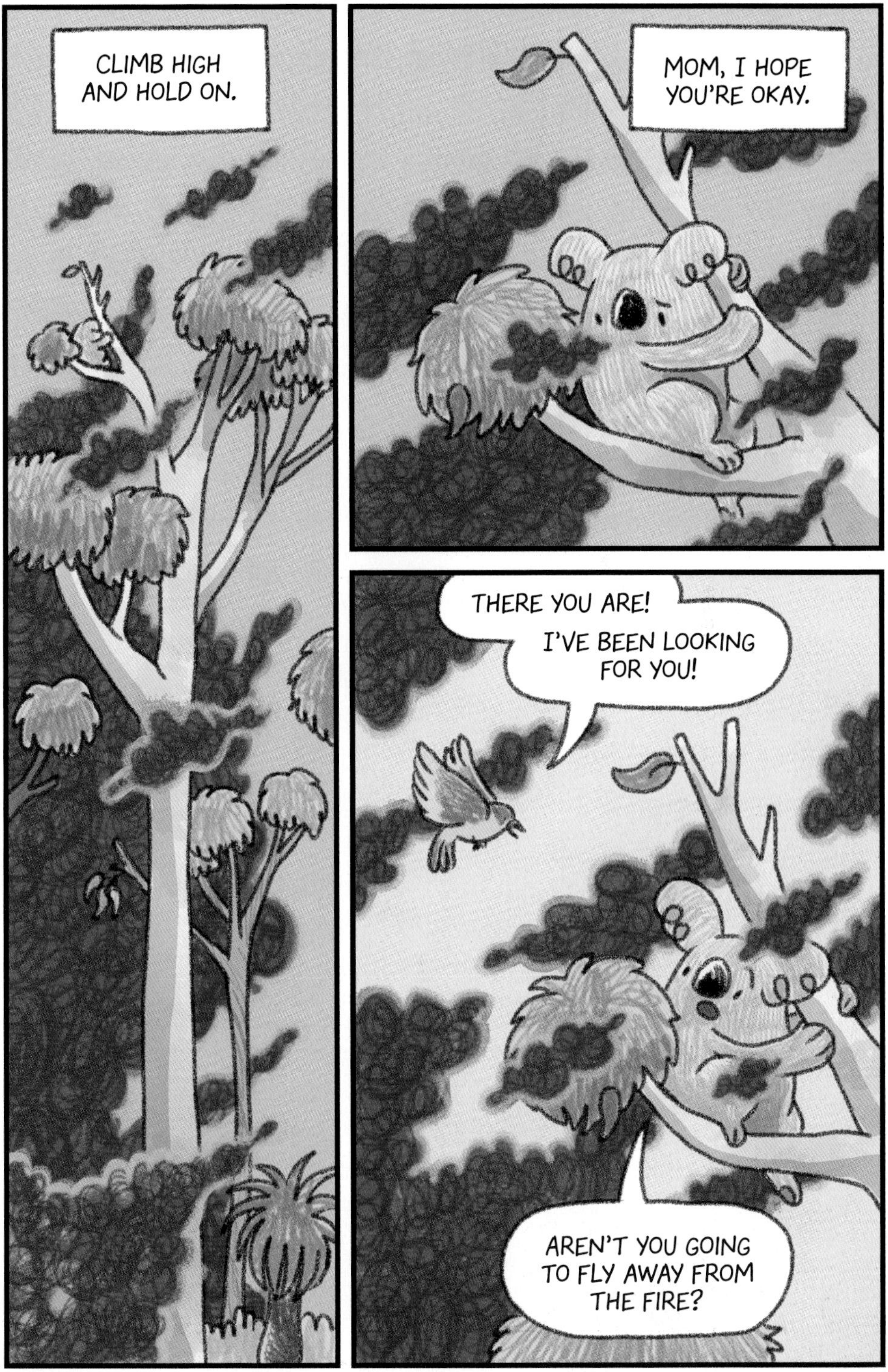

CLIMB HIGH AND HOLD ON.
MOM, I HOPE YOU'RE OKAY.
THERE YOU ARE!
I'VE BEEN LOOKING FOR YOU!
AREN'T YOU GOING TO FLY AWAY FROM THE FIRE?

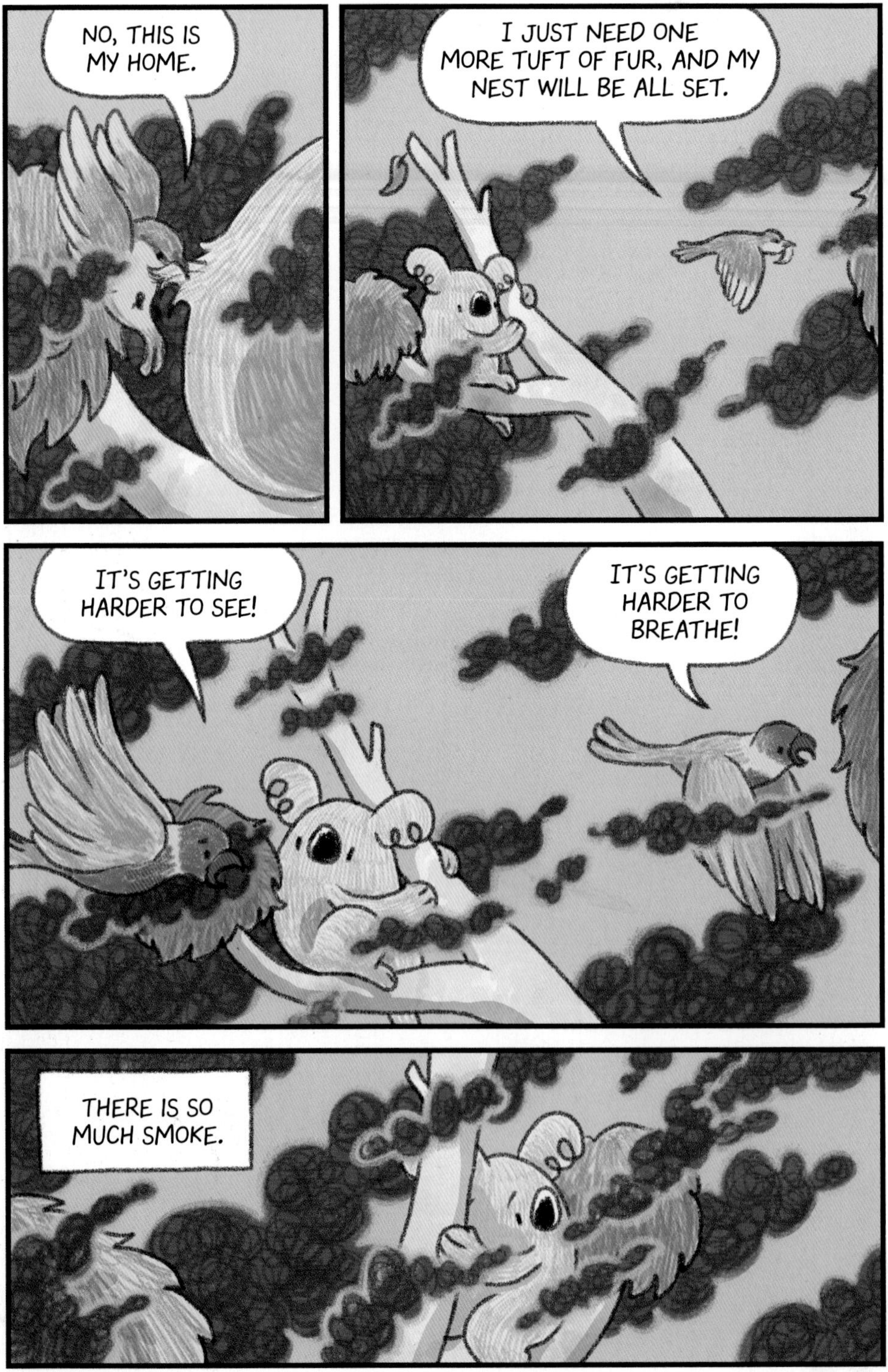
NO, THIS IS MY HOME.
I JUST NEED ONE MORE TUFT OF FUR, AND MY NEST WILL BE ALL SET.
IT'S GETTING HARDER TO SEE!
IT'S GETTING HARDER TO BREATHE!
THERE IS SO MUCH SMOKE.

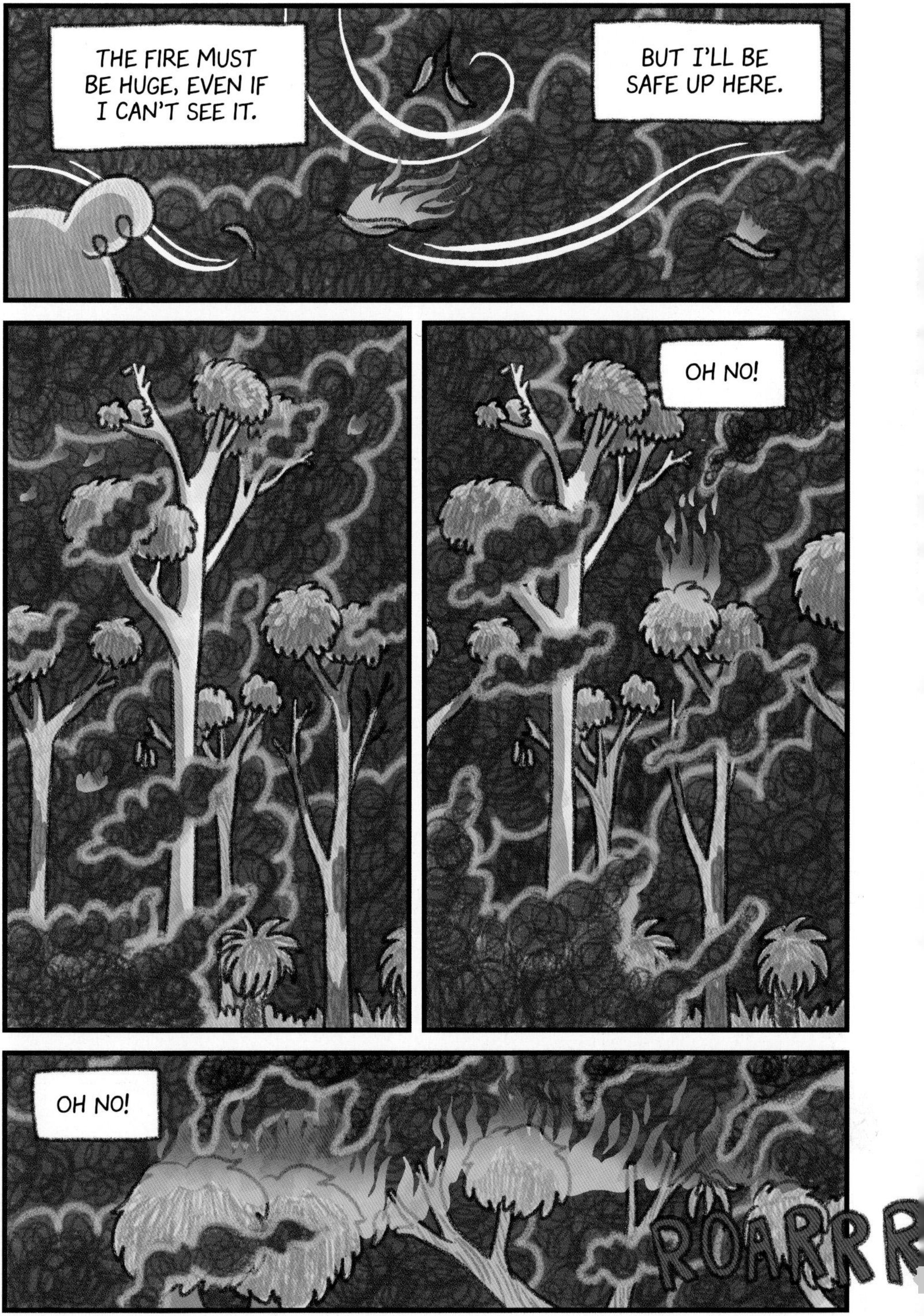
THE FIRE MUST BE HUGE, EVEN IF I CAN'T SEE IT.
BUT I'LL BE SAFE UP HERE.
OH NO!
OH NO!
ROARRR

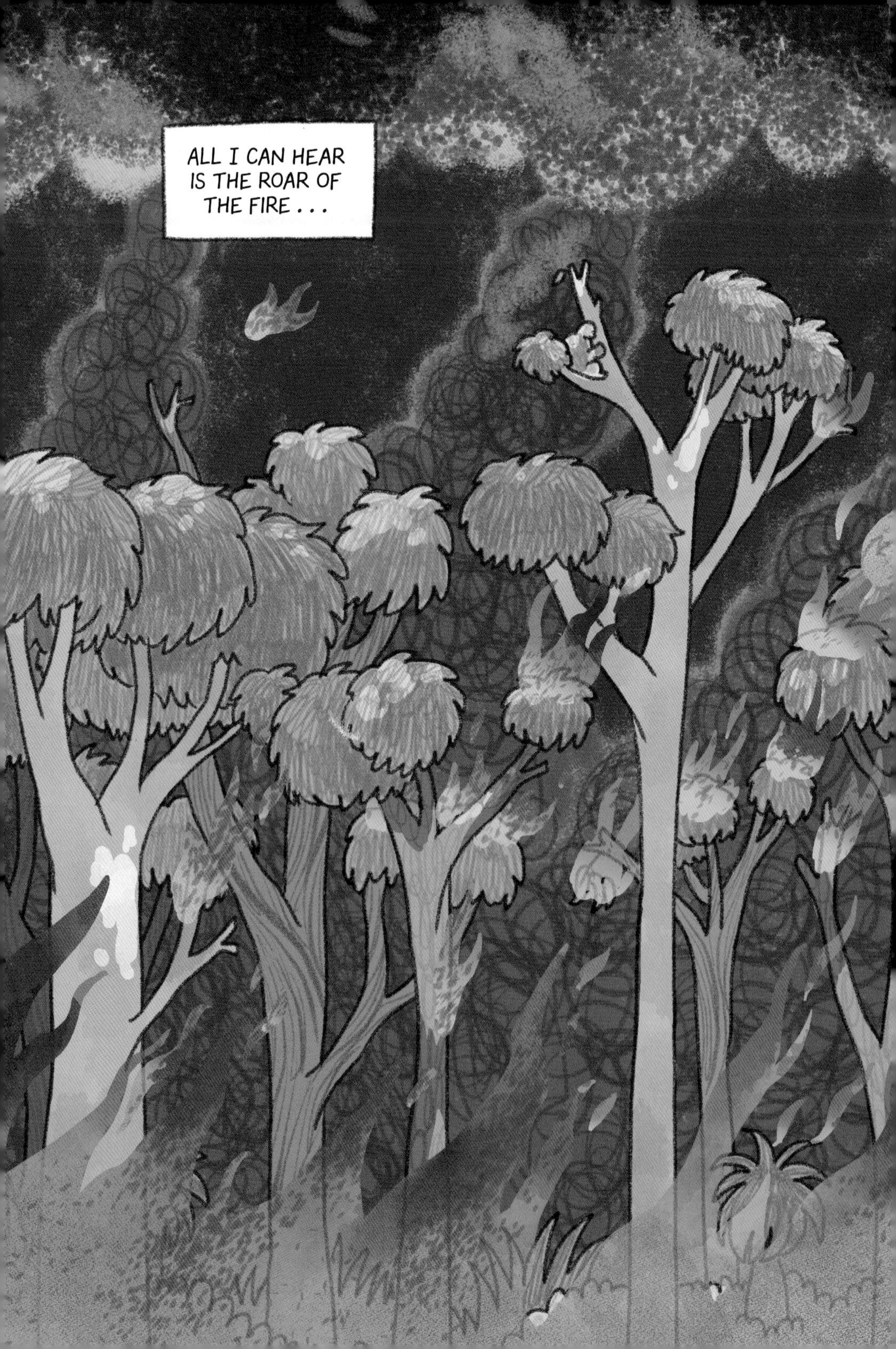
ALL I CAN HEAR IS THE ROAR OF THE FIRE . . .

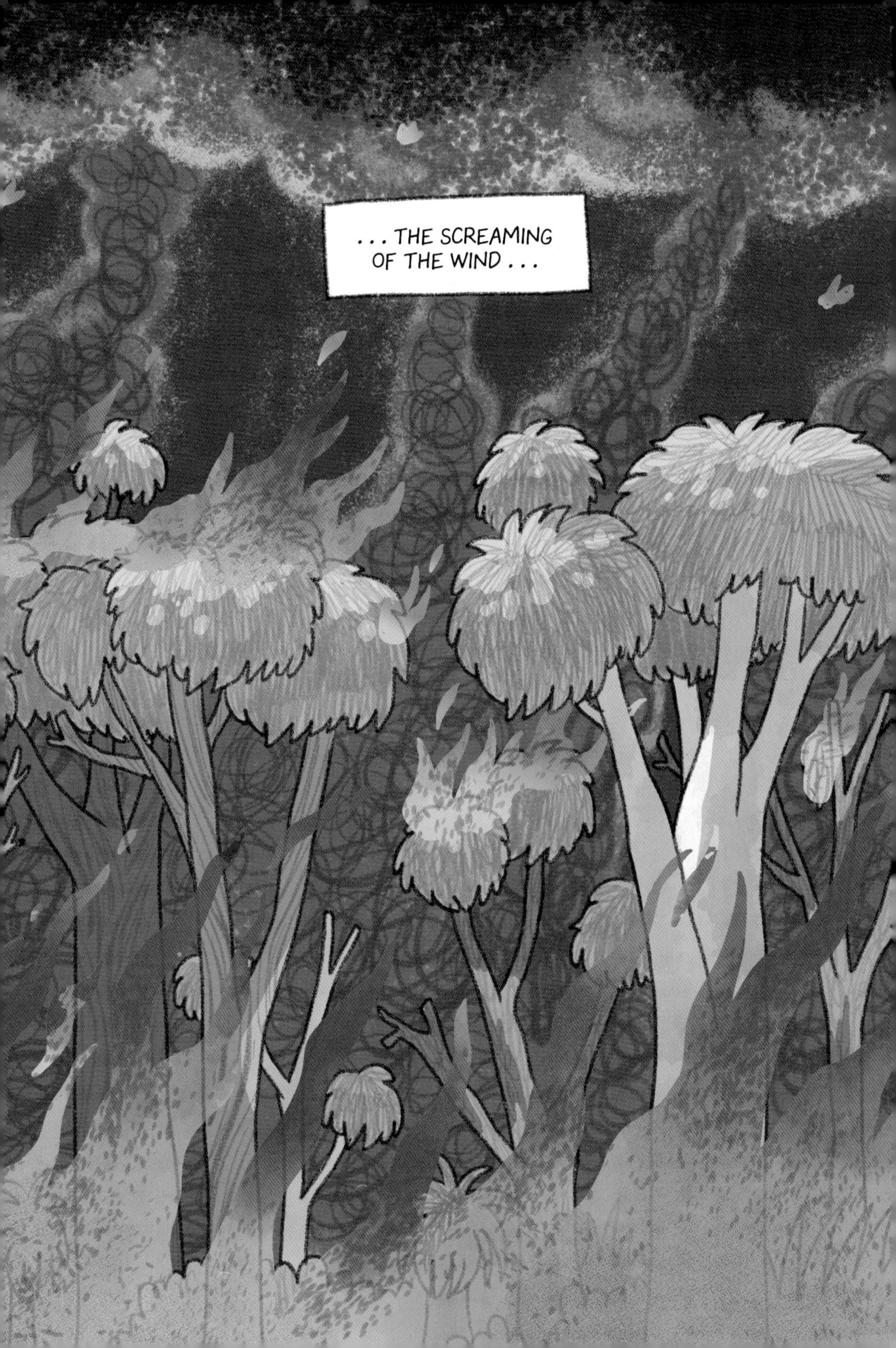
. . . THE SCREAMING OF THE WIND . . .

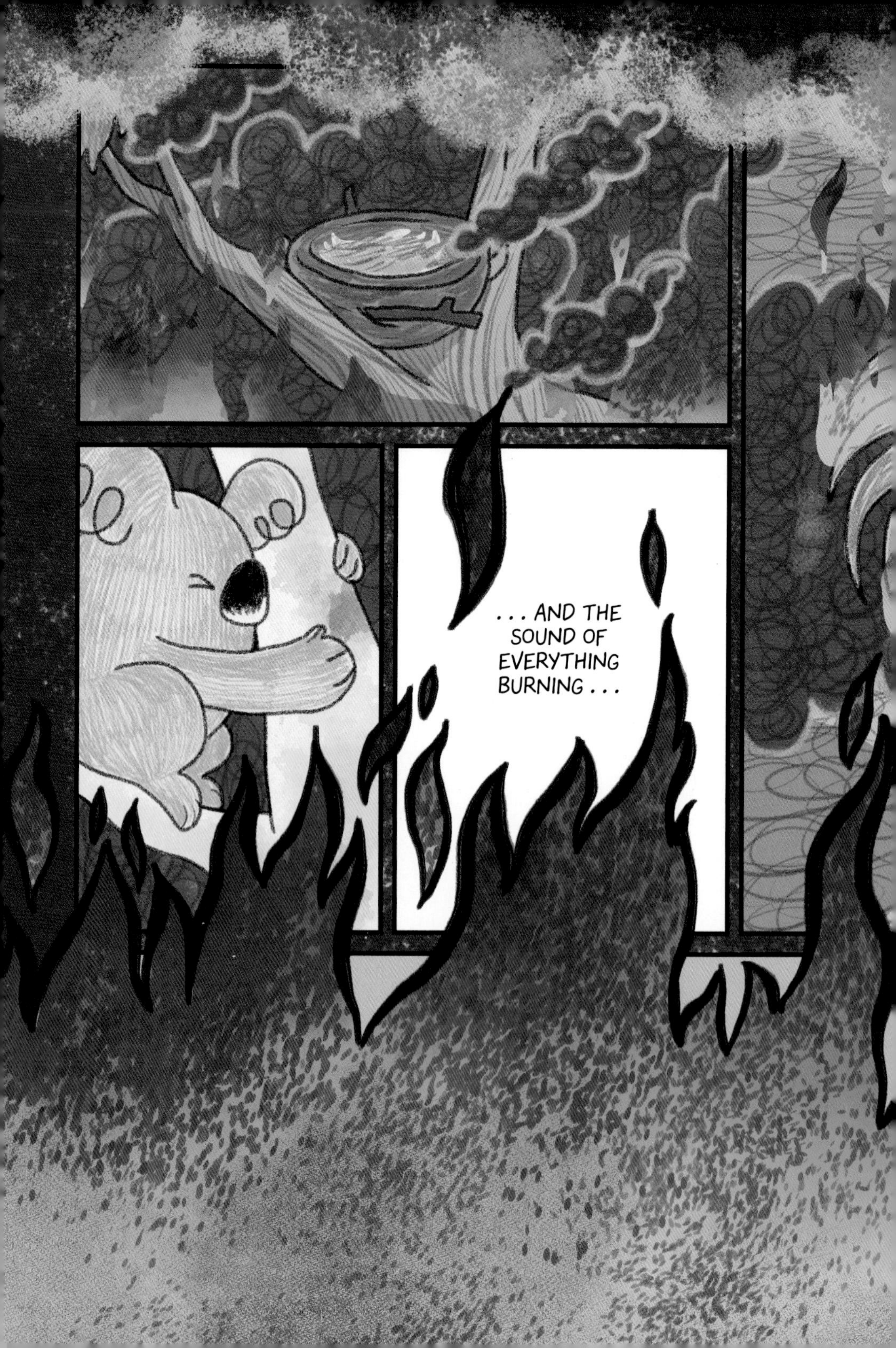
. . . AND THE SOUND OF EVERYTHING BURNING . . .

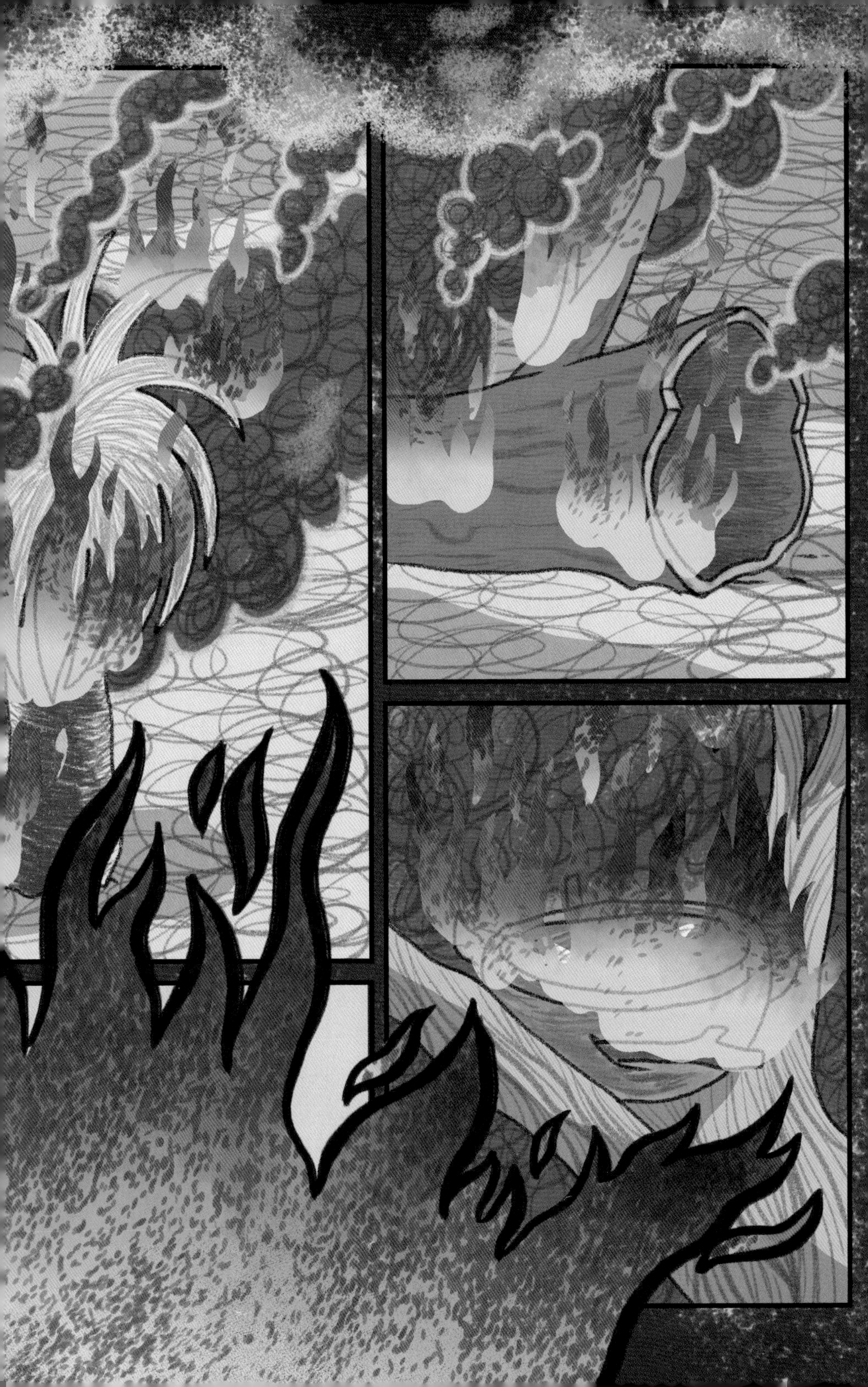

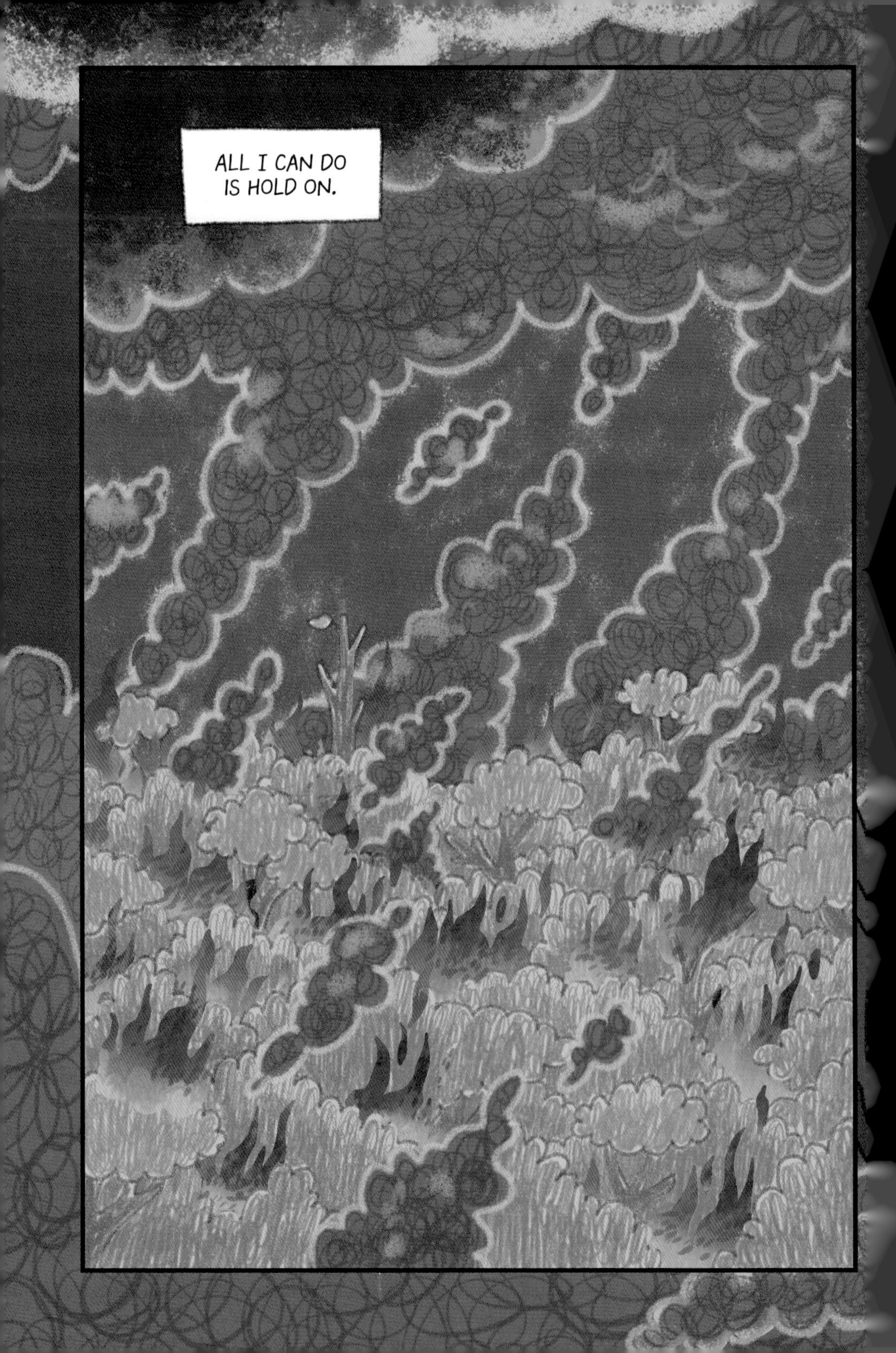
ALL I CAN DO
IS HOLD ON.

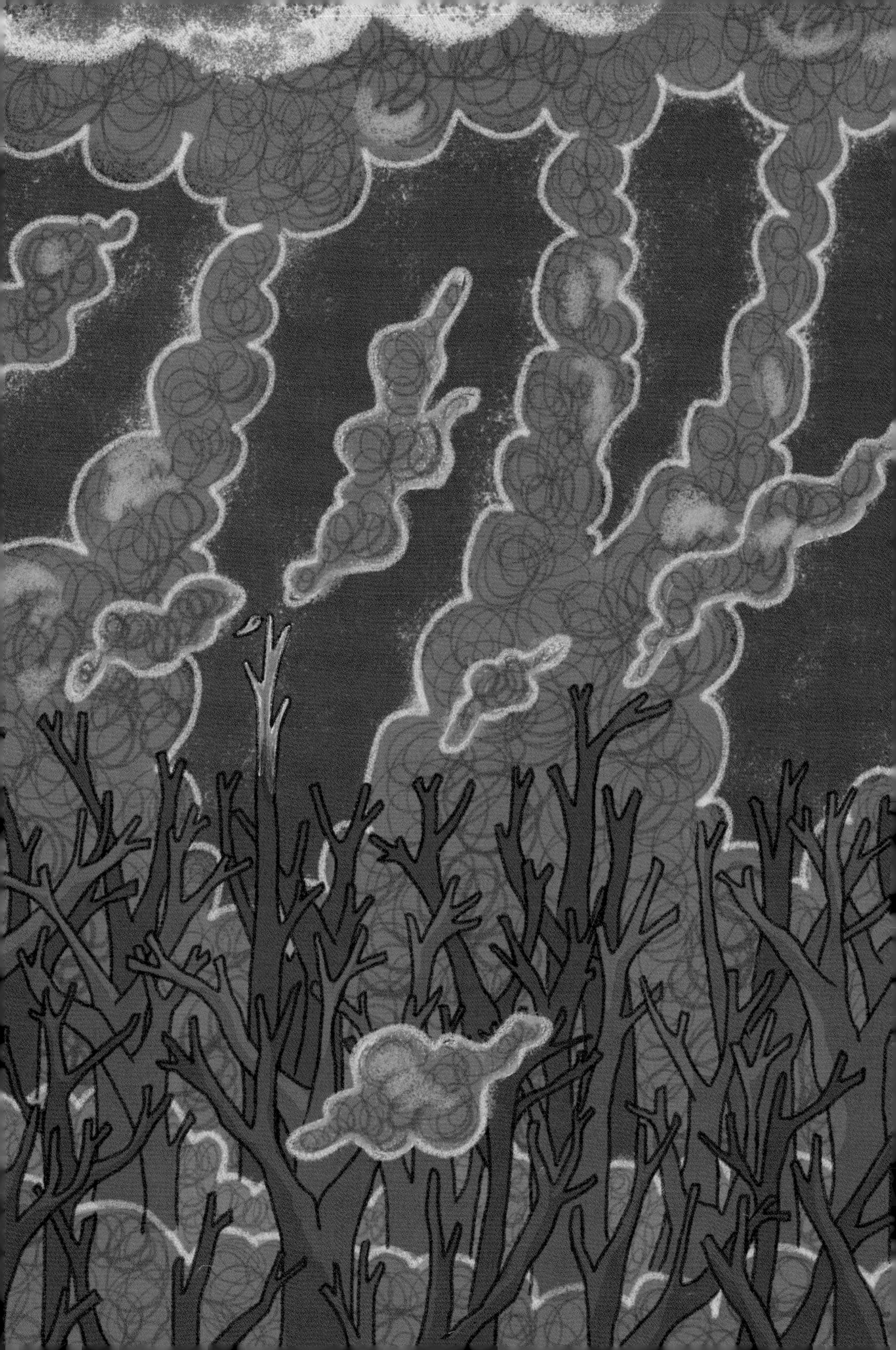

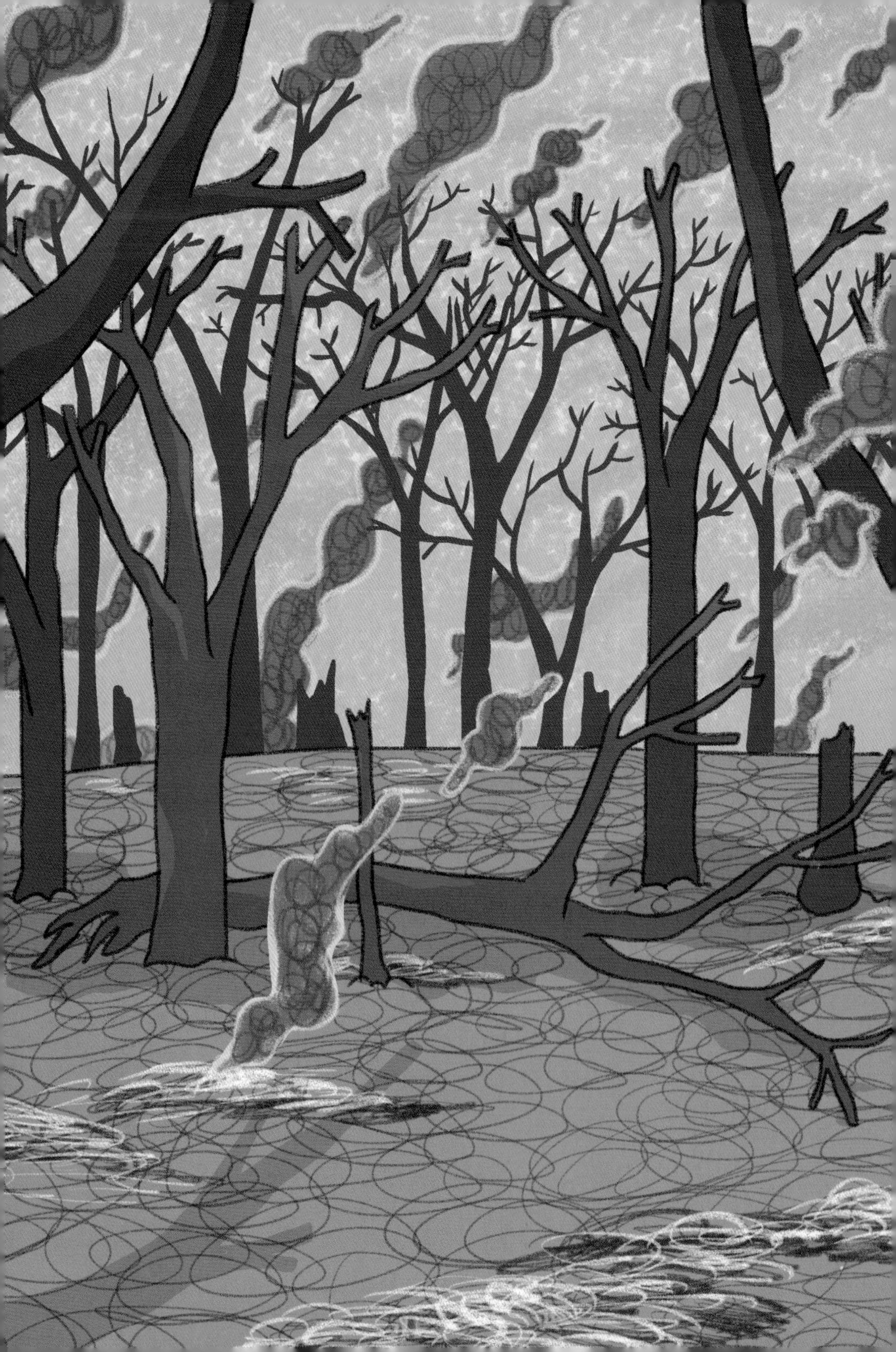

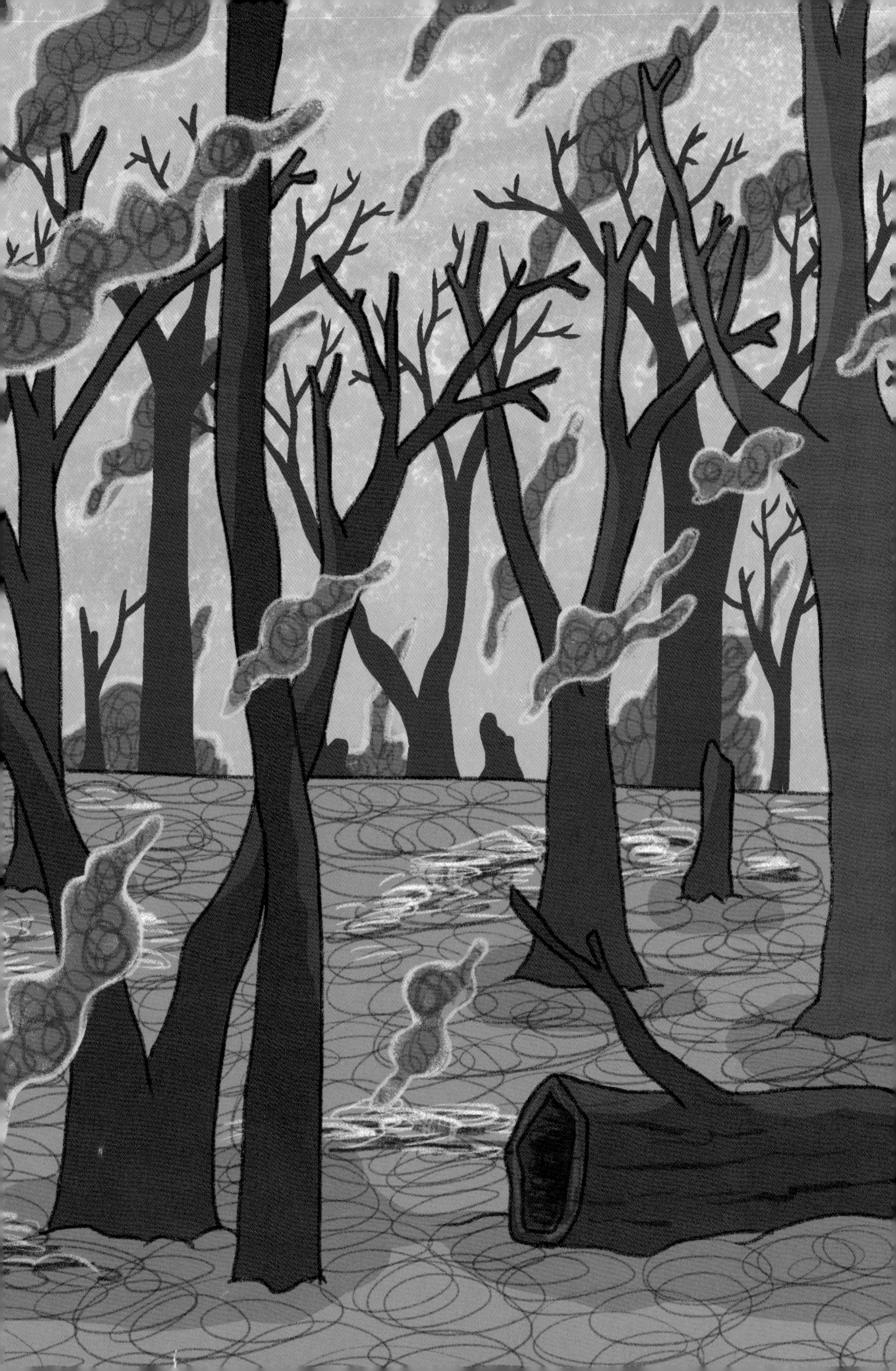

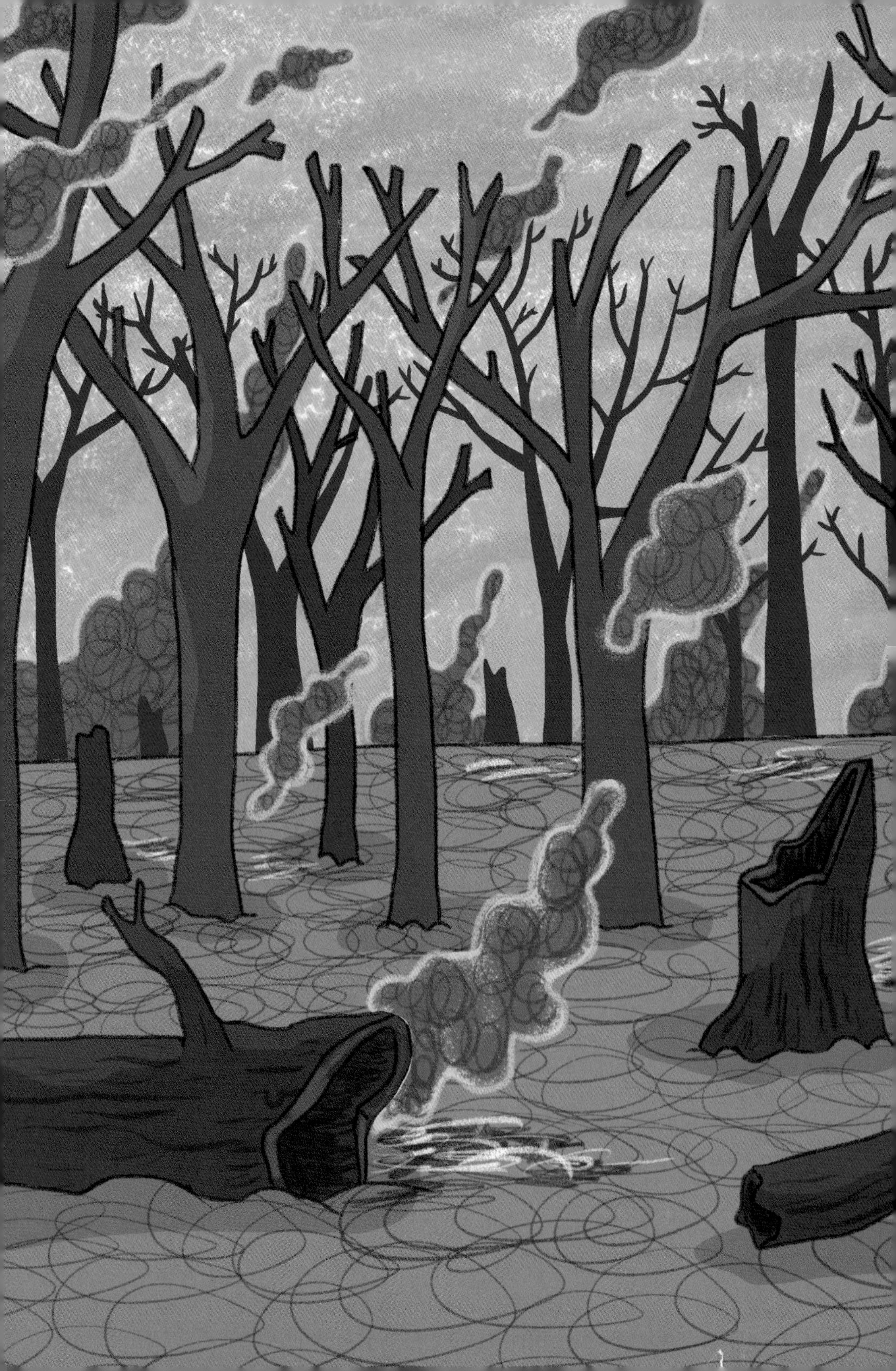

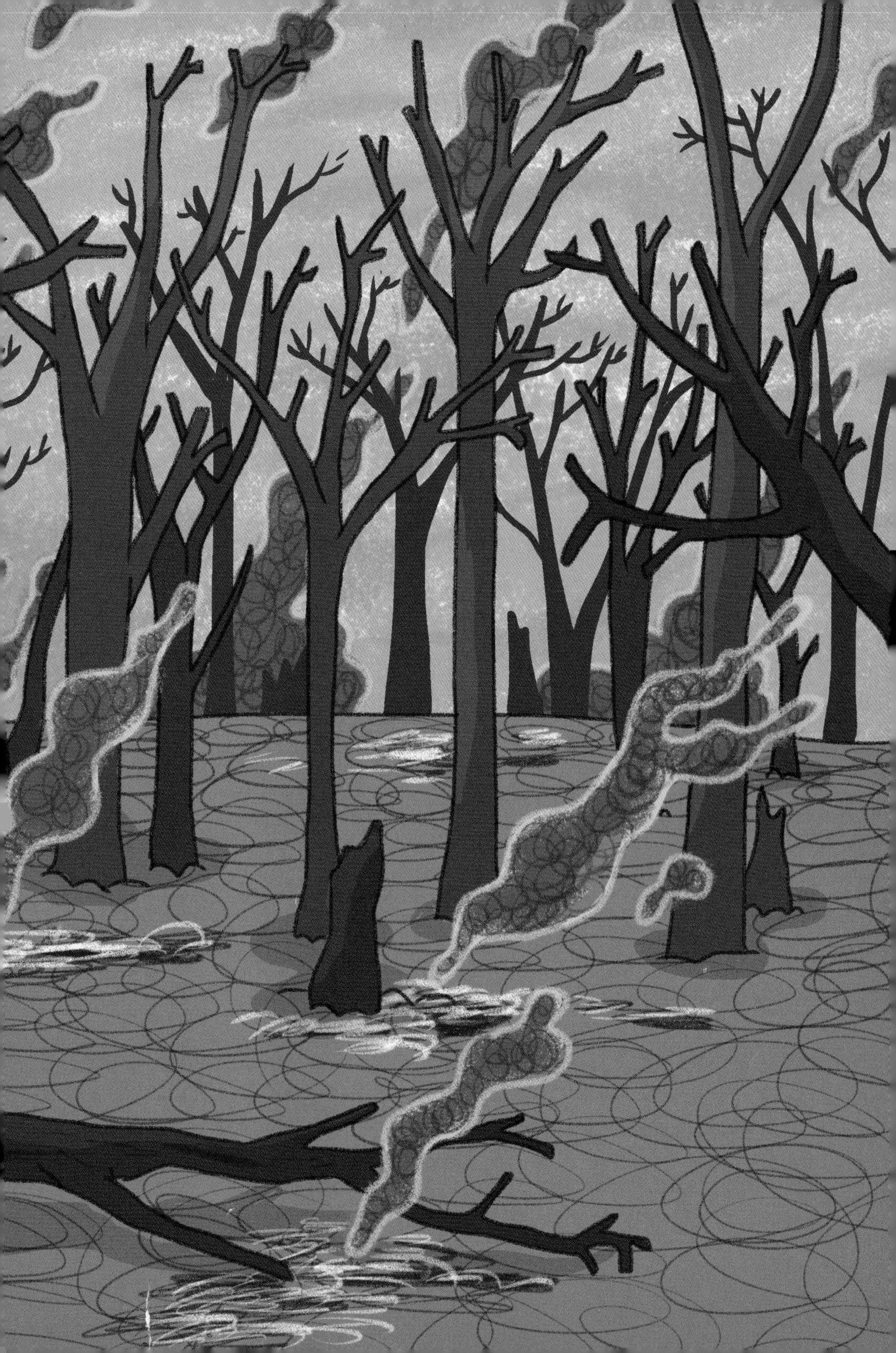

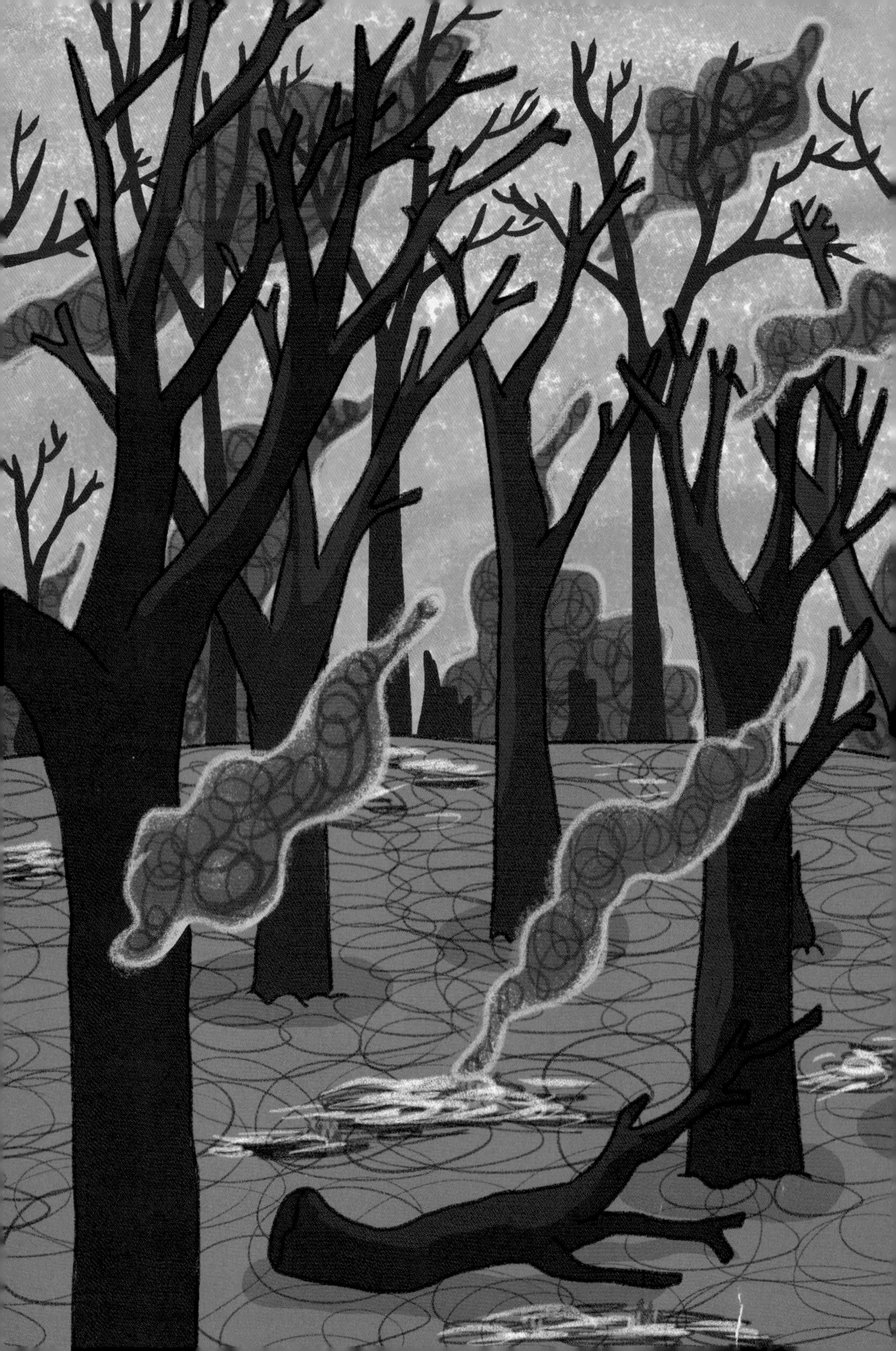

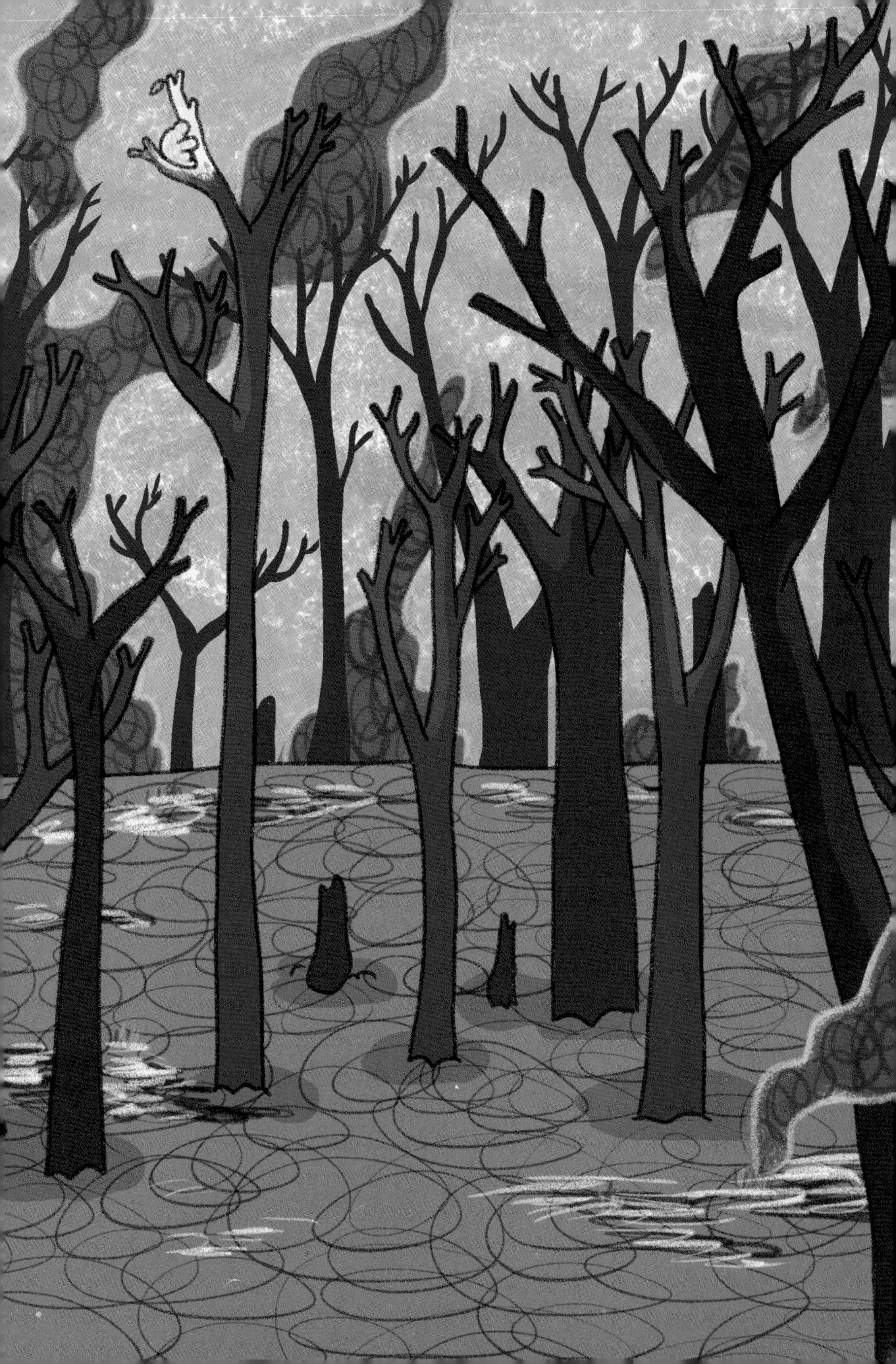

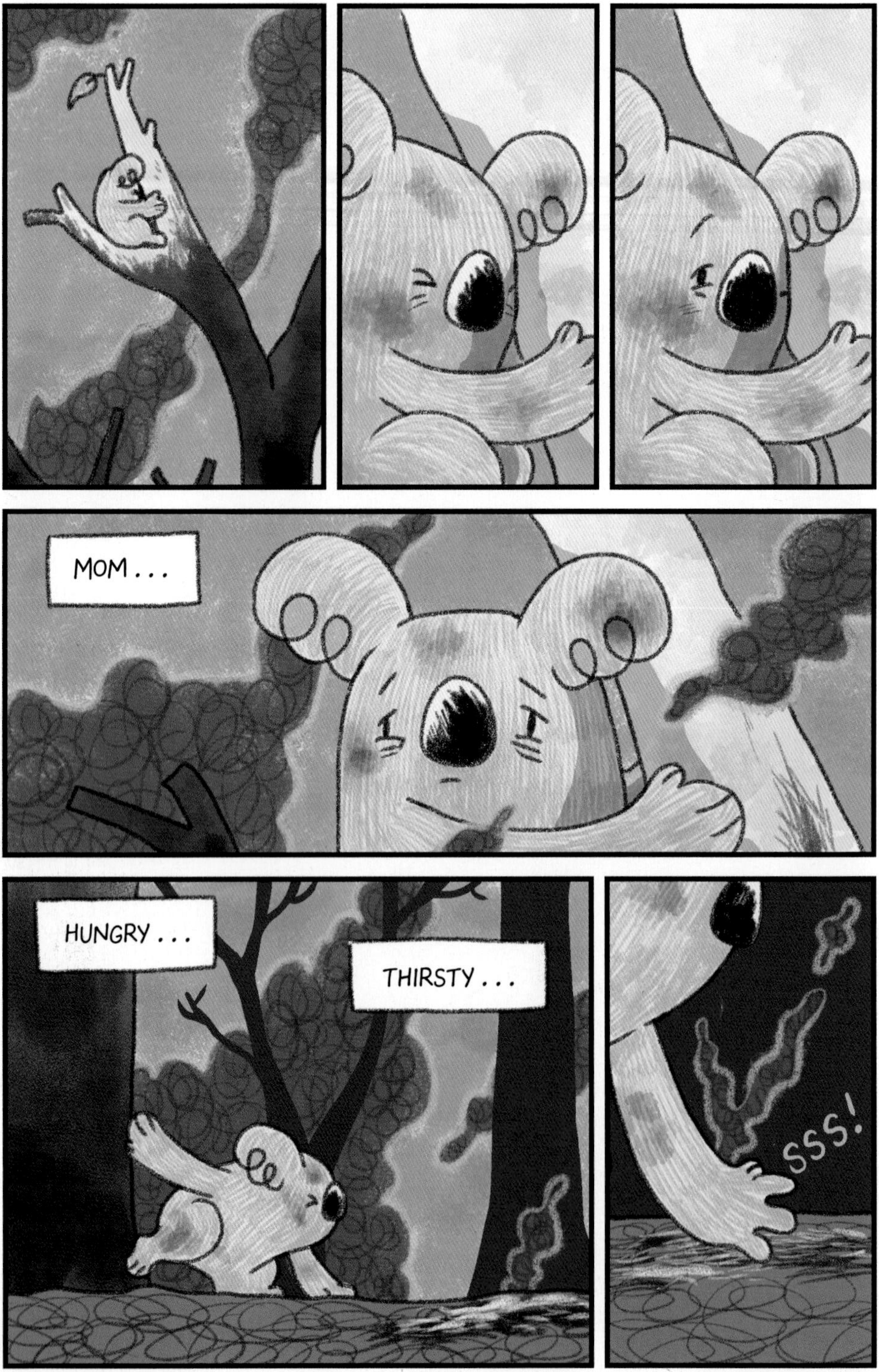
MOM . . .
HUNGRY . . .
THIRSTY . . .
SSS!

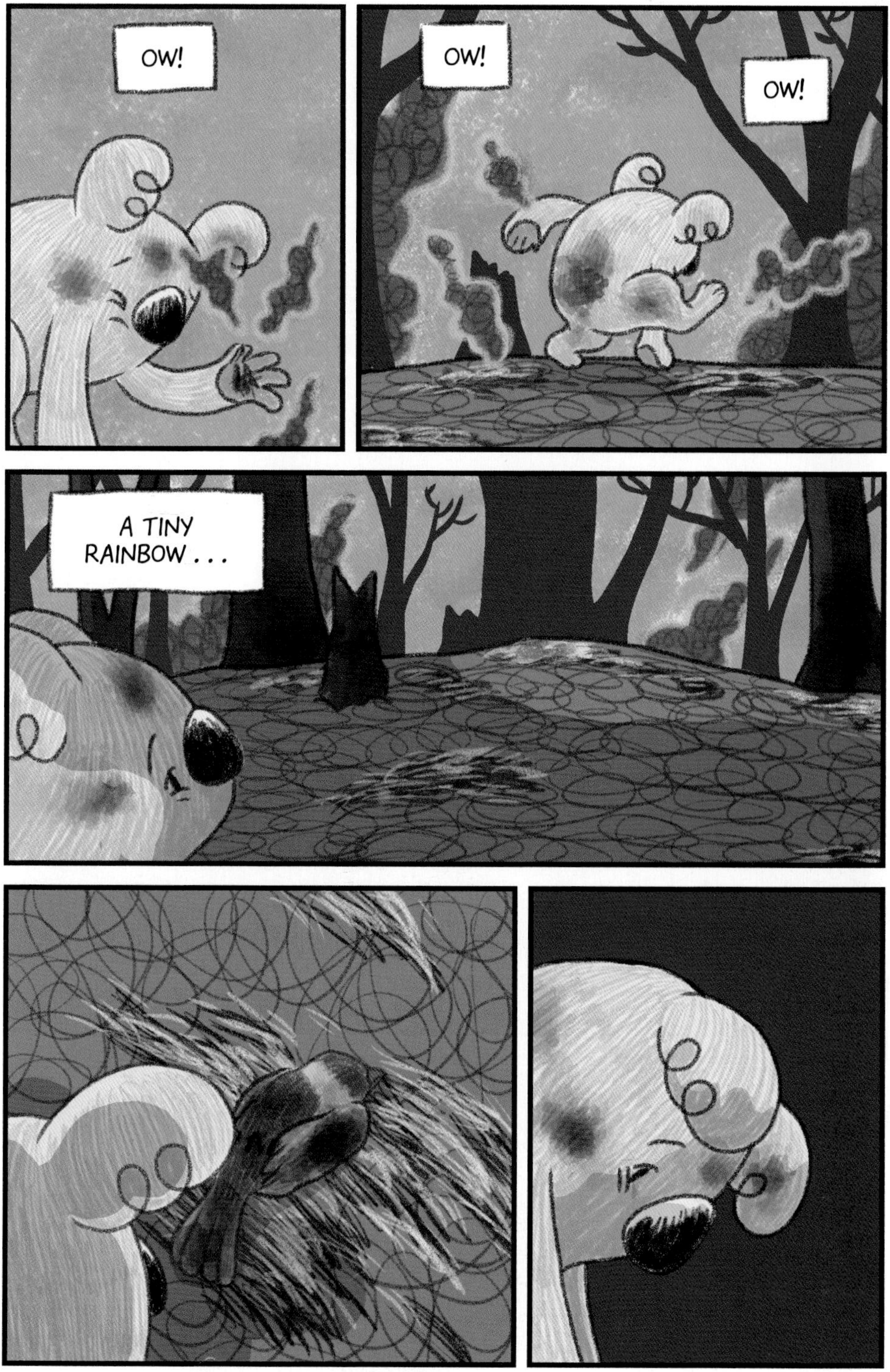
OW!
OW!
OW!
A TINY RAINBOW . . .

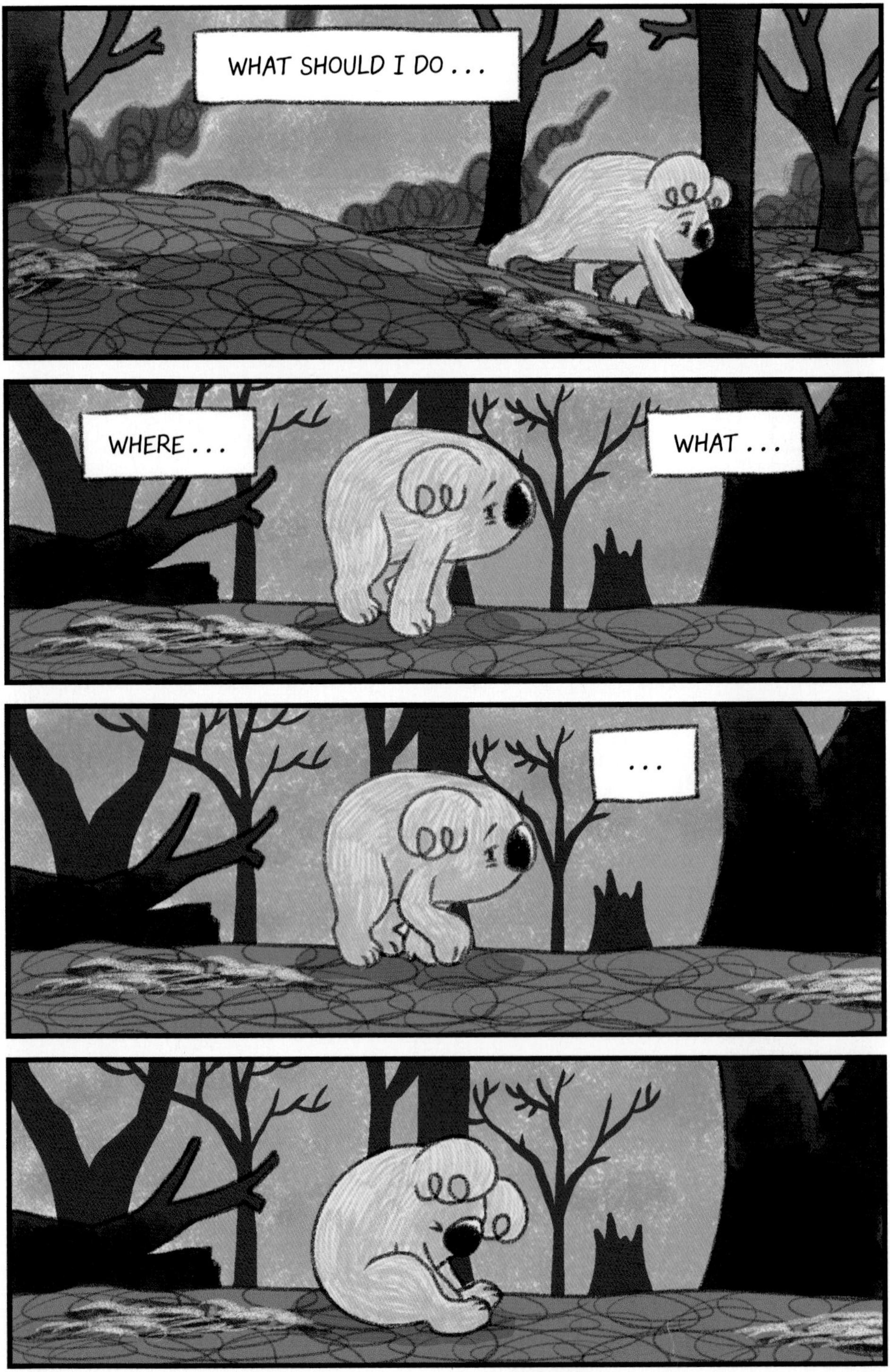
WHAT SHOULD I DO . . .
WHERE . . .
WHAT . . .
. . .

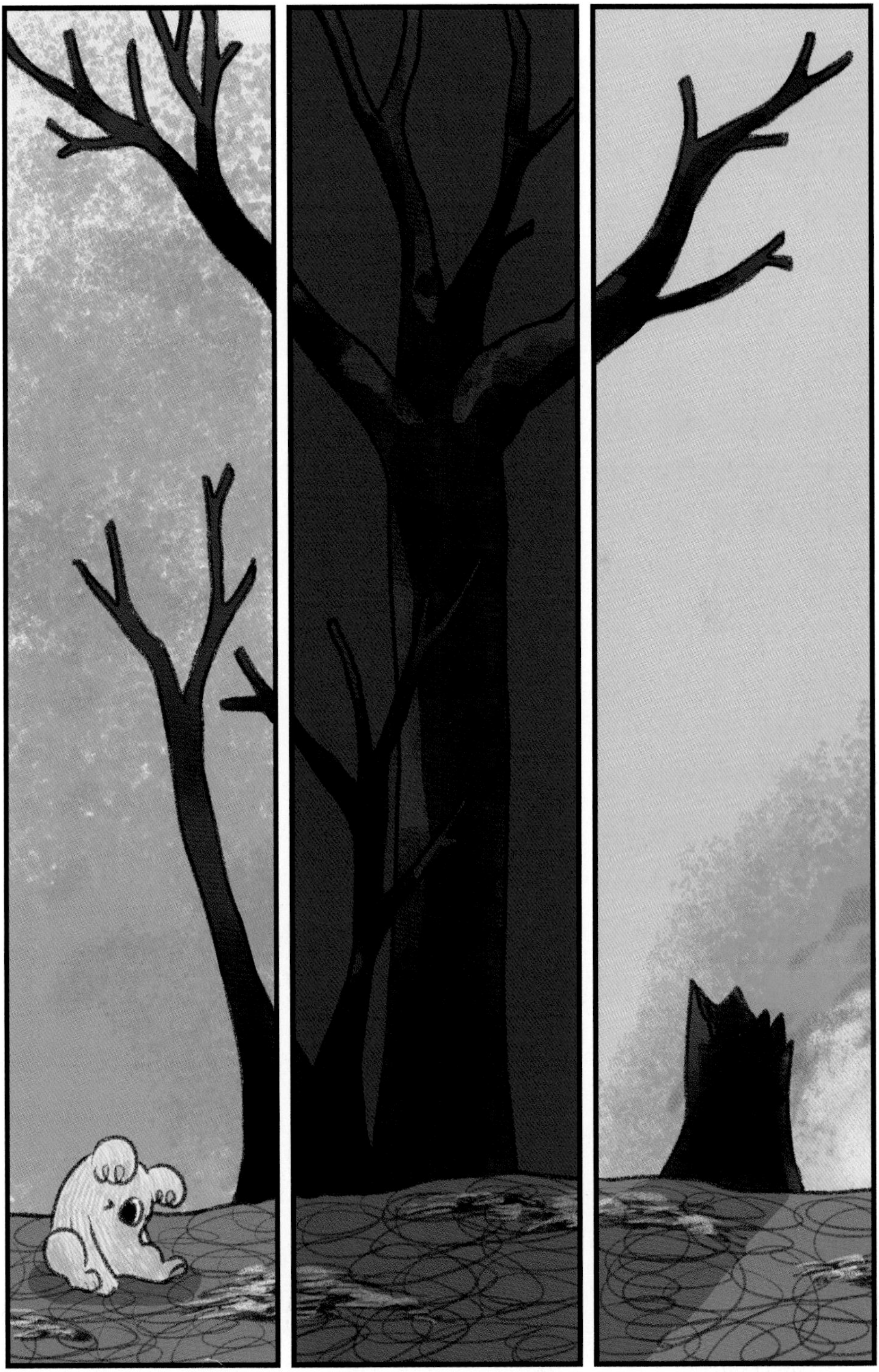

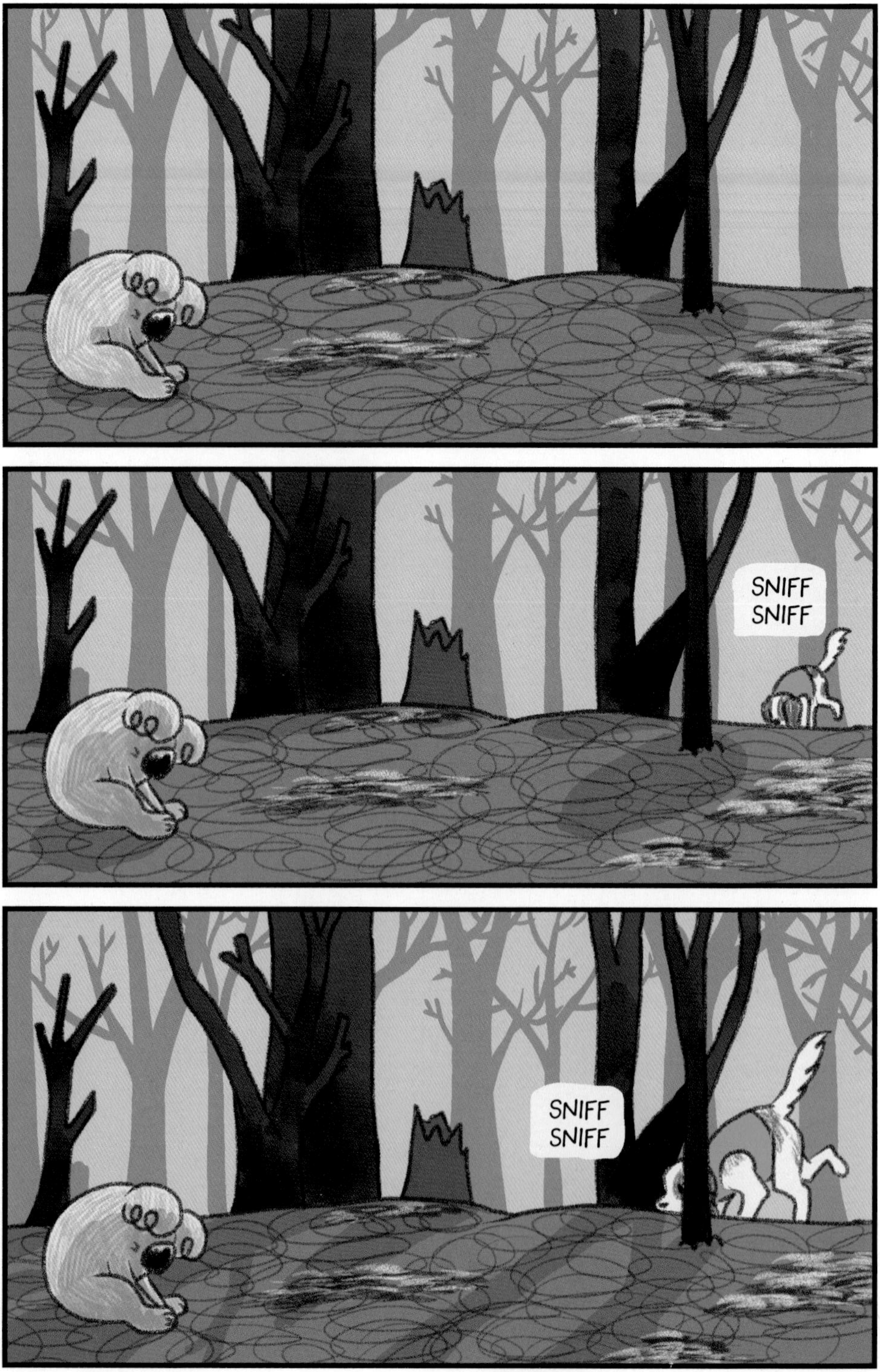
SNIFF SNIFF
SNIFF SNIFF

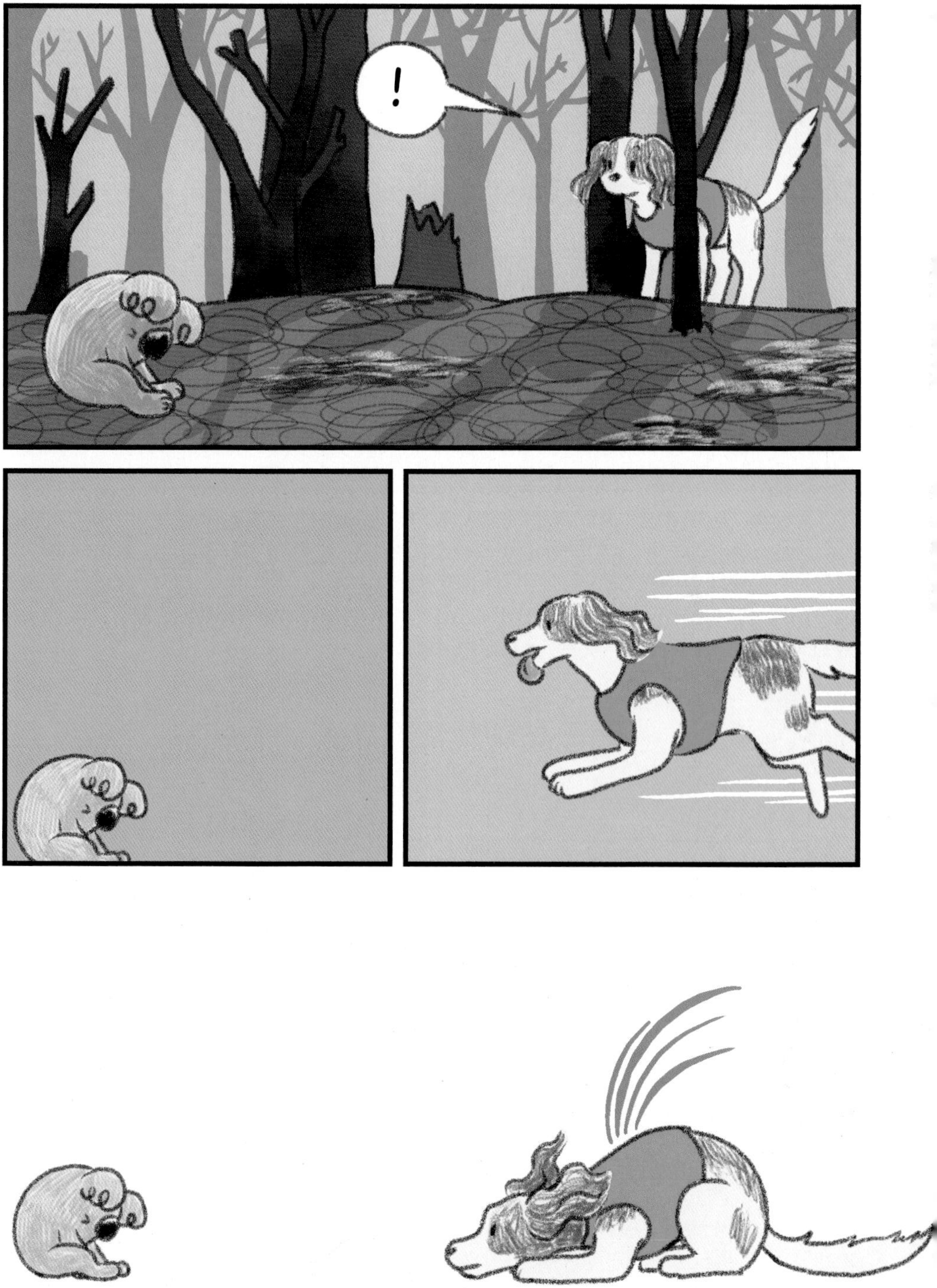
!

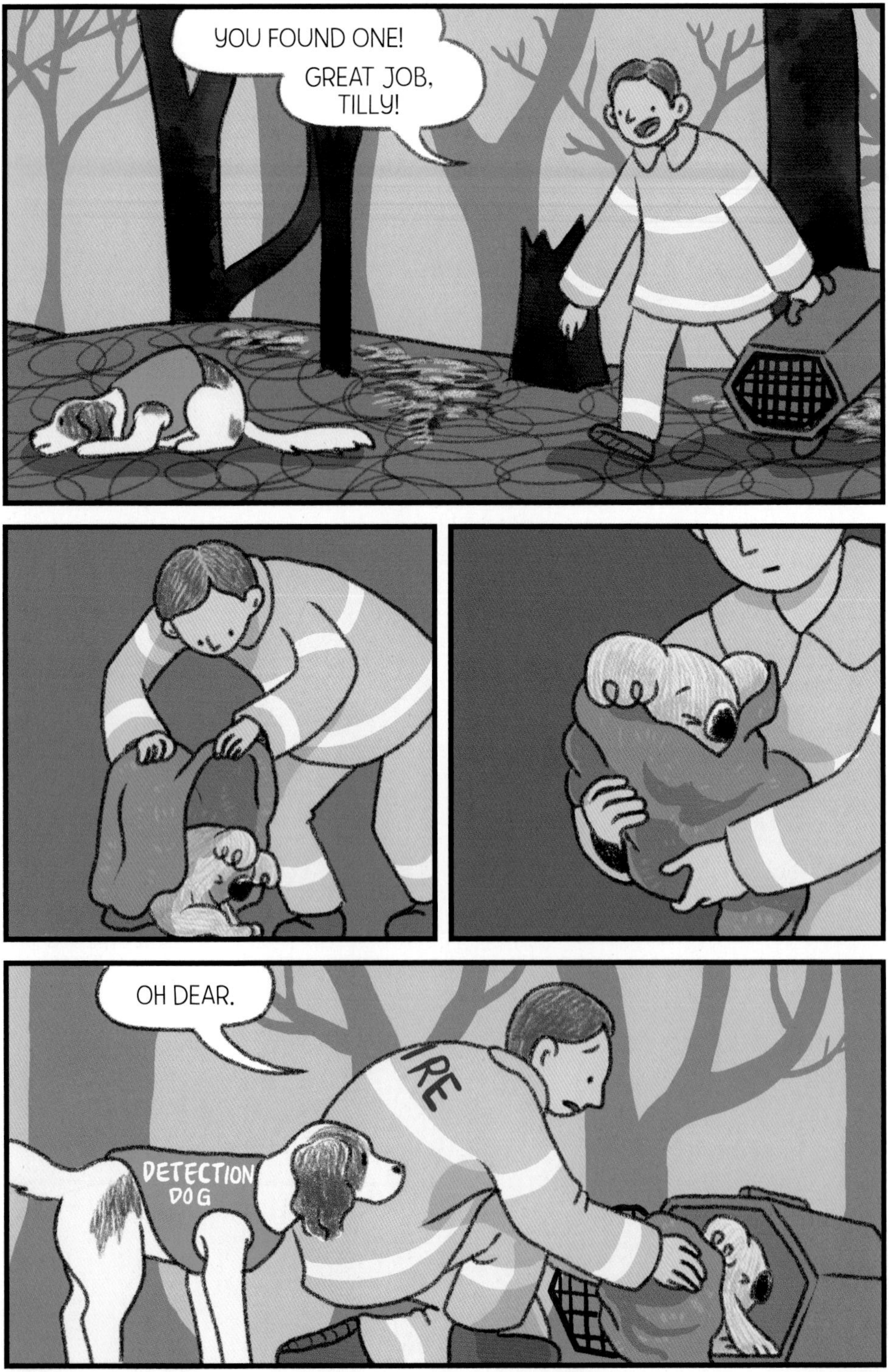
YOU FOUND ONE!
GREAT JOB, TILLY!
OH DEAR.
IRE
DETECTION DOG

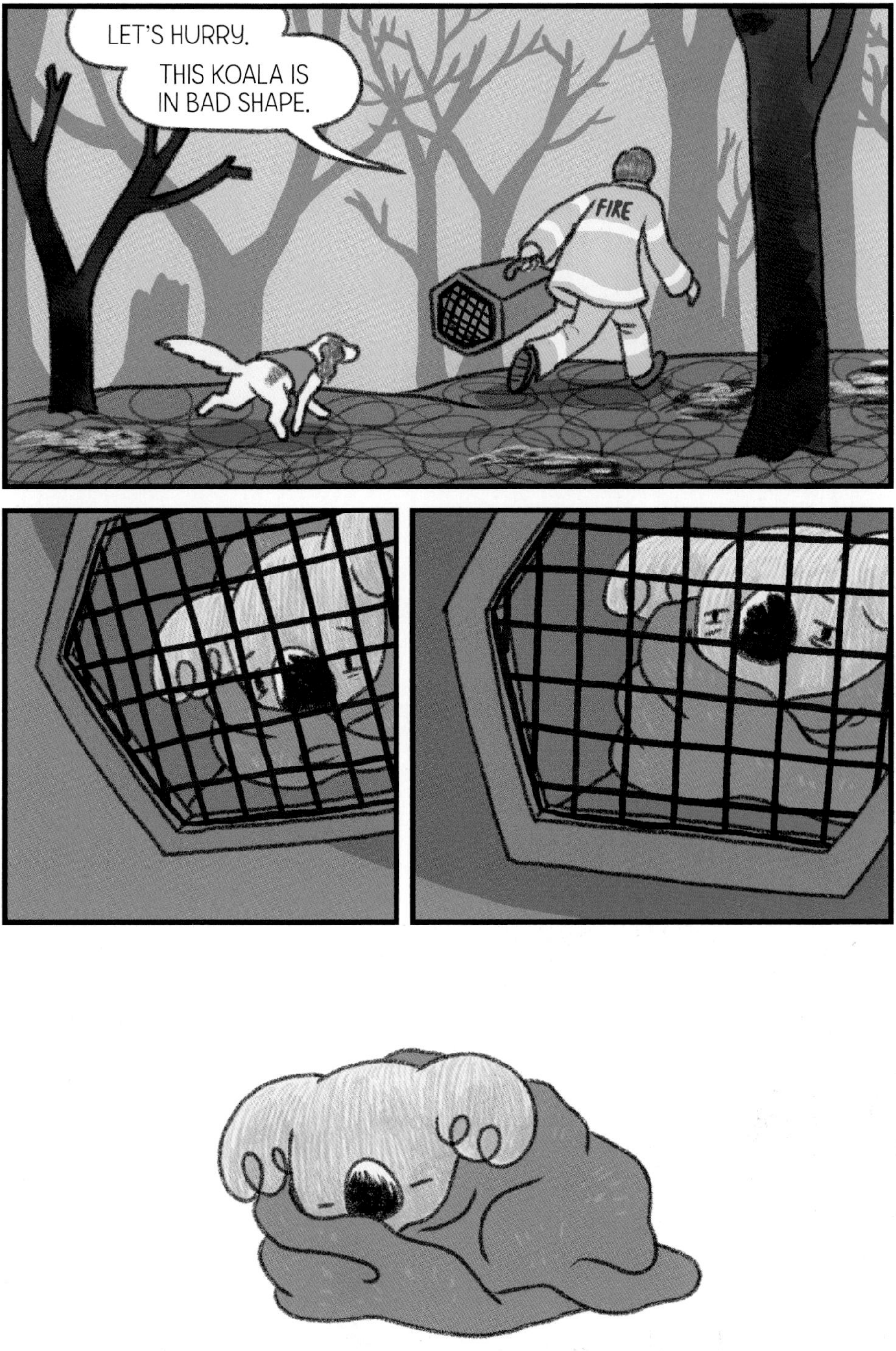
LET'S HURRY.
THIS KOALA IS IN BAD SHAPE.
FIRE

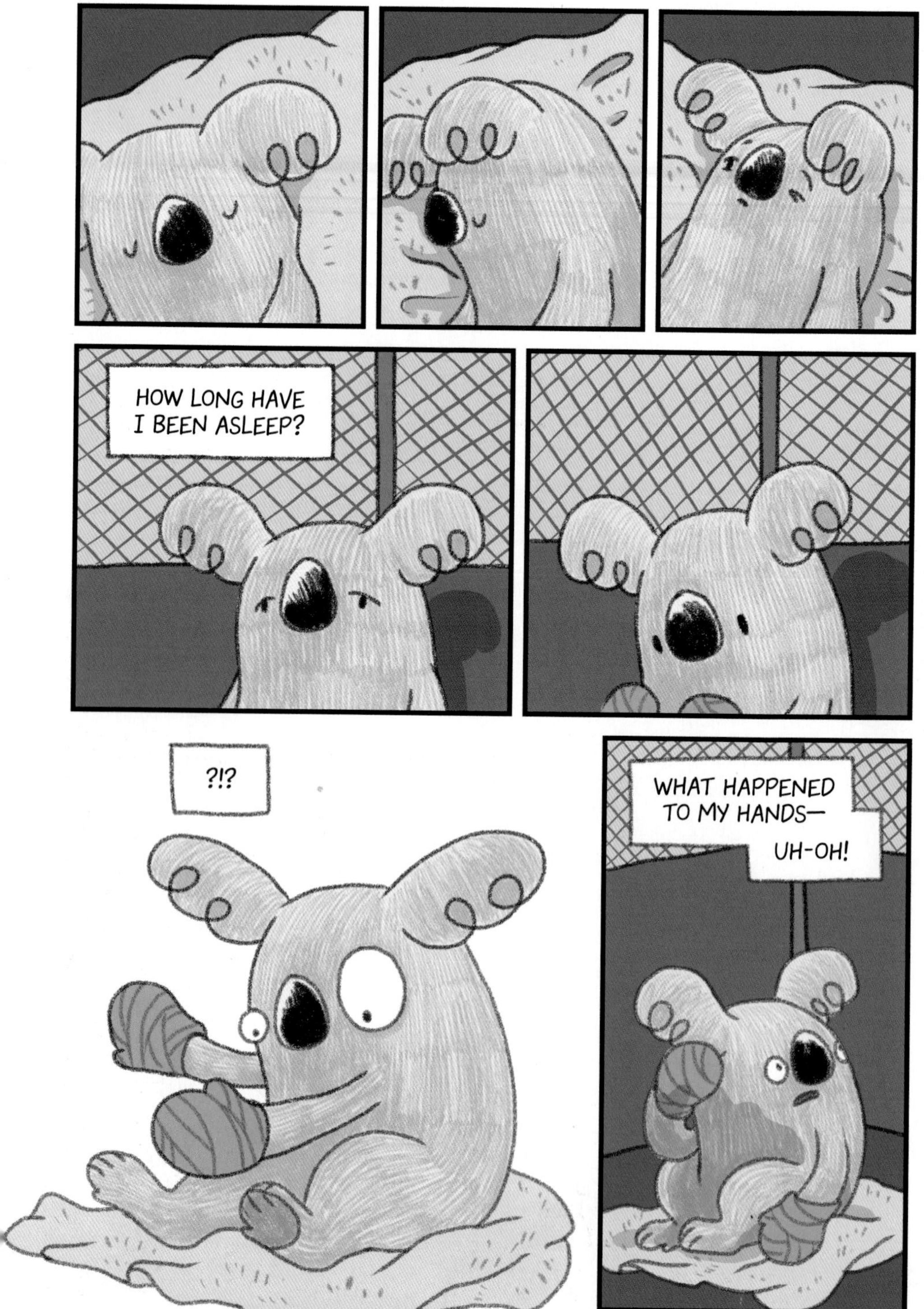
HOW LONG HAVE I BEEN ASLEEP?
?!?
WHAT HAPPENED TO MY HANDS—
UH-OH!

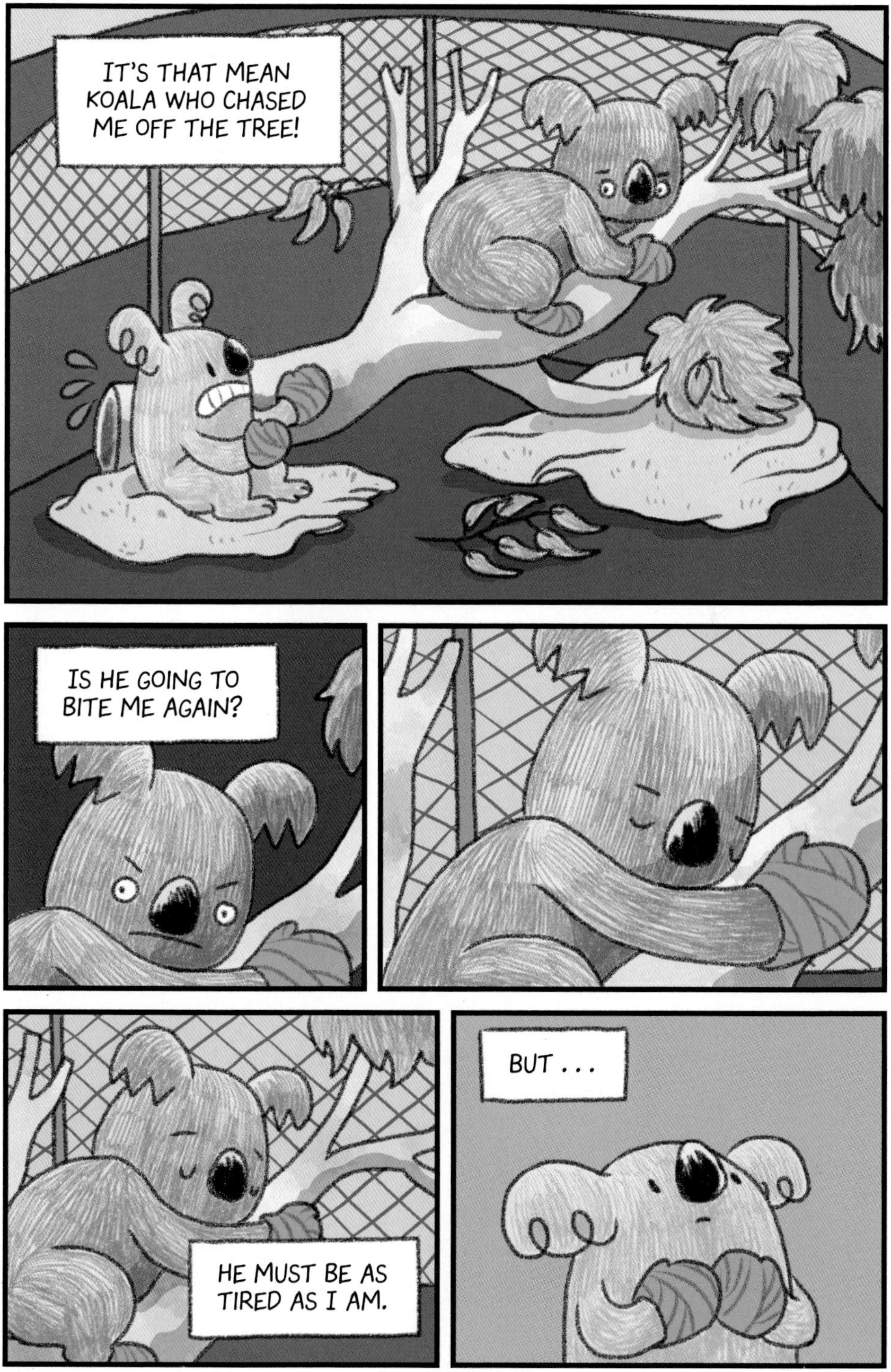
IT'S THAT MEAN KOALA WHO CHASED ME OFF THE TREE!
IS HE GOING TO BITE ME AGAIN?
HE MUST BE AS TIRED AS I AM.
BUT . . .

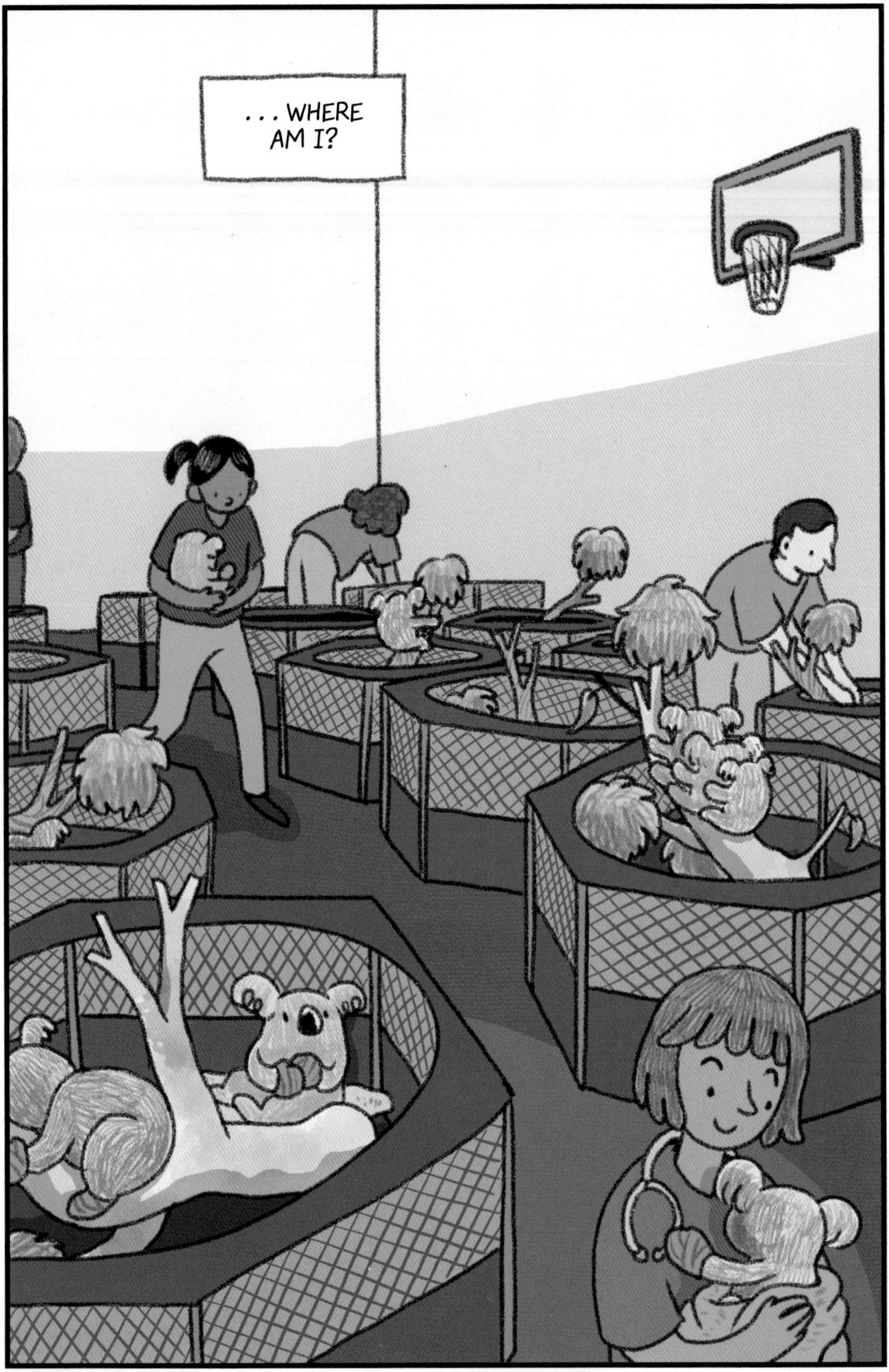
. . . WHERE
AM I?

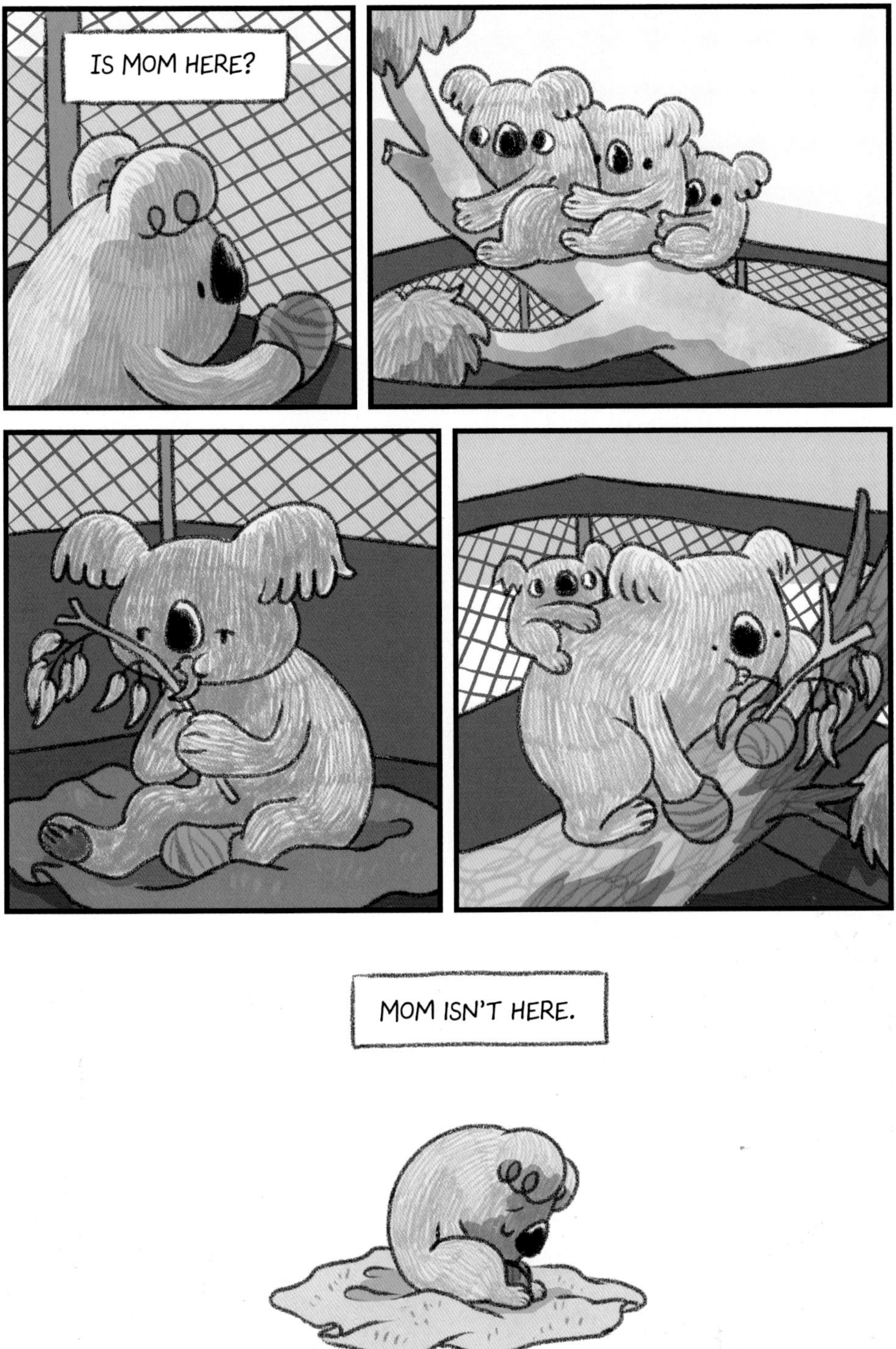
IS MOM HERE?
MOM ISN'T HERE.

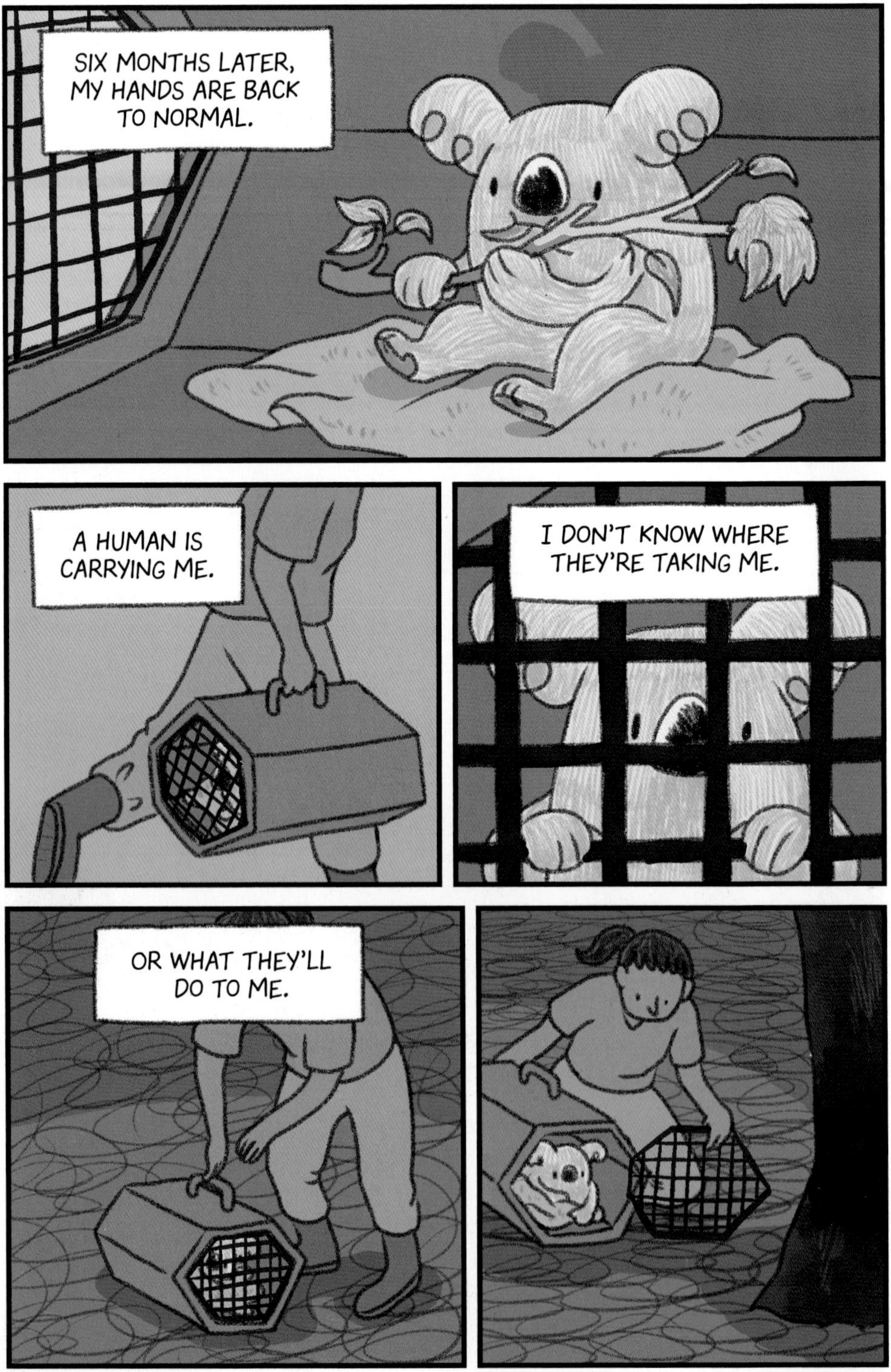
SIX MONTHS LATER, MY HANDS ARE BACK TO NORMAL.
A HUMAN IS CARRYING ME.
I DON'T KNOW WHERE THEY'RE TAKING ME.
OR WHAT THEY'LL DO TO ME.

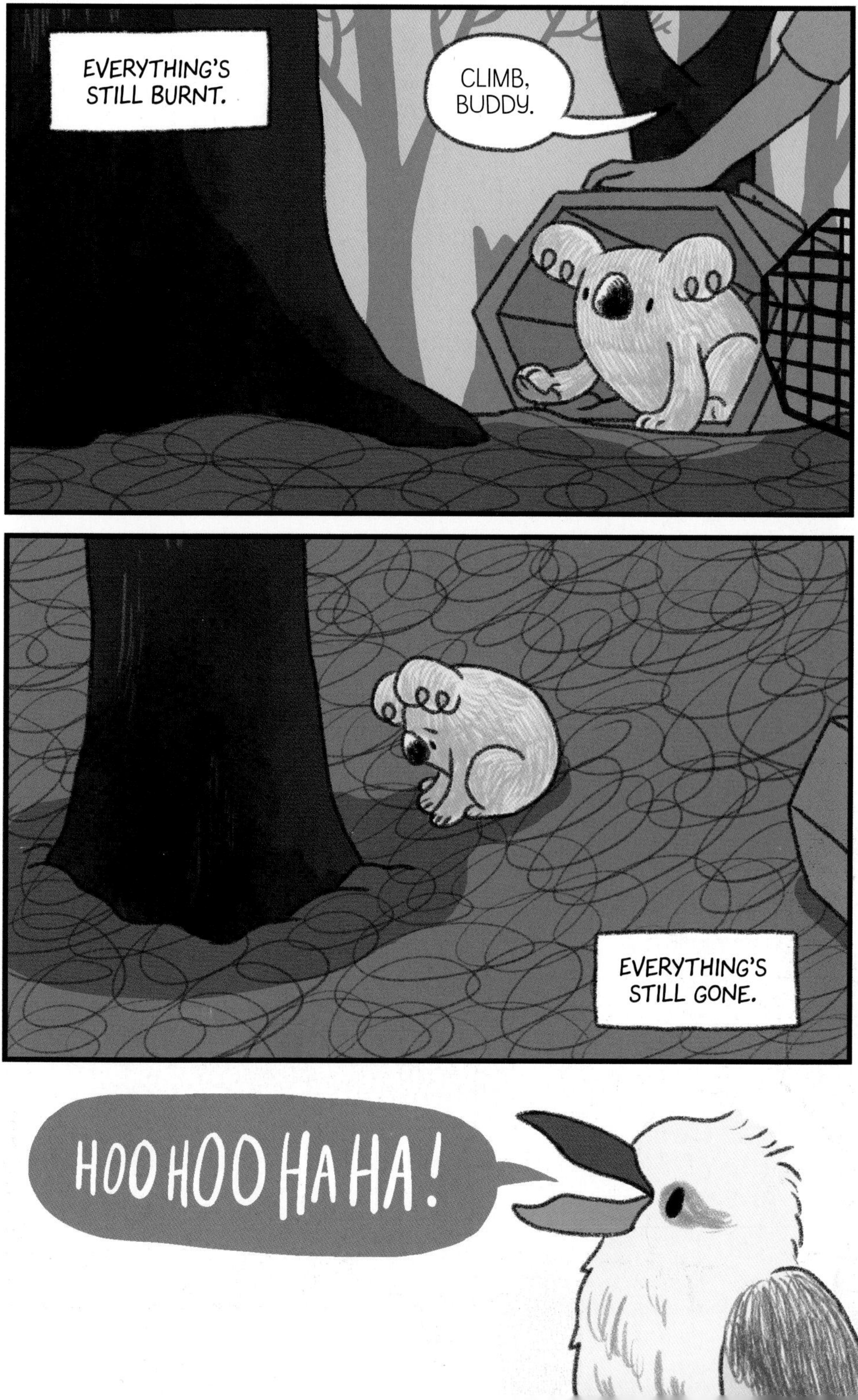
EVERYTHING'S STILL BURNT.
CLIMB, BUDDY.
EVERYTHING'S STILL GONE.
HOO HOO HA HA!

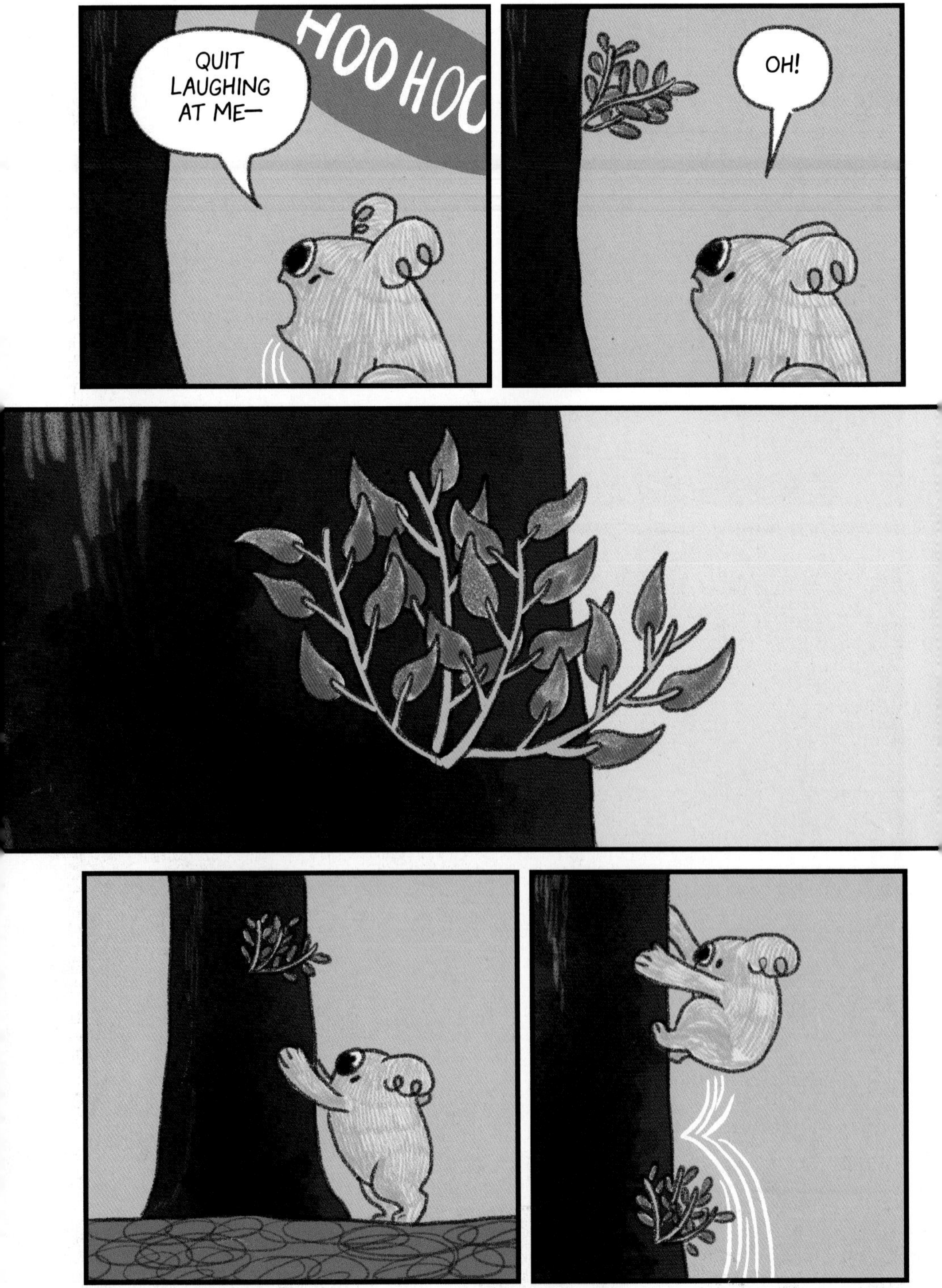
QUIT LAUGHING AT ME—
HOO HOO
OH!

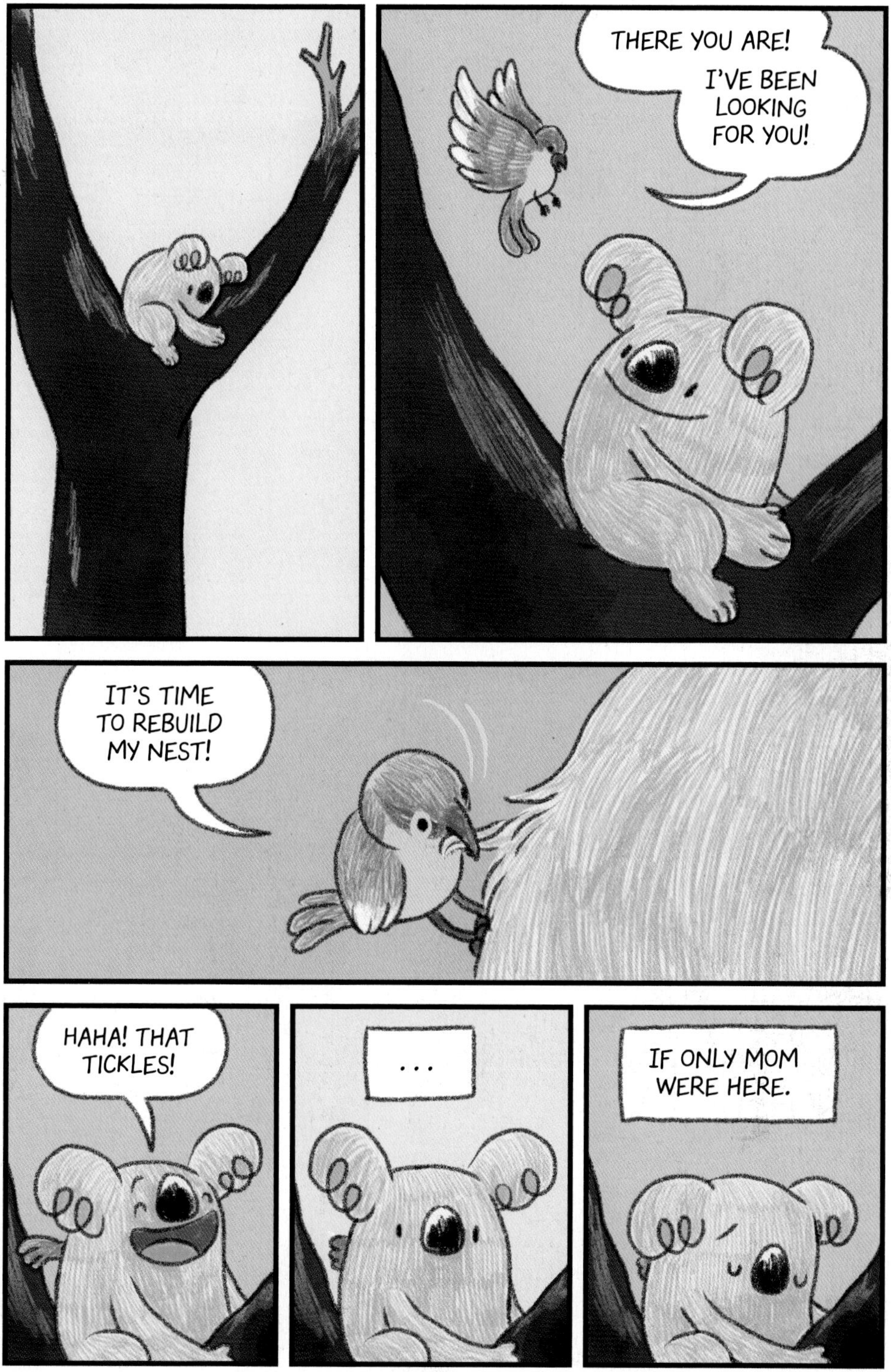
THERE YOU ARE!
I'VE BEEN LOOKING FOR YOU!
IT'S TIME TO REBUILD MY NEST!
HAHA! THAT TICKLES!
...
IF ONLY MOM WERE HERE.

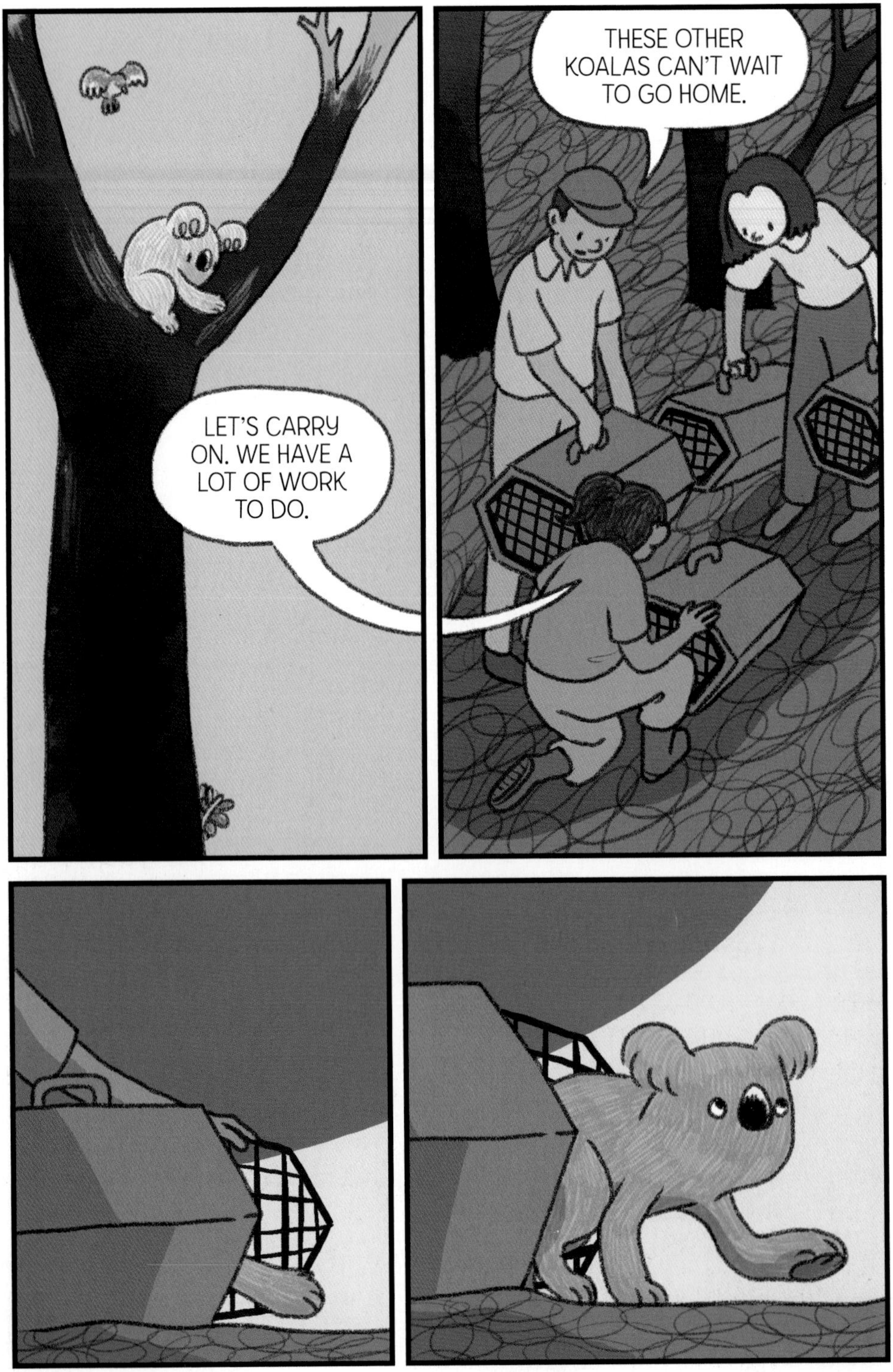
THESE OTHER KOALAS CAN'T WAIT TO GO HOME.
LET'S CARRY ON. WE HAVE A LOT OF WORK TO DO.

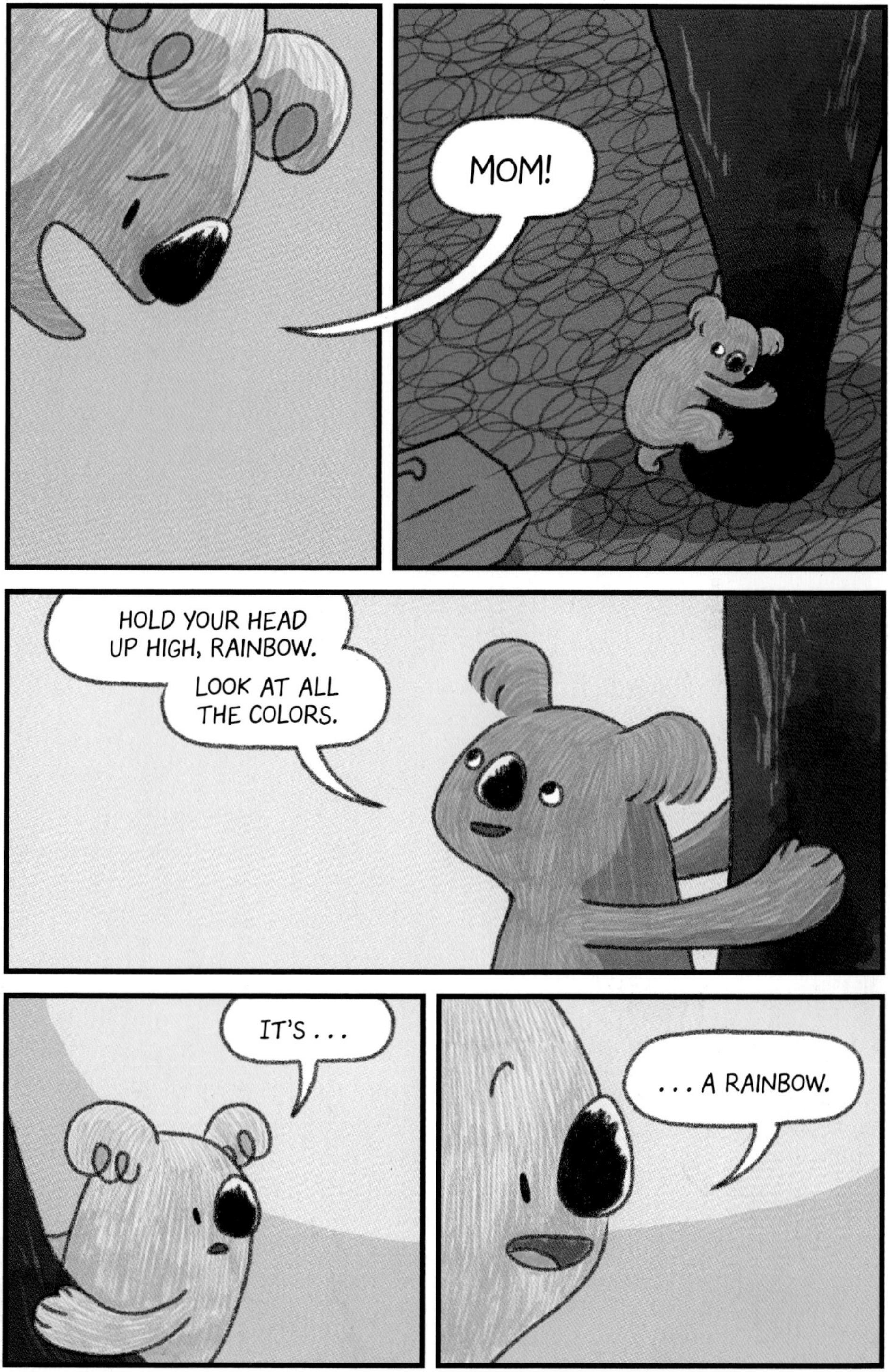
MOM!
HOLD YOUR HEAD UP HIGH, RAINBOW.
LOOK AT ALL THE COLORS.
IT'S . . .
. . . A RAINBOW.

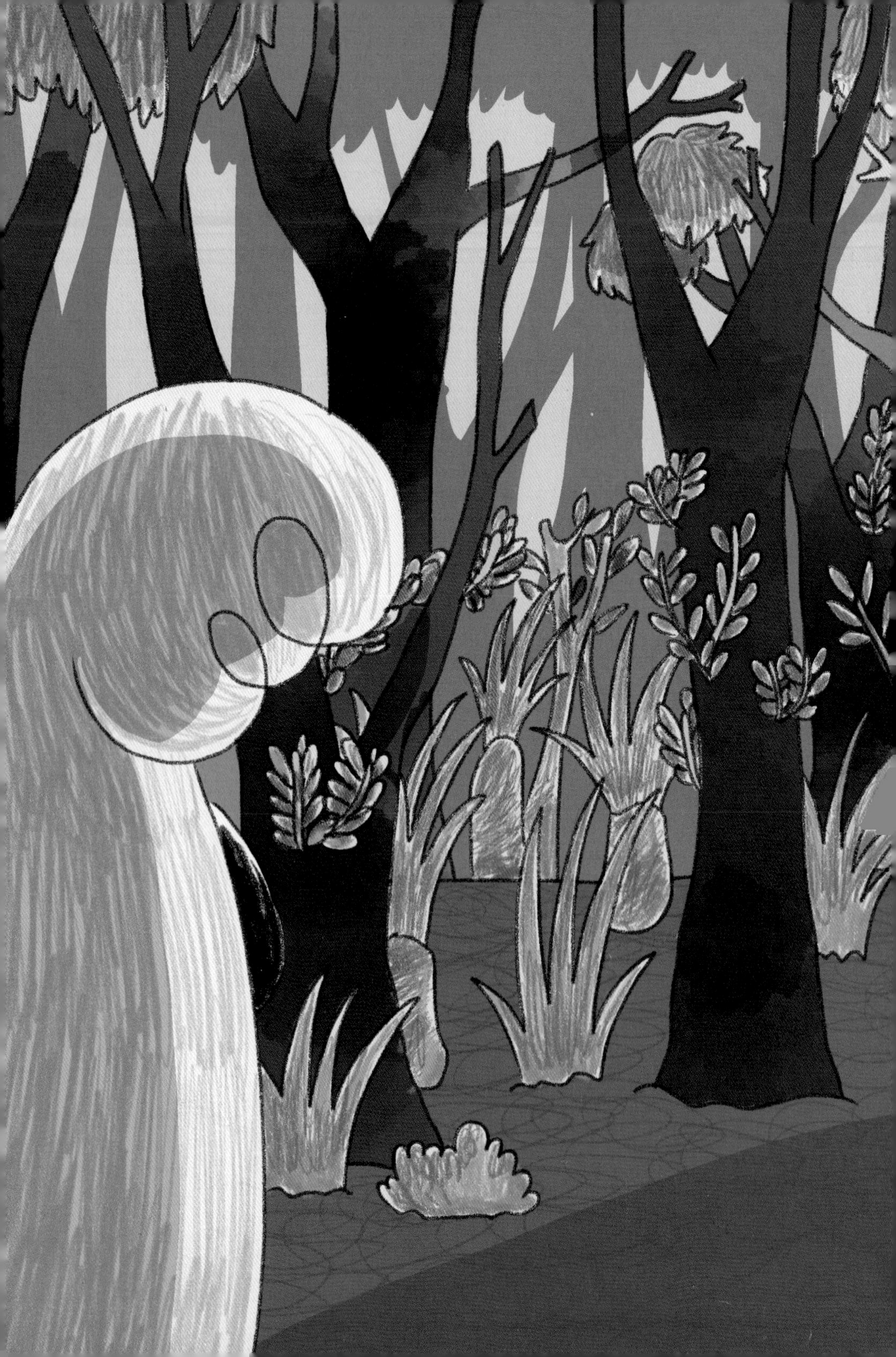

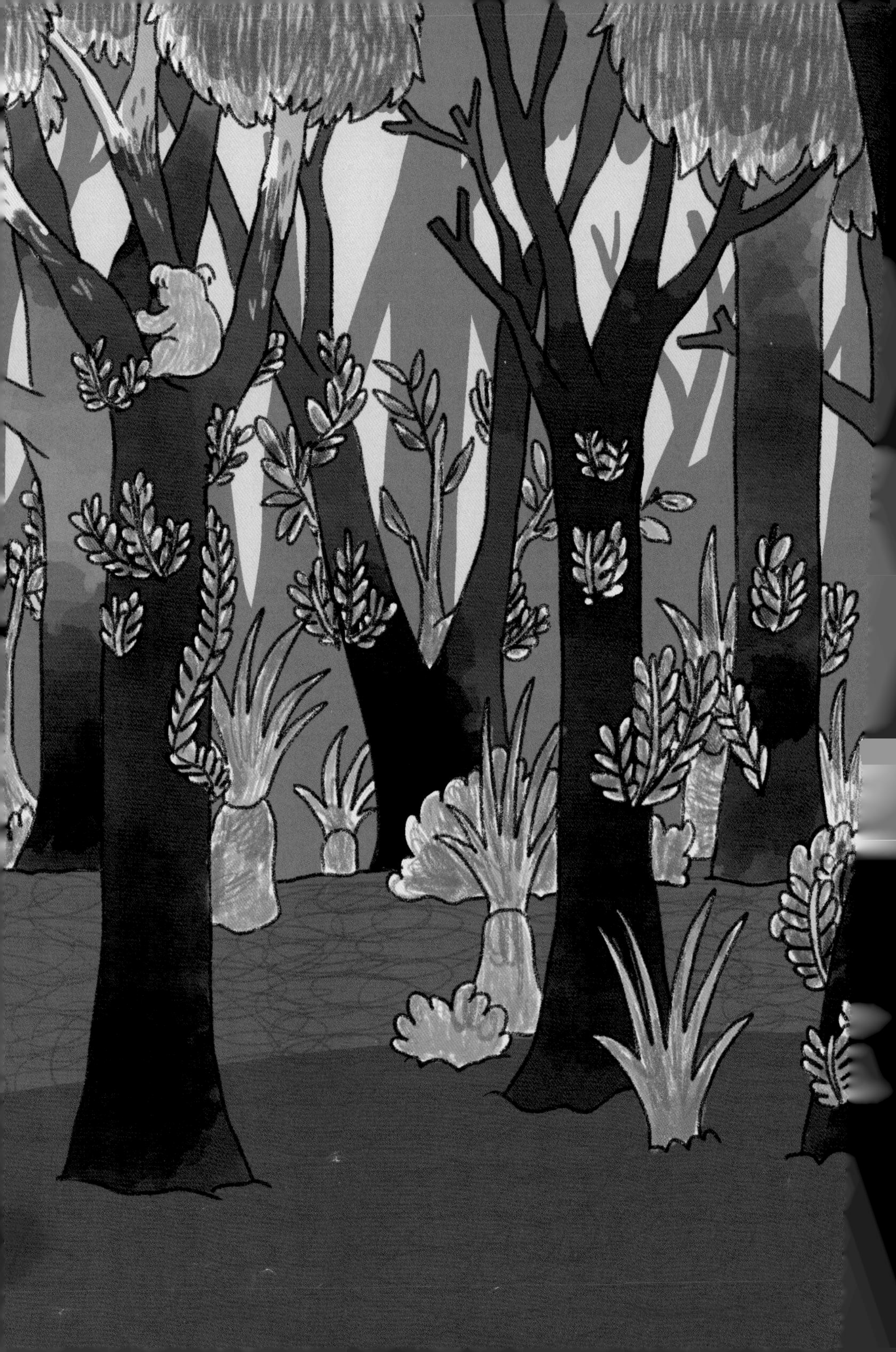

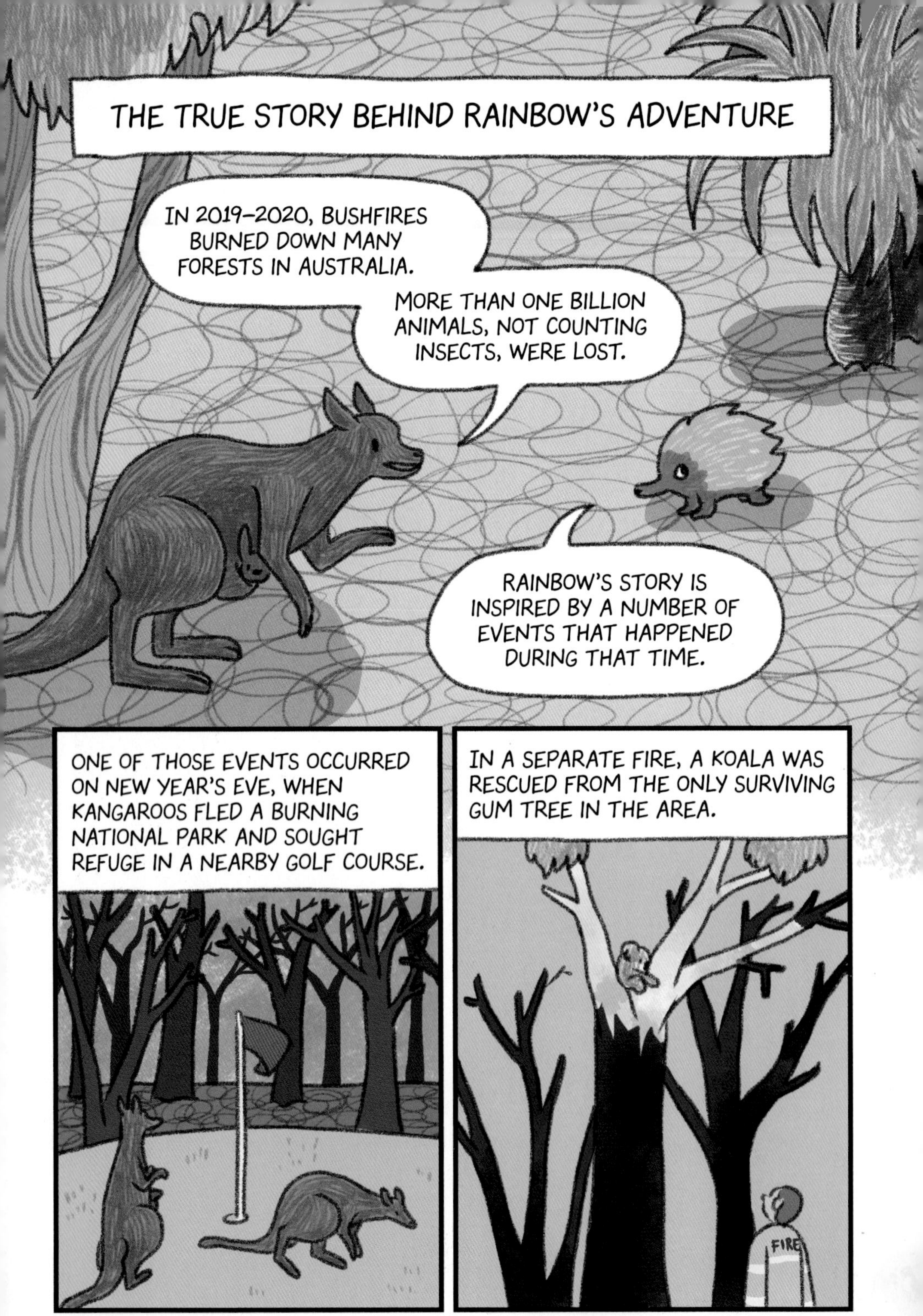
THE TRUE STORY BEHIND RAINBOW'S ADVENTURE
IN 2019–2020, BUSHFIRES BURNED DOWN MANY FORESTS IN AUSTRALIA.
MORE THAN ONE BILLION ANIMALS, NOT COUNTING INSECTS, WERE LOST.
RAINBOW'S STORY IS INSPIRED BY A NUMBER OF EVENTS THAT HAPPENED DURING THAT TIME.
ONE OF THOSE EVENTS OCCURRED ON NEW YEAR'S EVE, WHEN KANGAROOS FLED A BURNING NATIONAL PARK AND SOUGHT REFUGE IN A NEARBY GOLF COURSE.
IN A SEPARATE FIRE, A KOALA WAS RESCUED FROM THE ONLY SURVIVING GUM TREE IN THE AREA.
FIRE

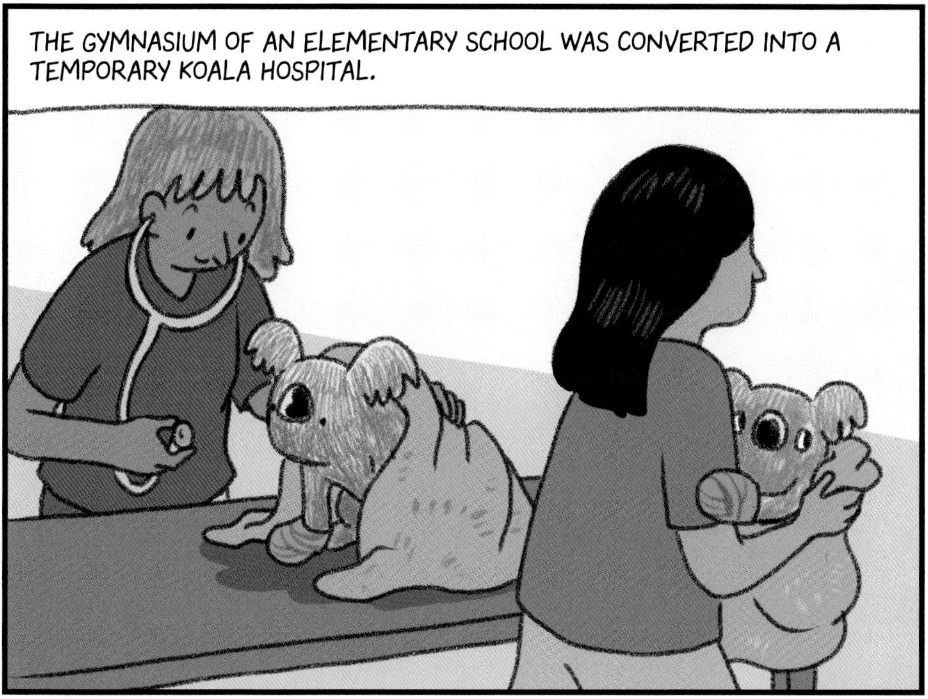
THE GYMNASIUM OF AN ELEMENTARY SCHOOL WAS CONVERTED INTO A TEMPORARY KOALA HOSPITAL.

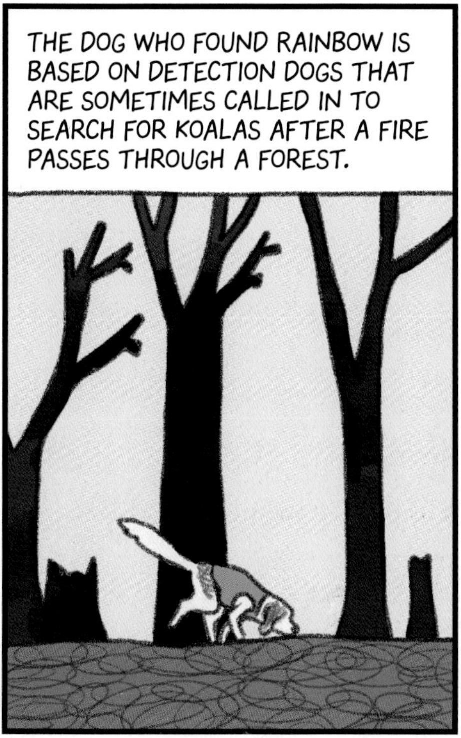
THE DOG WHO FOUND RAINBOW IS BASED ON DETECTION DOGS THAT ARE SOMETIMES CALLED IN TO SEARCH FOR KOALAS AFTER A FIRE PASSES THROUGH A FOREST.

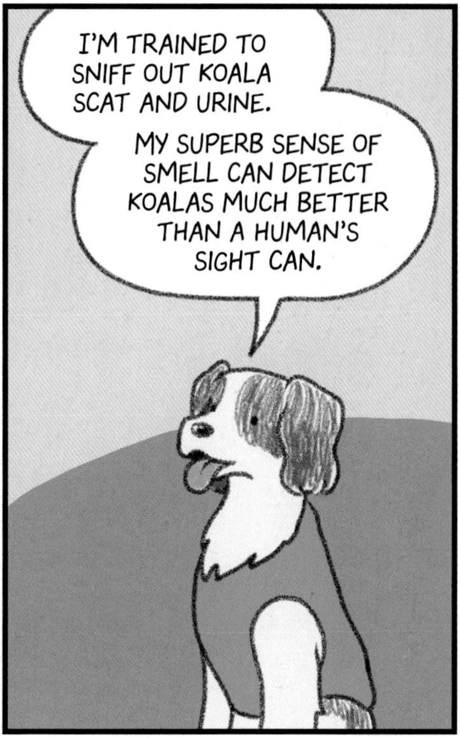
I'M TRAINED TO SNIFF OUT KOALA SCAT AND URINE.
MY SUPERB SENSE OF SMELL CAN DETECT KOALAS MUCH BETTER THAN A HUMAN'S SIGHT CAN.

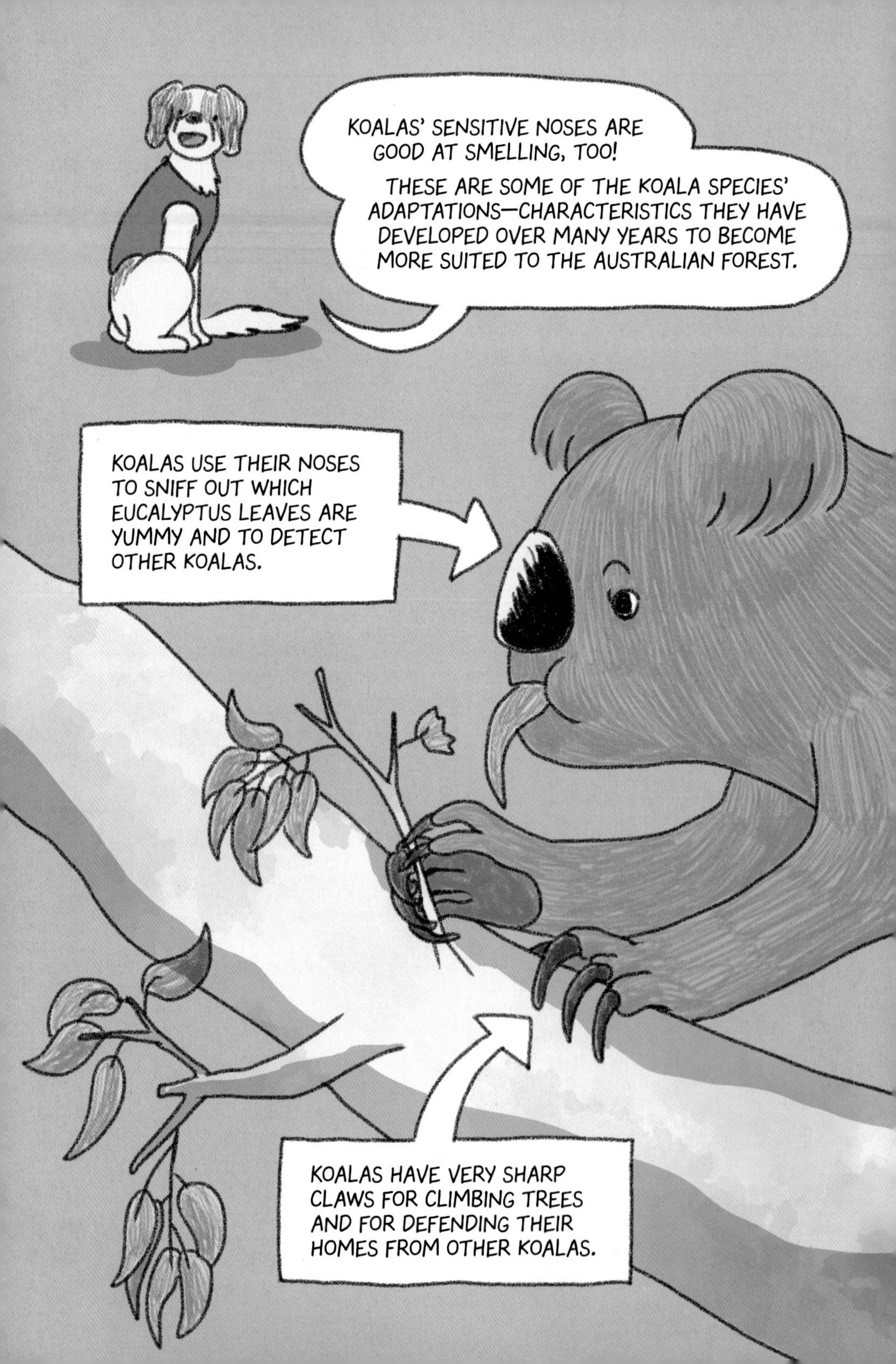
KOALAS' SENSITIVE NOSES ARE GOOD AT SMELLING, TOO!
THESE ARE SOME OF THE KOALA SPECIES' ADAPTATIONS—CHARACTERISTICS THEY HAVE DEVELOPED OVER MANY YEARS TO BECOME MORE SUITED TO THE AUSTRALIAN FOREST.
KOALAS USE THEIR NOSES TO SNIFF OUT WHICH EUCALYPTUS LEAVES ARE YUMMY AND TO DETECT OTHER KOALAS.
KOALAS HAVE VERY SHARP CLAWS FOR CLIMBING TREES AND FOR DEFENDING THEIR HOMES FROM OTHER KOALAS.

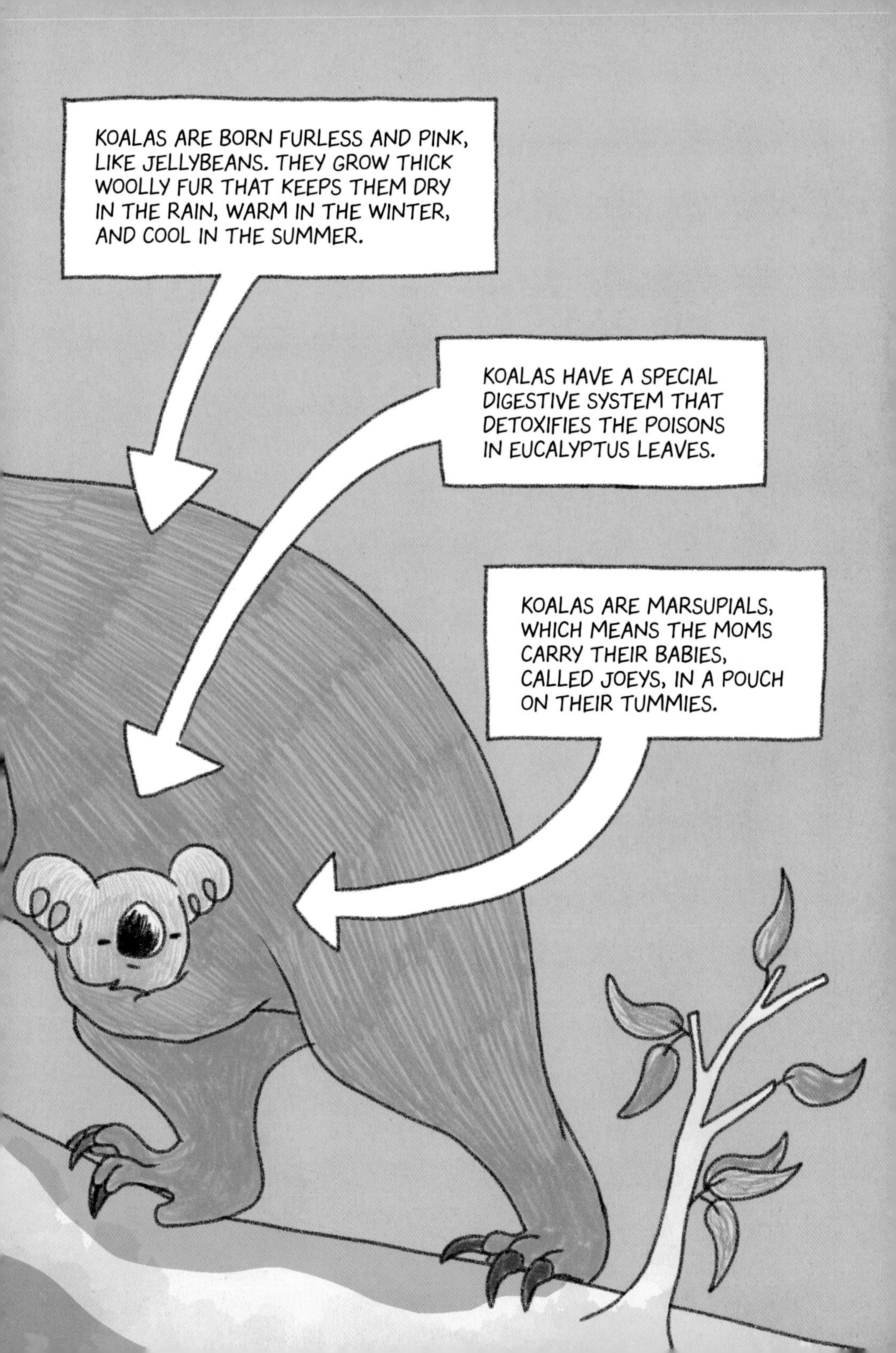
KOALAS ARE BORN FURLESS AND PINK, LIKE JELLYBEANS. THEY GROW THICK WOOLLY FUR THAT KEEPS THEM DRY IN THE RAIN, WARM IN THE WINTER, AND COOL IN THE SUMMER.
KOALAS HAVE A SPECIAL DIGESTIVE SYSTEM THAT DETOXIFIES THE POISONS IN EUCALYPTUS LEAVES.
KOALAS ARE MARSUPIALS, WHICH MEANS THE MOMS CARRY THEIR BABIES, CALLED JOEYS, IN A POUCH ON THEIR TUMMIES.

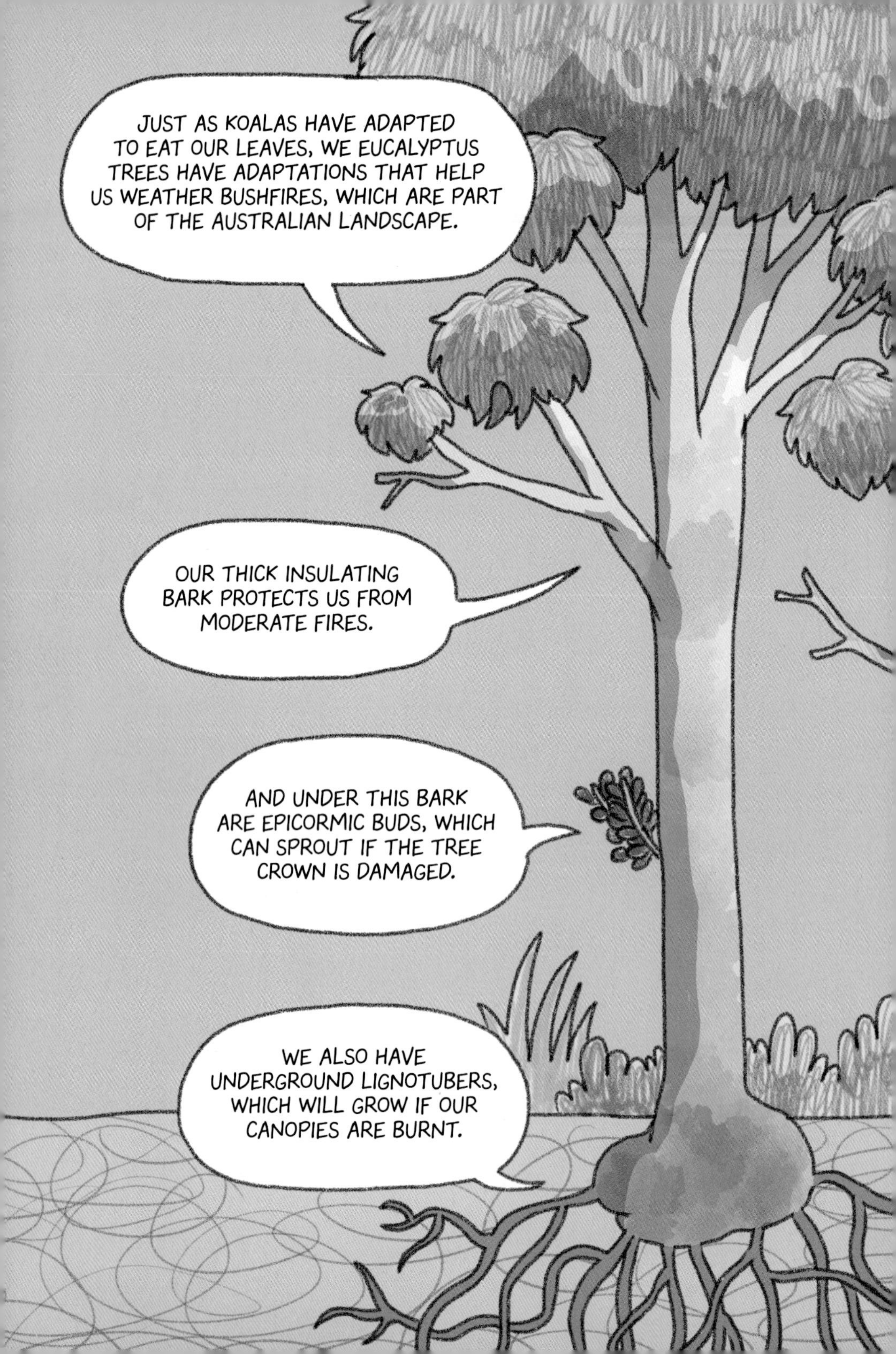
JUST AS KOALAS HAVE ADAPTED TO EAT OUR LEAVES, WE EUCALYPTUS TREES HAVE ADAPTATIONS THAT HELP US WEATHER BUSHFIRES, WHICH ARE PART OF THE AUSTRALIAN LANDSCAPE.
OUR THICK INSULATING BARK PROTECTS US FROM MODERATE FIRES.
AND UNDER THIS BARK ARE EPICORMIC BUDS, WHICH CAN SPROUT IF THE TREE CROWN IS DAMAGED.
WE ALSO HAVE UNDERGROUND LIGNOTUBERS, WHICH WILL GROW IF OUR CANOPIES ARE BURNT.

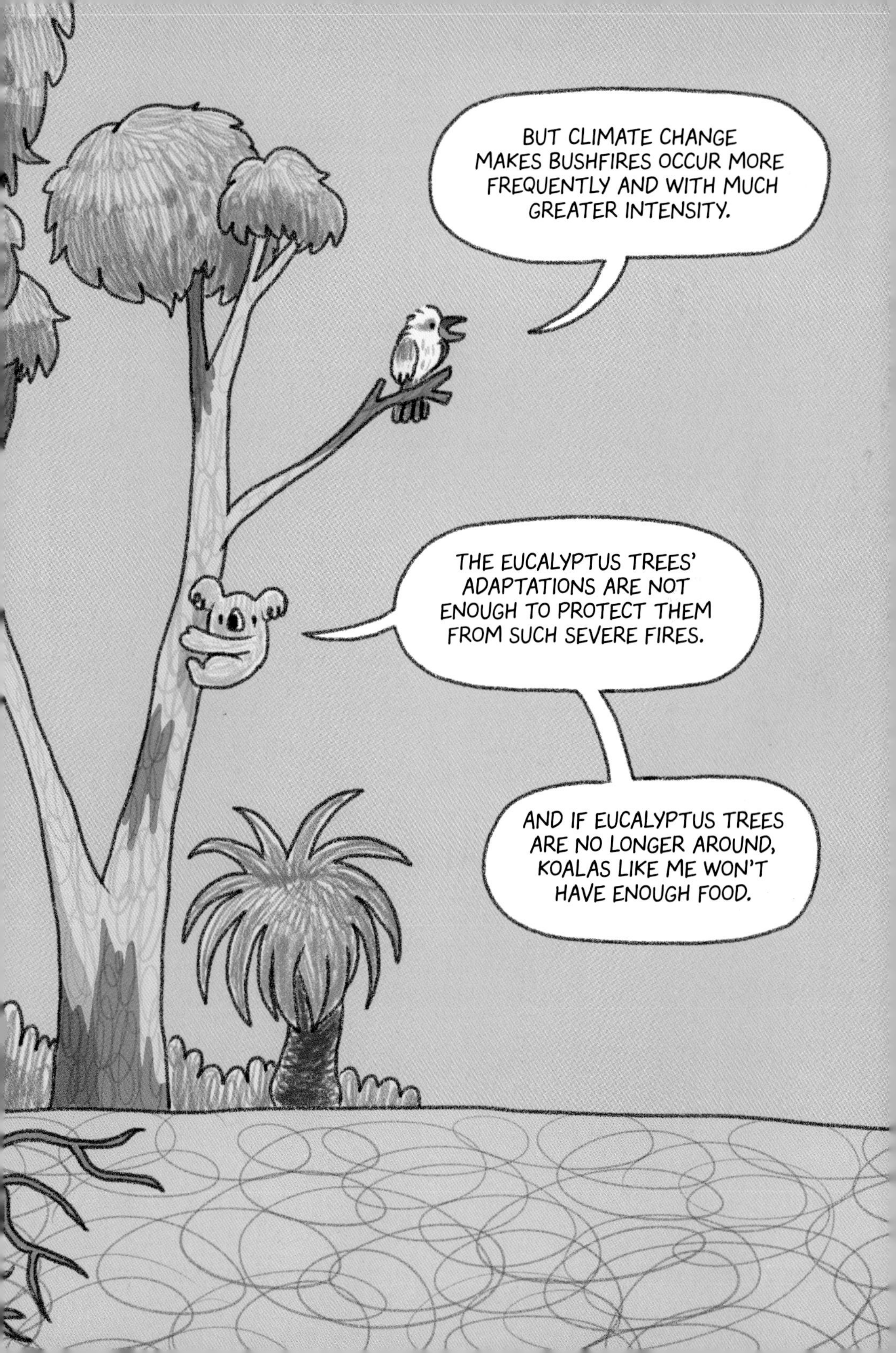
BUT CLIMATE CHANGE MAKES BUSHFIRES OCCUR MORE FREQUENTLY AND WITH MUCH GREATER INTENSITY.
THE EUCALYPTUS TREES' ADAPTATIONS ARE NOT ENOUGH TO PROTECT THEM FROM SUCH SEVERE FIRES.
AND IF EUCALYPTUS TREES ARE NO LONGER AROUND, KOALAS LIKE ME WON'T HAVE ENOUGH FOOD.

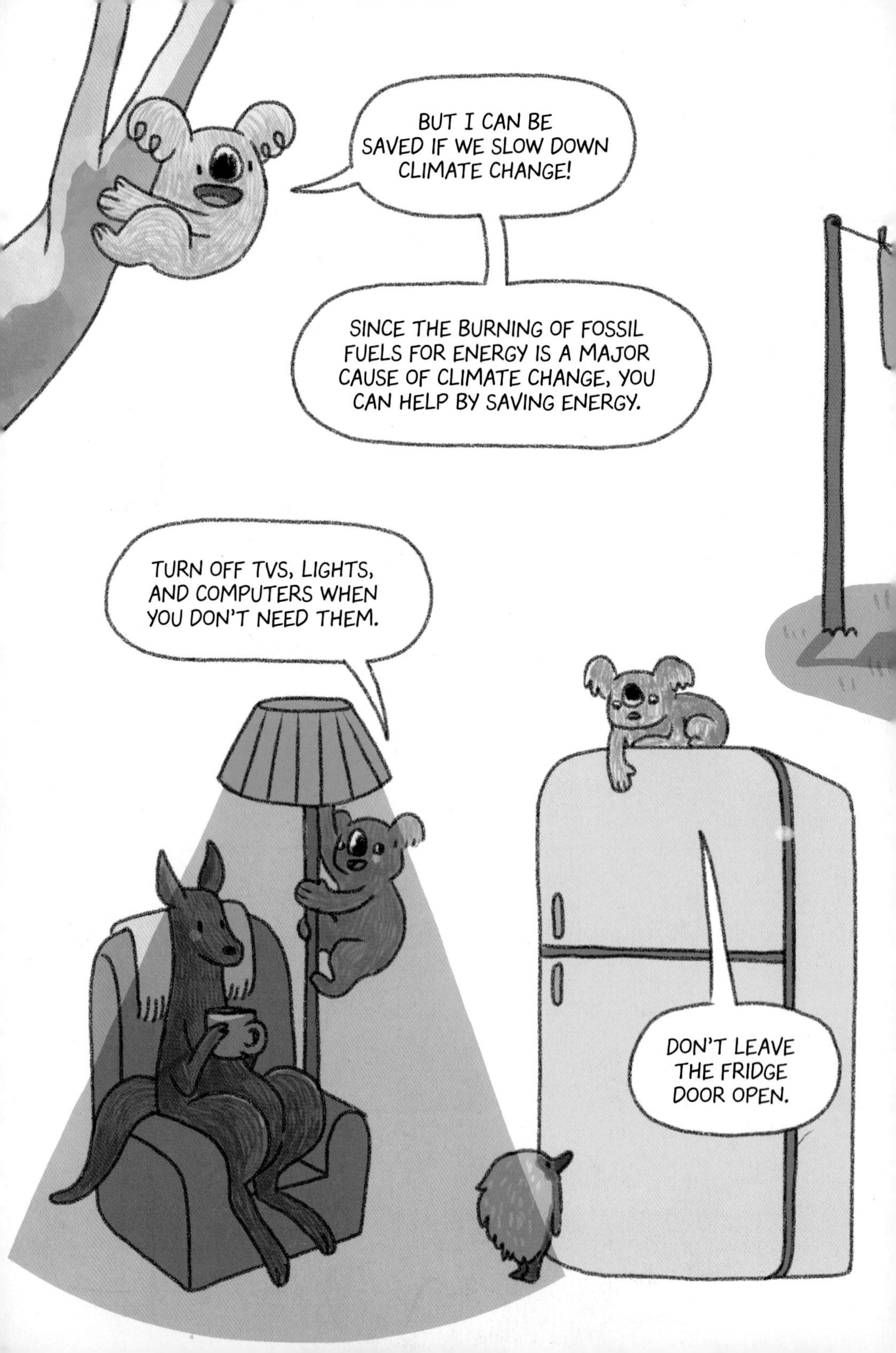
BUT I CAN BE SAVED IF WE SLOW DOWN CLIMATE CHANGE!
SINCE THE BURNING OF FOSSIL FUELS FOR ENERGY IS A MAJOR CAUSE OF CLIMATE CHANGE, YOU CAN HELP BY SAVING ENERGY.
TURN OFF TVS, LIGHTS, AND COMPUTERS WHEN YOU DON'T NEED THEM.
DON'T LEAVE THE FRIDGE DOOR OPEN.

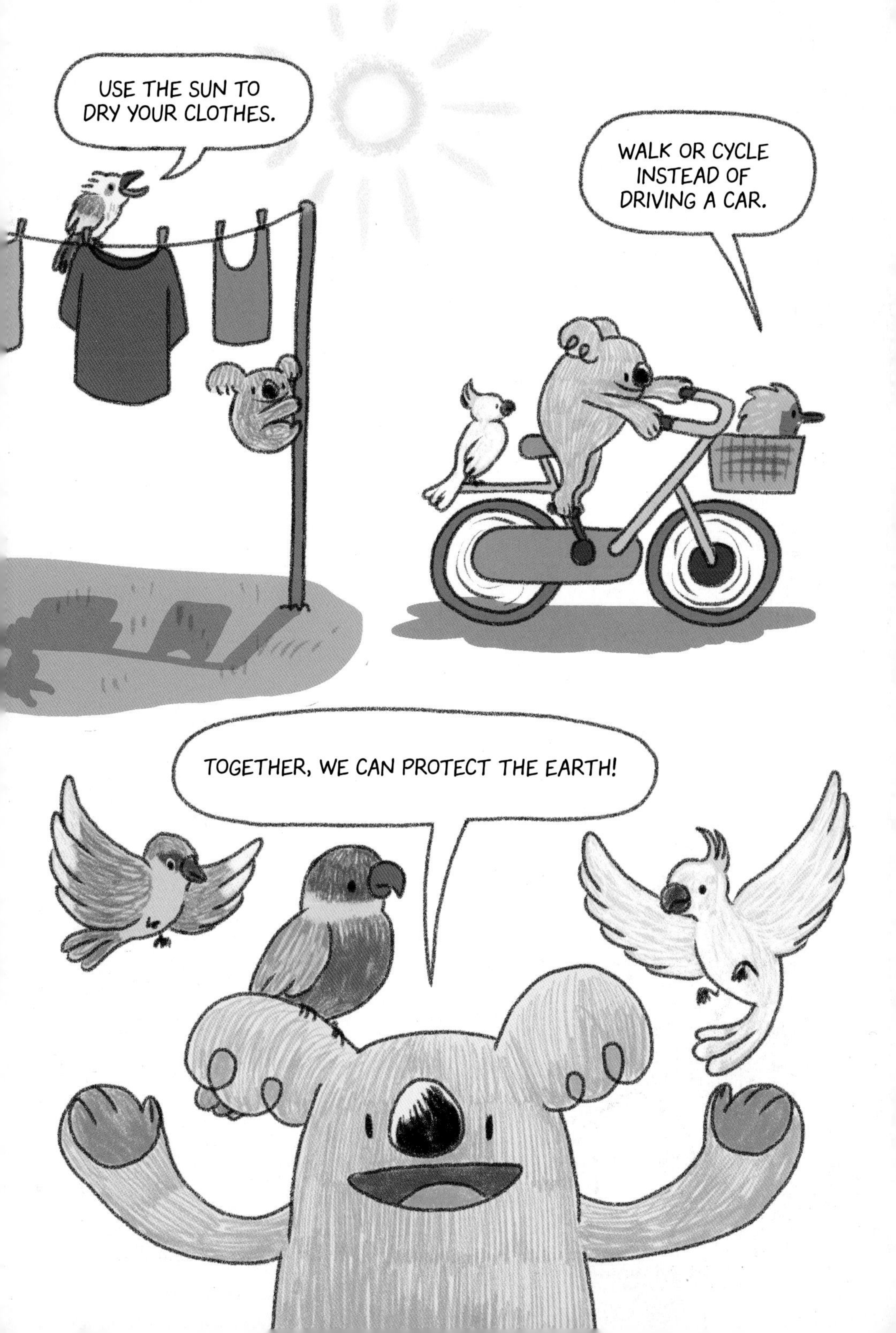
USE THE SUN TO DRY YOUR CLOTHES.
WALK OR CYCLE INSTEAD OF DRIVING A CAR.
TOGETHER, WE CAN PROTECT THE EARTH!

ARE YOU READY TO EMBARK ON ANOTHER EXCITING ADVENTURE?

STOMP INTO THE WILDERNESS IN:

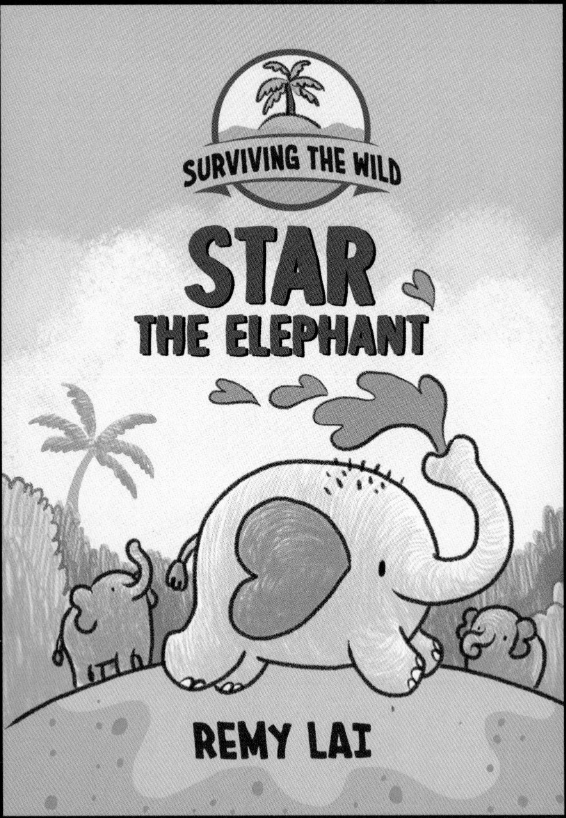
SURVIVING THE WILD
STAR
THE ELEPHANT
REMY LAI

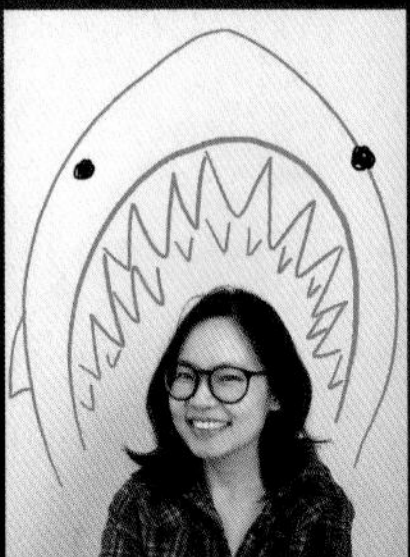

REMY LAI was born in Indonesia, grew up in Singapore, and currently lives in Brisbane, Australia, where she writes and draws stories for kids with her two dogs by her side. She is also the author of the critically acclaimed *Pie in the Sky*, *Fly on the Wall*, and *Pawcasso*. **remylai.com**